THE WIDOWER'S LIE

J. A. BAKER

B
Boldwood

First published as *Here Lies Alice* in 2022. This edition published in Great Britain in 2024 by Boldwood Books Ltd.

Copyright © J. A. Baker, 2022

Cover Design by Head Design Ltd

Cover Illustration: iStock

The moral right of J. A. Baker to be identified as the author of this work has been asserted in accordance with the Copyright, Designs and Patents Act 1988.

All rights reserved. No part of this book may be reproduced in any form or by any electronic or mechanical means, including information storage and retrieval systems, without written permission from the author, except for the use of brief quotations in a book review.

This book is a work of fiction and, except in the case of historical fact, any resemblance to actual persons, living or dead, is purely coincidental.

Every effort has been made to obtain the necessary permissions with reference to copyright material, both illustrative and quoted. We apologise for any omissions in this respect and will be pleased to make the appropriate acknowledgements in any future edition.

A CIP catalogue record for this book is available from the British Library.

Paperback ISBN 978-1-83561-238-5

Large Print ISBN 978-1-83561-237-8

Hardback ISBN 978-1-83561-236-1

Ebook ISBN 978-1-83561-239-2

Kindle ISBN 978-1-83561-240-8

Audio CD ISBN 978-1-83561-231-6

MP3 CD ISBN 978-1-83561-232-3

Digital audio download ISBN 978-1-83561-234-7

Boldwood Books Ltd
23 Bowerdean Street
London SW6 3TN
www.boldwoodbooks.com

If you reveal your secrets to the wind, you should not blame the wind for revealing them to the trees.

— KHALIL GIBRAN

For those who went before me, I've tried to keep you alive.

1

FEBRUARY 2018

It's always the dog walkers and the early-morning joggers that find them, isn't it? They begin their day full of hope, ready to greet the hours ahead with a smile as they step out into the crisp, morning air only to have those hopes dashed by their grisly find, their minds tarnished, the sight before them forever embedded deep within their brains.

The young woman stares down at the ground, realisation dawning. She thought initially that it was a stray shoe: a discarded trainer, one of many that litter this area, along with empty coffee cartons and crisp packets. She sees them all the time and wonders how they get there. Always one, never the pair. Babies' dummies, empty aerosol cans, mouldy food wrappers – she has stumbled across them all while out on her morning run, but this is different. She doesn't know how it's different, or why. It just strikes her as an eerie find. A shoe would slide down the embankment. It wouldn't just sit there, poking out from a pile of fallen leaves. It's the angle that worries and intrigues her. It's almost perpendicular. As if it's attached to something. Her skin prickles, ice sliding beneath her flesh.

She stands, stares up at it, her breath hot and sour, misting the air in front of her face: perfectly formed vapour clouds that appear in a small, pulsing orb before vanishing into the atmosphere. The mornings are getting lighter. Winter seems to have gone on for a hundred years. She shivers, thinks about carrying on with her run. It won't do her any good, standing here getting cold. She has to keep moving, keep the blood pumping through her veins, otherwise she will seize up, her muscles knotting, pain shrieking through her limbs when she tries to move. And yet there is something about that trainer – the angle of it perhaps – that doesn't sit well with her.

Moving closer, scrambling on her hands and knees to clamber up the bank, she can see even from a distance that it isn't a trainer at all. It's proper shoe – cream leather with a short, square heel. Mud has almost disguised it beyond recognition, clumps of dirt and rotted leaves sticking to its surface. It's an incongruous sight – the type of footwear somebody would wear to an office – smart, functional, not too glamorous. Not the sort of thing that gets lodged on a riverbank.

Her eyes are drawn to the steep, slippery incline above her, covered with moss and leaves and the general debris nature leaves behind after a cold, dark winter. Pressing on, she clambers up until the item is close to her face. She shivers and backs away a fraction, the thought of slipping never far from her mind. It's a steep gradient, almost vertical, requiring her to use her hands and feet to make the ascent. Her foot is lodged against the base of a tree that, along with many others nearby, appear to defy gravity. Standing upright, their deep root systems probably help to knit together this bank, stopping any erosion or landslips.

She shuffles ever nearer, one hand resting against the rough bark of the tree to steady herself while the other reaches down and brushes away the twigs and leaves that surround the shoe. Her hand hits something solid, something cold that makes her recoil. She lets out a shriek, hoping it isn't what she thinks it could be, yet knowing deep down that it probably is. This is a quiet, shaded area and yet she has never felt frightened or unsafe here. It's next to the river, just two minutes from the nearest village, but the canopy of trees and its deep-set location make it feel a million miles away from everything. It's peaceful, calming. And now this.

Her breathing is ragged, her skin flashing hot and cold simultaneously. She gives the soil and dirt and leaves one final push, sweeping it all aside to reveal a glimpse of dead flesh. It's a leg, its texture grey and mottled. She fumbles in her pocket for her phone, praying to a God she doesn't believe exists that she can get a signal.

Sweat rolls down her back. She is cold and clammy as she stares at the screen, panic biting at her. No bars. No signal. No way of getting any help.

Shit!

She clambers and crawls higher up the embankment on watery legs, her innards roiling, the image of the decaying limb burnt deep into her brain. By the time she reaches the top, her knees are scraped and bloody, her hands covered in leaf mulch. Strands of wet hair hang in her eyes. Sweat courses down her back.

Her phone springs to life. She cries out, her voice a loud echo. Relief blooms in her chest. She punches at the screen, calls 999, her voice a croak as she hears somebody speaking on the other end. A welcome voice. A helpful, soothing sound that eases the fear and helplessness that are currently slamming into her, violent blows that leave her winded and breathless.

'Body,' is all she can say before her legs give way and she collapses onto the wet grass. 'I've found a dead body.'

* * *

Man Jailed for Murder of Local Teacher

Phillip Kennedy, 40, of Wainwright Court, York, has been found guilty of murdering a local teacher. Her bruised and battered body was found on the banks of the River Ouse by an early-morning jogger.

Sophia Saunders, 38, a teacher, suffered severe head injuries and her body was dragged down an embankment before being covered with leaves and branches. She was discovered by an unsuspecting jogger who alerted the police to the grisly find.

Phillip Kennedy pleaded not guilty throughout the trial, lowering his head and weeping as the verdict was read out in court.

Judge Sebastien Ward said the killer would be shown no mercy and should expect to serve a long sentence for a heinous crime against an innocent woman.

Kennedy was led from the dock by police officers, turning only once to glance at the victim's husband who bore a dignified silence throughout the proceedings.

Sentencing will take place later this month.

The Yorkshire News, October 2018

2

A YEAR LATER

Alice

I see him before he sees me. I shuffle forward on unsteady legs, my hands trembling as he turns and looks my way. His eyes are blind to my presence, always glancing elsewhere, their unseeing stare shifting over and beyond me. This is always the way, me chasing after him, watching, waiting, hoping that one day, he will finally turn my way and sense that I am here. Weeks and weeks of longing for him to speak and acknowledge me. Anything. I will take any crumbs he decides to throw my way. That's how anxious I am for his attention. Does that make me sound sad and desperate? Probably. But that's because I am. I need him to want me, to be with me. It's just how it is.

The group of bodies moves out of the church, their voices a gravelly murmur. People turning, speaking to one another, talking in hushed tones, heads dipped together respectfully.

Only when we are outside does the noise level return to normal, people's whispers raised to their usual volume, their voices carrying over the warm air.

'How's your Mum? Still not well?'

'Yes, John's still working over at the big supermarket. Been there for over ten years now.'

'Lovely session, don't you think? Went really well.'

'My arthritis is getting worse by the week. Don't know how I managed to make it here today.'

The voices around me are no more than white noise as I scan the crowd for signs of him. He's disappeared. No hanging around for idle chat; Peter has vanished from the throng, heading away from the crowd before anybody has a chance to engage him in conversation. I admire him, being unwilling to become embroiled in the pointless, boring minutiae of other people's lives. The rest of us are all too polite to say no, to tell people that we have better things to do with our time than to stand and listen to their endless litany of ailments or be subjected to the mindless repetition of banal news about their lives; news that is insignificant and trivial to us and important only to them. We all have our damaged existences that we strive to conceal. Peter has his and I have mine.

I wonder if he has noticed me watching him from afar? I don't suppose he has. Why would he? He doesn't know me. Or at least, I don't think he does. I'm just another face in the crowd, another member of the group who is mourning the loss of somebody close to them. I know him, though. I definitely know him. We have a lot in common. It's just that he doesn't know it yet. For the past year, I've been wandering aimlessly through life, rudderless and confused, with nobody and nothing to assist me, to tell me that everything is going to be just fine. Nobody to stop me from collapsing in a heap. Until I realised that Peter attended the grieving sessions in church, that is. It gave me a purpose, knowing I could get close to him. It was a chance, possibly my only chance. Hope flourished within me. I had something to aim for, something tangible I could cling onto. Something that could turn my life around, make it worth living again.

Every week at the group sessions, I watch him: scrutinising his speech, his movements, every little thing about him. I need to know it all, to work him out, assess him. Become his judge and jury. Unlike me, he is able to speak coherently, to relax, converse with others in the group. Be himself.

I am not a gibbering wreck but choose to remain silent, convinced everyone can see my weaknesses and vulnerabilities, convinced they can see deep inside my soul, into the blackness that festers there, the simmering resentment at being left to cope on my own in this scary and often harsh and unforgiving world. Of course, we are all weak and vulnerable. That's why we're here. Peter stands out from the others. He's stronger, capable. It makes me wonder why he's here at all.

Every week as I watch him, I feel as if I am being drawn closer by an invisible strand. Each time I attend, I find myself trying that bit harder with my appearance, wearing more make-up, curling my hair. Not too much. Nothing too garish. It's a therapy group, not a pick-up joint. I don't want to turn up looking as if I am going clubbing. So instead, I wear perfume, brush my hair, do what I can to make myself noticeable and half decent without appearing too brash and brassy. Yet still he turns a blind eye, appearing to show little interest in anybody around him. Especially me.

I've never been particularly drawn to religion, finding churches often oppressive and unwelcoming, but knowing Peter would be there every week was enough to lure me through these doors and so here I am, trailing after him like a small child desperate for attention. And here he is, barely acknowledging my existence. I will keep trying however, and soon he will see me through his fog of misery and grief. Soon enough I will penetrate his armour, his invisible shield and then he will know who I am. I'll make sure of it.

I take a walk through the graveyard behind the church. It's peaceful here, filled with silence save for the whispering of the breeze through the trees and the distant chirrup of the birdsong. I like this place. It's sobering, a space for reflection and serious thought. A space where I can be me.

I kneel on the ground, the soil wet beneath my flesh, and turn to the graveside. I empty the vase of stagnant, foul-smelling water, flecks of dirt spreading next to my feet, and refill it at the tap next to the fence, then pluck out the withered flowers and rearrange the ones that still look half decent and haven't succumbed to age and decay, their stems still straight and not withered and wilting. It is as I am patting down the gravel that I hear his voice above me. It causes me to stop and suck in my breath. My skin prickles as I turn to see him standing next to me, looking down with a wry smile on his face. His eyes are dark and impenetrable, fathoms deep.

'I see you take good care of these people. This is a well-tended grave.'

I sigh and suppress a smile as I stare up at him, scrambling to rise from my haunches and wiping my hands down the side of my trousers. It's Peter. He's here, speaking to me, watching me. Actually acknowledging my presence. At long last. I've put a lot of work into this moment and now here he is. Finally.

'Thank you.' My voice is a low murmur. I want to look away but am afraid of missing something. This moment has been a long time coming. I want to see everything. Every single movement, every blink and twitch, every breath that exits his body. I need to see it all. I've earned this. I can't afford to make any mistakes, to lose this moment.

'We've met before?' He is smiling now, his eyes twinkling, his hand outstretched towards me.

I nod, trying to mask my enthusiasm, returning his smile. 'Yes, we have.' Surprised at how strong his grasp is, how cool and steady it is, I shake his hand. 'At the counselling sessions in church.' He's taller than I remember, a good six feet, perhaps more.

'I thought so. I knew you looked familiar.'

I want to tell him that I've been watching him for weeks and weeks and how has he not noticed me before now but remain silent, nodding instead and removing my clammy palm from his parchment-dry skin.

'I'm not sure how much they're helping, those sessions, but you never know with these things, do you?' My voice is croaky in comparison to his mellifluous timbre and my is vision blurred. I blink away the film covering my eyes and clear my throat. He must think me an idiot, this man. An idiot who is standing awkwardly, gazing up at him like a forlorn schoolgirl in the presence of her latest crush. I pull back my shoulders and try to inject some authority into my stance, flexing my fingers and jutting out my chin. I've waited a long time for this moment. Too long.

'I suppose you don't,' he says, looking away, his shoulders sagging slightly.

I stand, wondering what it is I've said. We were close to making a connection and now he has lost his initial impetus, his voice suddenly reedy and reserved. I need to get it back, that connection. I won't lose it. I can't. Letting it slip away isn't an option.

'I was wondering if you fancy a coffee? I mean,' he says, his eyes darting about the row of gravestones, 'only if you're not too busy. Or we can do it another time...' His voice trails off, his words swallowed by the fluttering of wings in a nearby tree. Two pigeons flap about on a branch, sending leaves falling to the floor. A grey feather floats through the air before landing at my feet. I bend down and pick it up, staring at it closely.

'Isn't that supposed to mean somebody who has passed away is thinking of you or is close by?' He lowers his eyes, his gazed fixed on the feather clutched between my fingers.

'An angel, apparently. From what I've heard, anyway. It means a guardian angel is watching over you.' Even as I say it, it sounds frivolous and foolish. I close my fingers over the small, silky object and throw it onto the ground, a small amount of embarrassment taking hold in me, my face flushing hot. 'An old wives' tale. Simple, silly nonsense,' I murmur as the crumpled feather blows away and is carried down the path and out of view by the warm, spring breeze.

'So,' I say, catching his eye again, 'how about that coffee?'

* * *

He works as a chief sales engineer for a national company, has a daughter called Lauren and is missing his wife terribly. He tells me this as we sit by the window in a small café on Roland Street and nibble at our complimentary biscuits. But of course, I already know all of these things; it's just that he doesn't know that I know.

I remain silent, my lips sealed, giving nothing away. I wonder if he sees the real me? There is no sign that he has noticed. That's good. It's exactly how I want it: to be elusive. Alluring. Secretive. I am the consummate liar. The woman he thinks he knows. Not the woman I really am.

'I'm so sorry,' he says, placing his cup down with a thud. 'I've not given you a chance to tell me about yourself. I've prattled on and on like a selfish arse.'

'It's fine, honestly,' I say softly. 'I don't lead such an interesting life anyway. Very little to report. No parents, no children, no partner. Just little old me.' I shift my gaze to the window, staring outside to the azure, cloudless sky. It's warm for springtime. Maybe we are in for a hot summer.

He sighs and folds his arms over his chest. 'There must be something you can tell me about yourself.' He pulls his chair closer and cocks his head to one side, grinning at me. 'Come on, I'm listening now. I promise not to interrupt.'

He looks insistent. Determined. So I relent and speak. I tell him how much I'm enjoying the sessions at church. I don't tell him that he's the reason I find them so appealing. I don't tell him he is the reason I attend. Instead, I tell him that I rarely venture out and that I enjoy reading, finding solace and comfort in my books, and that I like listening to music. I'm lying. I find books monotonous and music irritating, no more than white noise in the background, but felt the need to say something in return, something that will tell him nothing about me, about who I actually am.

'What was your partner's name?' He shifts in his seat, moving closer to me. I can feel the heat from his body, am able to smell the strong, slightly stale nicotine odour of coffee on his breath.

'Stuart,' I reply, swallowing down a swig of my latte.

He nods, smiles. A genuine, compassionate expression, not a thin-lipped grimace. I like that. No barriers. No concealed emotions. Makes it easier for me to get close to him. To get my own way.

'I think I recall you talking about him at the sessions,' he says casually. 'How did he die?' Peter shakes his head and lets out a long stream of air from between his pursed lips. 'Bit crass of me to say that. Sorry. I guess being so close to death has made me a tad insensitive.'

I suppress my sigh, keeping it trapped within my chest. He doesn't look or sound particularly sorry. 'Car crash,' I whisper, my hands clasped together on my lap. 'Stuart died in a car crash last year.'

He nods, turning away from me, scrutinising the clock on the wall. 'Sophia was murdered,' he says, his tone now dark, menacing even. The air around us thickens. I swallow and think of something to say. Anything to shatter the murkiness that has settled on us. I want to keep things light – need to if I am to succeed with this pursuit of Peter. I suppress a smile at my alliterative phrase. It has a nice ring to it.

'You must have loved her very much.' I resist reaching over and placing my hand over his. Too familiar. Too soon. It's all about timing.

'She was on her way home from an evening out with colleagues.' He lets out a small laugh, his voice bitter and cutting. 'A jogger found her body the following morning. I woke up to find her missing.'

His eyes are glassy, filled with unshed tears. I'll bet Peter isn't one for crying, bottling it all up instead, all those festering emotions bubbling within his gut. He stops, his Adam's apple bobbing up and down as he clears his throat and wearily runs his fingers through his hair.

'I'm really sorry to hear that.'

We sit in silence for a few seconds until he speaks again, his eyes once more full of their usual sparkle, his body straightening and springing back to life. 'Anyway, sorry for being morose and dragging you down. It's all in the past, isn't it?'

'We have a lot in common, you and I, it would appear.' I try to laugh, to inject some levity into the situation. 'Not what you'd call the easiest of topics, is it – death? Especially if it's the very thing that draws us together but we both know how it feels to lose somebody, don't we? To have that void in our lives that needs filling.'

Peter nods and gives me a bright smile. I feel easy in his company, as if we have known each other for the longest time. This is good. This is exactly how I want it to be – lacking in any kind of tension or awkwardness.

'Thanks for the coffee,' I murmur, my heart starting up as I wait for his response to my words, hoping this isn't it. I've waited a long time for this man to notice me. Please don't let this be the end of us before we have even begun.

3
LAUREN

The days are long without her. I do kind of miss her. I know Dad does too. We wander around this house, rattling around in it like a couple of strangers, barely noticing one another. I don't know how it's meant to be after somebody dies, but I didn't expect it to feel like this. There are self-help books for people who've just had a baby, or people who need some sort of stimulus to exist, the sort of people who need help to get their life in order by using those silly motivational phrases and relaxation techniques, but I've yet to see any guide books on how to get through the day after a family member dies. So we just get up every morning and go about our daily business, heads down, tongues too tied to speak to one another.

It's sad, really. We used to be so close, Dad and me, but now things feel so difficult. I want to open up to him, hear him talk freely about Mum, about anything really, but no matter how hard we try, the words just won't come. He's afraid of speaking to me, that's what it is. Afraid of what might come spilling out of his mouth, and I can't talk to him because I don't know what it is he wants to hear, what he wants me to say that will make everything better for us.

I don't cry about Mum dying. I can't. I won't. Dad does on occasion. I hear him sometimes when he thinks I'm asleep. It's a soft sobbing, not a howl or a self-pitying wail. Just a gentle sound that tells me he's still grieving.

Sometimes, Grandma calls over, but truthfully, she causes more problems than she solves. Her remit seems to be cleaning things that don't need cleaning and moving things around so we can't find them the following day. Last week, she called over while we were both out and cleaned and moved all the crockery around into different cupboards.

'Easier for you to find it,' she had said later, on the phone. 'You had all your plates mixed up with your cups and saucers. I've separated them all into colours and sizes. And by the way,' she added as an aside, 'pyjamas and dressing gowns need washing as well, you know. Not just left hanging on the backs of doors for weeks and months at a time.'

She's actually really lovely and we know that this is her way of trying to help us out but sometimes, it drives me insane. I shouldn't complain. Dad isn't the tidiest of people and it saves me having to continually pick up after him. I like cleanliness and order, strange I know for a seventeen-year-old, but that's just how I am, a hygiene freak, whereas Dad can wreck a room just by looking at it. Still, we've always rubbed along together nicely without any real arguments worth speaking of. Maybe opposites do attract after all.

Dad going to church is a new thing and I'm not sure how I feel about it. He always claimed he was an atheist so this U-turn in his thinking is a bit a shock and not something I could ever have predicted. It's a massive shock, actually. Many men in his position would turn to drink, spending their days propping up the bar in the local pub, or go out running, or smash a ball around a squash court to vent their anger and grief, but Dad appears to have turned to God instead. It makes me uneasy and I've tried asking him about it but he just waves me away with a half-hearted smile.

'It's just somewhere to go where nobody bothers me,' he said the last time I tried to probe him.

He's busy at work, I get that. He works for a cut-throat company in their sales department selling engineering parts and from what I can gather, they are an organisation who show no interest in grieving employees and their difficult personal home lives. It's a hectic occupation and during the day, he has hardly any time or energy to think about our circumstances so I imagine some downtime and solace is much needed and perhaps the church provides him with just that. I'm not denying him it; I'm just concerned that somebody will attach themselves to him, some overzealous religious person who wants to indoctrinate him, twist his mind round to their way of thinking. If I'm being truthful, I'm afraid he'll become so besotted by the church that he'll forget all about me. Does that sound selfish? It probably does but Dad and I only have each other. We can't afford to drift apart.

Mum was a Catholic but a lapsed one. She came from an Italian family so it was a given that she would carry on the faith, but she didn't. Her parents still live in Italy and have weird little religious artefacts all over their house. Mum would laugh when they sent photographs, saying that they'd added to their collection again and that they had more crucifixes than the Vatican.

It must be tricky for them though, being so far away, but Dad has said that their faith has helped them through. He's probably right. Maybe that's what drew him to the church. Or maybe it was something else that he doesn't want to talk about. Something that he wants to keep secret. Maybe one day, he'll talk to me about it, or maybe he won't. Maybe we'll continue wandering around this house in a fog of secrecy and confusion, the subject of Mum's murder a massive, unscalable wall between us. It's probably better that way because for all everyone thinks their marriage was a terrific one, solid and impenetrable, there were things that people didn't see, acts of injustice that set them apart. I love my dad, I really do, but a part of me thinks that this church attendance for the grief counselling is just a ruse, a way of concealing what he really thought before Mum was murdered.

I'm no mind reader or fortune teller, I'm just a young girl for God's sake, but I'm not thick and I do know this – had Mum not died, my parents would probably now be living apart, their marriage too fragmented to ever be put back together. I once read that it's easier to move on with your life after a death than it is after a divorce. Perhaps Mum dying has been easier for us to handle than having her live apart from us. Apart and with somebody else who isn't my dad.

4
ALICE

A warm glow settles inside me as we part. I stand and watch Peter as he leaves the café, heads off down the street and disappears amongst the crowds. It took him a while to ask to see me again but we got there in the end. I nudged and hinted, gently pushed him into a corner until he relented and we agreed to meet next week after the session at church. Same time, same place. This café is hardly the height of sophistication and elegance with its vinyl seats and Formica tables, but it's a start.

Behind me, the coffee machine whirrs and sizzles, chairs scrape across the tiled floor, people chatter. A myriad of everyday noises that help soothe me. For all I have waited for this moment, for Peter to finally notice me, now it has happened, I am both nervous and excited in equal measure, my stomach clenching and unclenching, my skin rippling with delight and dread. I take a deep breath to steady myself, repeating over and over that this is my chance to start again, to claw back some of my life. The life I had before it was cruelly and thoughtlessly torn apart. I think back to the devastation, to the unending heartache that was almost the undoing of me. I bite at my lip, knowing that I deserve some semblance of normality as much as the next person. I deserve to be happy. And I was for a while. I had Tom, and then I didn't. Now there's just me. And Peter. A dart of something resembling happiness bolts through me. Not yet, though. I don't want to push things too quickly or too far.

I stand, feeling as if the watching world can read my thoughts, and leave the café, enjoying the breeze outside as it passes over me, caressing my hot skin. Crowds bustle past, the street remarkably busy for a Sunday morning. I suppose most places open on a Sunday now. No difference between a religious day and any other day of the week. Life has changed – the pace faster, people busier. Too busy to notice the likes of me. I prefer that. I like the anonymity that busyness brings. My life is my life and nobody else's. Heartache, loss and death have taught me how to be private, how to lose myself in a crowd of one.

People pass by me as I make my way home, their eyes glued to their phones. They weave through the crowds, deftly and rapidly, never looking up, never noticing me. I am a ghost in their presence, a wandering soul, searching for the things I lost. Constantly scanning and scratching around for the things that have been taken from me.

The house is cool as I let myself in. The blinds remain closed, everything a wash of light grey. I prefer it this way. It helps clear my head, allows me to breathe properly, the air clean and pure, not sullied by sunlight and warmth. Just me and my thoughts. Me and my loneliness.

I stare at the bare walls, at the plain furniture and wonder where it all went wrong. I am living a half-life, a watered-down version of myself. But not for much longer. Things are ripe for change. No more diluting my existence. I can start again, focus on Peter, focus on me. Become once again, the person I used to be.

The walls are cool as I trail my fingers over them, thinking about the past and how it almost robbed me of my future. Being on my own has been miserable. I've survived but it hasn't been easy. I used to have a family, a life, until things turned sour that is, like curdled milk: the scent of it never leaving me, a foul stench trailing in its wake. The unshakeable odour of death and loneliness. Of grief and anger.

And then there's this house. So many memories, a combination of good and bad, delightful and dire. I should have moved, done the right thing. Learned to start again. But I didn't. I'm still here and he is everywhere. Everywhere and nowhere. The bricks and mortar, and furniture holding onto his memory, his soul embedded in them. And yet I'm still very much alone. For now.

My job is menial and mind numbing, but it pays the bills – bills that were automatically taken care of by my husband when he was here. I'm now employed as a nanny for a wealthy couple. It sounds easy but being a nanny for people who have high expectations for their children is exhausting. As well as caring for their children, I'm also left lists of tasks to do such as doing the laundry and tidying the children's bedrooms. My employers rarely speak to me, leaving instead notes for me on the sideboard, directing me to the required tasks. Only once did the lady of the house stop to talk to me, commenting on my hair, something that made me flinch.

'Is that your natural colour, Alice?' she had said in her usual dispassionate way. 'I think a darker shade would look better on you. That blonde looks too forced and doesn't sit well against your pale skin.'

I had bristled at her words, my hackles rising in defence. It is both rude and insulting to say such things to people. I don't suppose she thinks of me as a person, certainly not a real one, the type that she socialises with. I'm the paid help, somebody who happens to occupy the same space as her, somebody who takes care of her children because she, it appears, cannot be bothered to do it herself. They're easy enough to handle, the youngsters, and she certainly has lots of time on her hands but seems incapable of or, rather, unwilling to spend time with them, preferring for me to take charge and interact with her offspring. But then, she pays my wages so I suppose I shouldn't complain. Without that income, I don't know where I would be. It's the chores that get to me, chores that I didn't expect to have to do when I signed the contract. They are demeaning. Insulting. However, the money she pays me allows me to have a roof over my head and a steady income and I suppose that's what matters. I no longer have my husband of course, but that is something I have had to learn to live with. Jack and Elizabeth Downey giving me heaps of housework to do pales into insignificance compared to what I have endured in the past year.

I think of Tom, the only relationship I have had in the past year until meeting Peter, and my stomach shrivels. Batting those thoughts away, I slump down, the chair sighing under my weight as I settle into it and curl my feet up under my backside, my back arched against the softness of the cushion. Today has been a successful day. Peter spoke to me. We have a future date, albeit in a coffee shop that serves stale biscuits on chipped plates, but a date is a date and I should be thankful for that small fact. The future starts here. I just hope it's everything I ever hoped it would be: a chance to restore some balance in my life.

Despite it being mid-morning, I am overcome with a bout of weariness that digs into my bones. Being sociable is exhausting. Keeping up the pretence is draining. I've never been much of an actress. I have had to practise and hone my skills to get thus far.

I close my eyes and sleep carries me away to another world where my husband is still here and our relationship isn't unspooling and coming apart at the seams, our marriage, our family disintegrating before my eyes while I stand by and watch helplessly, unable or perhaps unwilling, to try to save it.

5
PETER

He can't explain it, the lure of the sessions in church. They were recommended by a well-meaning colleague who knew little of Peter's life except that he had lost his wife in the most tragic way imaginable. And so, at a loose end one weekend, he went along, sceptical, fully expecting to leave the place feeling far worse than when he entered. But he was surprised to find that talking and listening to others about their personal experiences and grieving processes actually helped. He had spent that last year full of anger, convinced a greater power somewhere was punishing him, wreaking havoc with his life. The sessions have helped him quash those thoughts, helped him calm his nerves and extinguish the fire that has raged deep in his belly for the past twelve months.

Making friends at the sessions was never his intention but it appears he has bonded with Alice, who lost her partner at around the same time he lost Sophia. He decided to escape the crowds that had gathered outside the entrance by taking a wander around the graveyard behind the church, and bumped into her. She's attractive enough. He never noticed it before and thinks that perhaps he has been blind to everybody and everything in the past twelve months, grief and guilt smothering him, obliterating everything. Meeting somebody there had never been his intention but they chatted, had coffee and have death of a close one as a common bond. Hardly your average, run-of-the-mill shared interest but it is what it is. Something about her drew him in and as a result, they are meeting for coffee again next week. She's a friend. That's all she is. Just a friend.

Lauren is upstairs when he arrives home. They need to speak. Not about anything in particular. They just need to speak more often, to dig themselves out of the rut they have become entrenched in. It's not healthy living like this and it's especially not good for Lauren. She's a young girl. Actually, she is no longer a girl and is rapidly turning into a young woman. At seventeen years of age, she has more nous, common sense and integrity than he could ever hope to have. Considering her age and situation, he thinks she is pretty damn amazing.

'Dad?' She leans over the banister, her hair hanging loosely around her face in chunky ringlets.

'Yeah, it's me,' he says, trying and failing to inject some joviality into his voice. Sometimes, even greeting people is an uphill struggle. But this is Lauren, his daughter and none of this is her fault. None of it. She deserves better. 'Listen, honey. How about we go out somewhere for lunch for a change?' The words are out of his mouth before he can stop them. He doesn't regret it. Sometimes, it's better to let things take their own course, not put too much effort into forethought and planning. It clouds things.

There is a brief hiatus, a second or two that feels much longer than that before she replies, her voice almost a squeak. 'That sounds great! Where were you thinking of going? Have you booked anywhere?'

She's right. It's Sunday. Most places will be full to bursting. Being spontaneous does have its downfalls. This is the first time he has ever suggested such a thing and now he runs the possibility of letting her down. Again. That happened a lot when Sophia was alive. He swallows down those thoughts, blots them all out. A fresh start, that's what they need. And if not now, then when?

'Just a minute. Let me have a look.' He scrolls through his phone, checking all the local restaurants and pubs, checking reservations and stops at the one that has a table available. The Half Moon Inn. Sophia's favourite. His heart hammers out a small beat in his chest. He clamps his jaw together, telling himself to stop it. Lauren needs to get out of the house for a while. They both do. They need to talk, be normal again. Be a proper father and daughter. A father without a wife, a daughter without a mother. He punches in the number, speaks to the person on the other end, and reserves a table for 1 p.m.

'Right,' Lauren says, her voice lighter than he has heard for many months when he tells her that they're good to go. 'I just need to get showered and changed. I'll be twenty minutes.' She pounds her way around her room right above him. He smiles, unfamiliar feelings of normality slowly returning. The sounds above his head take him back to a time when things seemed brighter, a time when Sophia was still alive.

He checks his watch and glances in the mirror. It feels like such a long time since he took any interest in his appearance. There seemed little point but now is the right time to do something about it. If Lauren can make an effort, then so should he. He stands there, his own reflection staring back at him, his features coming sharply into focus. He sees things there that make him ashamed, things nobody else can see. He blinks and looks away.

Twenty minutes later, they're both showered and dressed and standing at the front door, ready to go.

'Dad. You look...' She steps around him, eyeing him up and down as if he is a lab rat about to undergo some sort of experiment. 'You look great. I mean, really healthy.'

'For a change, eh?' He gives her a wink and she smiles. His stomach flips. She resembles her mother so much. He realises then that that is one of the reasons why he's been avoiding her, keeping his eyes lowered every time she passes him in the hallway, or getting up and heading into the kitchen whenever she enters the living room. Guilt travels through him, swirling in his gut like acid. He hasn't been a terrible dad but he hasn't been a good one either. Lauren is still young. He is a grown man. They need each other. It isn't her fault she bears such a striking resemblance to the woman who used to be his wife. The woman who made him feel complete and yet utterly empty at the same time. He thinks back to the arguments, the suspicions. The furtive glances she gave to her phone when she thought he wasn't looking.

'Right,' he says, grabbing his keys from the console table that has been there since they moved into this place over twenty years ago. 'Your carriage awaits, young lady. And my stomach is empty. Let's go.'

6

LAUREN

'I went for coffee with somebody today.'

I feel as if I'm falling, the floor coming away beneath me. Dad had coffee with somebody? 'Oh my God! Really?' My voice is croaky, gravel filling my throat. I sound like one of those lads at college whose voice is in the process of breaking: half man, half boy. 'Who? And where?' I'm in shock. Dad going out for a coffee with somebody is a good thing. It's just unexpected, that's all. And well overdue. That much I do know. It's been a long and lonely year.

'Just a friend from the church.' He fiddles with the menu, straightening it, rearranging the condiments, twirling his fingers around the rim of his glass.

It's a female, I just know it. It has to be. He can't bring himself to look at me. 'A friend, eh?' I smile, picturing a tweed-wearing librarian type or a middle-aged woman in Victorian-style, lace-up boots and a high-necked, frilly blouse, wearing a stern expression and clutching a bible in one hand and her pearls in another, permanent outrage etched into her expression.

'Yes,' he says with a knowing grin, 'a friend.'

'So, is this friend a man?' I glance down at the menu then back at Dad, who is now watching me intently, 'or a woman?'

His voice is soft when he replies. Gone is the desperate, hard-edged tone that he has used since Mum's death. This is something gentler, more appealing than the brusque growl that has been his way for the past twelve months.

'A woman. And before you say anything, she is just a friend.' His hand is outstretched, his palm in front of his chest. 'I met her at church and she also lost her partner at the same time as...'

Even now, he can't bring himself to speak about it, to broach the subject of Mum's death. I wish he would. I really do. I want him to mention her and just get it over with. It feels as if we can never move on from this point until he accepts what happened. I mean, what the hell does he talk about at those grief sessions anyway? If he can talk about it there, why can't he talk about it to me, his daughter, his only child? Mum is dead and we need to accept that fact. *He* needs to accept it. We have our lives to live. Does that make me sound cold and unfeeling? Perhaps it does, but life when Mum was alive was far from perfect. This is our chance to start again.

A familiar itching takes hold on my skin, flames burning just beneath the surface. 'At the same time that Mum died. Is that what you were going to say?' There, I've said it, got it out in the open.

He nods, his mouth a thin line. I feel guilty for being so blunt with him but one of us had to say something. I'm sick of tip-toeing around the subject. I reach over and take hold of his hand. It feels big and hot against my own skin, his fingers long and slender. 'Look, Dad. I think it's great that you went out for coffee. It's time for us to start living our lives again. In fact, I think you should take lots of people out for coffee. Hundreds, even. And I hope they're all glamour pusses who wear short skirts and boob tubes, not some doddery old frump that wears long, grey dresses and has their glasses perched on the end of their noses like some judgemental old bint.'

He laughs and looks away. I swallow and clear my throat. Saying all of that about him dating some other woman was never going to be easy, none of this was, but it had to be said. And now the words are out there, now we've broken through that invisible barrier, we can start living again. Not before time.

'Now then, Peter, good to see you here. Are you ready to order yet?' Norah, the middle-aged waitress who has worked here for as long as I can remember, is standing by our table, her smile warm. She is genuinely pleased to see us and that helps me to relax. In her hands, she holds a notepad and a pencil. She looks at us both, her eyes flicking back and forth as if she is watching a particularly frenetic game of tennis.

'Norah, it's lovely to see you too. Tell you what, I think I'll have the chicken. What about you, sweetheart? You know what's safe and what isn't by now, don't you?'

I look at the menu, searching for the things that I know are nut-free, thinking how much I would love a vodka and lime but knowing also that Dad wouldn't approve and also knowing that they wouldn't serve me. 'I'll have the same, thank you.'

Norah smiles and nods, giving us both a sly wink. She continues to stand beside me, her smile now a rictus grin. 'Any more drinks?'

'Not for me,' I say through gritted teeth, thinking of the night I spent in this place trying to get served and being refused because they knew I was underage, Norah continually shaking her head and smiling at me while I pleaded with her like a desperate schoolkid, which is what I actually was. How embarrassing. And I'm still underage. The humiliation is never-ending. Roll on my eighteenth birthday.

'I'll have another lemonade, please.'

She eventually leaves, shuffling away to the other side of the restaurant. I let out a sigh and take a swig of my drink, hoping we can now start being more open with one another.

'Sophia loved this place.' Dad is looking around wistfully, an expression almost resembling happiness in his eyes, making it harder for me say what it is I want to say. 'I asked her to marry me in here.'

I know this story. I've been told it a thousand times or more. Years before Mum died when he would tell this tale, I used to roll my eyes at him and tell him to shut up and that it was a boring story and that his banter was boring as shit. My face burns at the memory. I like to think I've grown up since then, developed a more sensitive side to my nature.

When she was alive, they always would come here, him and Mum, for their wedding anniversary meal. Actually, I'm surprised he managed to make it here at all without getting maudlin and upset. His rose-tinted memories are making it harder for me to speak openly about Mum, about what I knew of her life.

There were things I discovered about her shortly before she died. Things that Dad should really know. Maybe he already does. She wasn't the saint everybody thought she was. They didn't know her that well. Not really. I did and I'm sure that deep down, Dad did too, it's just that death has blinded him to who she really was. He's obviously blinkered to it all but I'm not. Perhaps I'm a little less forgiving, or perhaps me being younger allows me the privilege of being able to see things without the hindrance of those rose-coloured glasses that have given her saint-like qualities. Whatever the reason, there is one thing I do know and it is this: Sophia Saunders had secrets. She may have brought me up and cared for me but sometimes, I lie in bed at night wondering if I ever really knew her at all.

* * *

'I don't want to talk about this right now, Lauren.' Dad's hands grip the steering wheel. I bite at my lip. I should have expected this really, this reaction. She was his wife. People do take on saint-like qualities after they die. I get that. I mean nobody wants to speak ill of the dead, do they? Not unless it's some mad dictator like Hitler. I'm not really sure why I said anything. I should have stayed silent, kept my words to myself. My timing is all wrong. Stupid. Sometimes, I'm such an idiot.

I lean back against the headrest, a hollow feeling in the pit of my stomach despite being a pig and having eaten a full plate of chicken, roast potatoes and gravy. I try not to think about it any more. I should just let it be. Mum is gone and we're now on the path to having a life again but those words are out there now. There's no taking them back. I've got to speak my mind, to clear the air and untangle the knotted thoughts that clutter up my head.

'Dad, she wasn't who you thought she was, that's all I'm saying.' There, I've said it again. I can't seem to help myself.

He drives on in silence, his face set like stone. I don't even know why I'm saying this, why I've cornered him into having this conversation. It's just that sometimes, I become furious at him for being so committed to her memory and refusing to allow anybody else into his life. But maybe now that's all going to end with this new friendship he has forged. Maybe now we can allow somebody else into our life and move on from Mum's murder. We've been on repeat for too long and I think it's time to change that pattern.

I decide to leave things alone, to let him get on with his life while I get on with mine and hope that at some point, our paths will cross and we can become a proper family again. A family without Sophia's memory infiltrating every corner of our lives.

7
ALICE

'No, you can't have any more snacks. Your parents will be home soon and they're taking you out for dinner.'

I suppress an eye roll as Fionn slinks off into the playroom. If it was my decision, they would both be allowed the occasional piece of fruit or a yoghurt or even a bag of crisps but their parents strictly forbid it and as much as it pains me to do it, I have to stick to their rules. They're children for God's sake, not robots. I sometimes think that Jack and Elizabeth think less of their children than they do of me, and that takes some doing.

I'm pretty low on their agenda. Their children aren't much farther down the ladder than me. We are all practically scraping our bellies on the ground.

I continue folding the laundry, heat billowing off the linen. Perspiration stands out on my face. I rub my hand across my forehead and let out a long, frustrated sigh. It's too warm for such chores. Were it not for the fact that Jack and Elizabeth are due back, I would take the children out to the park, let them run and play; let them have some fun and just allow them to be free of the constraints placed upon them by their overbearing parents. They are bored here in the house and forbidden from playing in the garden. No ball games. No trampolines. No paddling pools. Nothing that suggests children actually live here. Too many precious plants and flowers out there that could be ruined. Gardens are meant to be played in, but not in this household apparently. Poor Fionn and Yasmin. And poor, poor me.

It's another hour before Jack and Elizabeth arrive home, sailing through the door looking cool and composed. Sweat blooms under my armpits as I finish cleaning the windows in the children's bedrooms. I empty the soapy water down the sink and rinse out the bucket, watching as the soap suds swirl and glug before disappearing down the drain.

'Where are the children?' Elizabeth rarely greets me, instead barking out commands and questions about Fionn and Yasmin and asking if my jobs have been completed in her absence.

'In the playroom. I think they're bored.' I can't help myself. I shouldn't speak to my employer in such a brash, undiluted tone but something about this woman doesn't sit well with me and today, I am all out of patience.

I expect a dressing down for my arrogance and lack of respect but receive just a dark look as she brushes past me to see her offspring. Jack hangs up his coat and heads upstairs, his eyes averted away from me. I often wonder if he even notices that I'm here.

On impulse, I walk over to where he has hung up his coat and slip my hand into the inside pocket. I have no idea why I am doing such a thing. I guess I am tired and pissed off and want to see if he is as perfect as he appears. Getting hold of any of Elizabeth's personal effects is too difficult but this man is a little less anal with his belongings. Their bedroom door is always locked, as is the study. This only makes me more curious. It makes me wonder what it is they're hiding.

Inside his pocket is a receipt. I lift it out and glance at it, my stomach coiling and churning when I see the figures listed there. Over £300 for a meal. I shouldn't be shocked, knowing how these people live their lives, but it still roots me to the spot. It's for a restaurant in town – Maison. I know of it but have never been inside. It's not for the likes of me. Far too expensive. Far too exclusive. Perhaps this is where they've been all this time, wining and dining in the most opulent restaurant in town while I carried out their menial chores – washing and ironing their clothes, scrubbing the kitchen floor and cleaning their windows. How the other half live. A furnace strikes up inside of me, a spark of envy at how easy, how luxurious and comfortable their lives are compared to my miserable existence.

When Phillip was around, we could have afforded such luxuries. Not that he was ever interested in visiting those types of places, but still, the disparity in our circumstances since losing him sticks in my craw. And when I say he wasn't interested in visiting those places, what I mean is, he wasn't interested in visiting them with me. But that's a different matter. A story for another time.

'Alice, why don't you take the rest of the day off?'

Jack's voice causes me to jump. I crumple up the receipt and stuff it in my pocket. He won't miss it. It's not as if they need a piece of paper to keep check of where their money goes. What's £300 to these people? It's small change to them. Chicken feed. To me, it's a week's wages. I can put the receipt back tomorrow.

'Are you sure?' I spin around, my face flushed, my chest, my torso, hot and clammy.

Jack is still upstairs, his head peeking over the banister. 'Yes, absolutely. We can manage here just fine. We're going to spend some quality time with the children.'

I cringe at his use of that phrase. *Quality time*. What does that even mean? It's a trite expression trotted out to assuage people's guilt for ignoring their progenies. I find myself wondering what their idea of quality time is, doubting that it involves anything remotely interesting or child-orientated. They neither know nor understand their own children.

'Okay, well I'll see you tomorrow then.' I am out of the house before he has time to change his mind, the receipt a deadweight in my pocket. I have no idea why I took it. Jealousy, perhaps. Or maybe it was just because I can. These people are so frivolous with their spending, their lives, their children. They will hardly notice a missing receipt for a horribly expensive meal. They hardly notice me wandering around their house every single day so a little bit of missing paperwork isn't likely to trouble them.

I walk by Jack's car which is parked out the front of the house and am tempted to gouge it as I pass, to dig at its sleek, black paintwork with a sharp implement. Their spending and ostentatiousness are a slap in the face to people like me. People who will always have to be thankful for the meagre scraps that life throws their way.

And then I think of Peter and my heart skips a little. Attending those sessions was worth it. They may not have helped me with my emotions in any conventional sense, but they have put me one step closer to Peter and that's got to be a good thing, hasn't it?

The sun burns my neck as I leave the leafy suburbs and head home to my humble abode closer to the centre of town. I put all thoughts of my absent other half to the back of my mind. He's gone now and although life is a damn sight harder without him around, if I'm being honest, it's also a relief. No more arguments, no more worrying. No more name calling and accusatory remarks. And yet I hate this life he has left me with. I resent him leaving me to cope on my own. I hate the bitter memories that swill around my brain. I hate all of it and yet I don't hate him. I miss him so much, it's like a physical ache that cuts me in two. Would I have him back? Absolutely not. I miss the idea of him and also without wanting to sound too mercenary, I miss the money. He had a good job. We never had to worry about our finances. All I ever worried about was his movements, keeping track of where he was and more importantly, who he was with. That was nearly the undoing of me.

Bitterness at the hand life has dealt me swells in the pit of my stomach. Some would say I deserve everything I've got. I would tell those people to shut their mouths and leave me alone.

I think of Peter and wonder how much longer it will take him to get over the death of his wife? Months? Years? I'm hoping it's the former. I'm hoping he sees beyond his grief and allows me into his life. I've worked hard to get to know him. I pray he doesn't turn me away and leave me out in the cold. I don't think I could handle another blow. I need this opportunity. I need to get even.

8
PETER

Lauren is right. Of course she is. He's in denial. It's a form of self-preservation. He's protecting himself. Covering his tracks with his behaviour, his acts of total dedication towards his wife as a type of deceit. He knew what was going on before Sophia died. Who she was with. Both he and Lauren know it. It sits between them, a huge, opaque obstacle, stopping them from getting on with their lives. At some point, they will have to climb over it. He just didn't expect it to be now.

He turns the corner, the car violently leaning to one side. Placing his foot on the brake, he glances at Lauren before turning his attention back to the road. 'Why don't you have some friends over sometime?'

'Friends?'

He can feel her eyes boring into him as he leaves go of the steering wheel and changes gear, slowing down as they approach the traffic lights just outside of town. 'Yes. Friends,' he replies lightly. 'You know, those people that you spend time with who aren't related to you.'

She laughs and he is relieved she has understood his stab at humour. Humour that has been absent from their lives for so long now, it feels alien to him.

'Okay. When?'

'Anytime you like. I just think it's time for us to start living again. You especially. You're young. You need to get out and meet people. I've got my church sessions but it occurred to me that you're stuck at home on your own.' He smiles, hoping he hasn't overstepped the mark and inadvertently insulted her. That isn't his intention at all. They are both treading water here. It's time to build up their strength and confidence and get back in the deep end.

'Are you going to continue going to church, Dad?'

Peter can see her concerned expression in his peripheral vision. She thinks he's had some sort of epiphany and has had a complete about-turn in his thinking. He hasn't. It's just that he doesn't want to reveal to her the real reason why he attends. Initially a recommendation, it's now something he is compelled to do for reasons he cannot or will not explain. Even to himself. That's the hardest part – coming to terms with it, having to listen to that small, still voice in his head that tells him daily how he needs to attend to assuage his guilt. Maybe he should start believing. If only he could. It might just silence that voice.

'Maybe. Maybe not. This isn't about me. It's you I'm worried about. I'd like to see you getting out and about, meeting people. Having fun.'

Having fun. What a phrase. Easy, light. Relaxed. It feels like an age since they have had any fun in their tiny little family. There is a great big hole where their smiles and laughter used to be. Lauren deserves to have fun and so much more. She deserves the happiness and closure that he himself is searching for.

'There's a party at Lacey's next weekend. I wasn't going to go but maybe...'

'Please go, sweetheart.' He sounds desperate. He doesn't mean to. It's just that he doesn't want his girl to become lonely and isolated. No more sitting in her room texting. No more brooding and solitude. He thinks Sophia would agree that it's time they both started living again. She certainly did plenty of it before she died. Now it's their turn. Maybe there is a form of life after death after all.

* * *

By the time the weekend arrives, he is worn out. Work is hectic, the travelling up and down the A1 to meetings in Birmingham, an exhausting trudge. One of these days, he will look for another position, one that doesn't involve so many needless journeys. One that is more fulfilling, less gruelling. Travelling from home on the outskirts of York, to Birmingham two, sometimes three times a week is enough for any man. More than enough.

'So, what do you think?' Lauren is standing in front of him, hands on hips, expectancy on her face. She has curled her long, dark hair into thick ringlets and is wearing a pair of jeans and a green, floaty top that matches her eyes. She looks so much like her mother, it pains him. So many memories. So much hurt.

'Sensational.'

'Sensational? Dad, you sound like an ageing rock star. Since when do people say something or somebody looked sensational?' She laughs, her eyes glistening as she points her finger at him, a playful expression on her face. 'You really need to up your game, you know. Get to grips with everyday language and terminology. You're stuck in a time-warp, old man.'

'I don't want to. Quite happy as I am, thank you, being stuck in this time-warp. It's nice in here. Familiar and comforting.'

'It must be. Look at you, all alone in your own special, antiquated little world.' She is laughing even harder and shaking her head at him.

'I'm not alone. There are loads of us here. It's a great place. People are pleasant to one another. They still have manners and use words like sensational.'

'Well,' she says, looking more relaxed and happier than he has seen her in a long while, 'you're welcome to it. Would somebody as quaint and polite as you fancy giving me a lift to the party?'

* * *

The place is bouncing as they pull up outside. A sliver of anticipation pushes through him, darting through his veins, nestling under his skin. 'Be careful, yes?'

She rolls her eyes. This is something she used to do a lot, something that irked him but he managed to ignore. This time, he doesn't dismiss it. He thinks of drugs and alcohol and young men and their capabilities. He thinks of the food.

'Have you got your—'

She opens her bag and inside is her EpiPen, lying at the bottom amongst the detritus – bits of old tissues, lipsticks, discarded tampon wrappers, something else he has had to learn to deal with as a single dad. Every day brought a new challenge. He had no idea how much Sophia did for them both until she was no longer around to do it. And then he recalls the other side of his wife: her furtive ways, her indiscretions. He shuts his eyes, opens them again and turns to face Lauren.

'Please tell me it hasn't expired?'

She looks at him from under her lashes, dark and silky, just like Sophia's. Jesus Christ, she is everywhere. Everywhere and nowhere. Will this ever end?

'Dad, it hasn't expired. Now you will stop worrying. Go home and pour yourself a glass of wine?'

'I can pick you up later if you like?'

She sighs and leans over to give him a kiss. 'I've got friends in there. We'll get a taxi together.'

'Right,' he replies dolefully. 'Make sure you're not the last one in the cab.'

She lands a punch on his arm and widens her eyes. 'Stop it! Go home old man and get drunk. Watch a film on TV. Ring a chatline. Anything! Now begone before I slap you again.'

She steps out of the car, blows him a kiss and saunters up the path. This was his idea, this party. His idea for Lauren to start socialising again. This is another part of single parenting he hadn't accounted for – worrying for both of them with nobody at home to talk to, nobody to listen to his fears and anxieties. Nobody to tell him to go to hell when he asked the question he never thought he would ever have to ask about whether or not his wife was sleeping with another man.

But that's over now. A thing of the past. He can move on without having to monitor her movements, without checking her phone. She's gone. Her lover is in prison for her murder. What more is there to be said?

9

ALICE

He's not coming. I feel sure of it. I cornered him last Sunday, forced him into this. He's had a full week to mull it over and now he's not going to turn up. I missed the counselling session at church. I couldn't face it, sitting there opposite him as he tried to catch my eye, watching and waiting for him to subliminally tell me that he no longer wants to be associated with me. I don't blame him. He doesn't know me. Not really. He doesn't know why I'm here, what my intentions are. I'm not even sure I know that myself, not the full endpoint of it all. I just know that I need to strike up a relationship with him, become a part of his life. And then it will all fall into place.

My phone buzzes. I lift it out of my pocket and stare at the screen. Another missed call from Sandra and two texts. I turn it off and slip it back into my pocket. I don't have time for her or anybody else from that period of my life. It's in the past. I've moved on.

The door opens behind me, warm air wafting my way. I don't turn around. I don't want to be disappointed when I'm faced with somebody who isn't Peter. I've waited a long time for this moment and it seems it may not happen after all.

'Another latte? I see you beat me to it.' And there he is, standing looking down at me, his eyes shining. And he's smiling. I haven't scared him off. I haven't sent him running in the opposite direction. He's here. With me.

'That would be lovely, thank you.' My chest tightens as he goes to the counter and orders our drinks then comes back and slips effortlessly into his chair.

'You made it.'

'I made it.'

'I thought perhaps you weren't coming. Thought maybe I'd scared you off.' I smile at him and he smiles back. This is easier than I anticipated.

'I didn't see you at the grieving session.'

'Ah yes. I thought that maybe it was about time I stopped going. It's been a year now. Time to move on, I think.' I divert my gaze away from his, keep my voice even. Try to conceal my innermost thoughts. He hasn't recognised me. My deliberate changes in the last year have served me well.

There is a moment's silence before he replies, his voice dry and husky. 'Perhaps you're right. Maybe it is time to move on.'

'I'm sure it is.' I look up at him again, try to soften my voice, my posture, to welcome him into my world. My upside down, damaged little world. If only he knew.

He grins. 'My daughter was out last night. She didn't get in until turned 2 a.m. and I couldn't sleep until I heard her key in the door so you'll have to excuse me if I appear a bit tired.'

I nod to indicate my comprehension at his words even though I don't have any teenagers and have no clue how it would feel to lie awake nights worrying about them. I've lain awake worrying about many other aspects of my life, but never given any thought to how I would deal with teenagers of my own. I suppose now I will never find out. My body clock is ticking, the hands racing around the face at an almighty speed. Too late for me now. Everything is too damn late.

'So, I decided to have a lie-in this morning and am moving at half-speed which explains why I'm a bit behind time.'

'Good for you. I would have done the same myself had I been able to sleep.' I glance away, stare out of the window, knowing he is watching me, knowing he is trying to work out what is going through my mind. Trying to work out what it is that stops me from sleeping. If only he knew. We wouldn't be sitting here in such close proximity, being gracious and courteous if he did. He would walk away in the opposite direction, vowing to never see me again. I bite at my lip and lower my gaze.

'How do you fancy a walk after we finish our coffee?' He is still watching me, waiting for my reply.

'That would be lovely,' I say quietly, sipping at my latte, steam billowing off it in tiny tendrils.

'There's a footpath that runs behind the church. We could go there. That's if you want to?'

I nod, trying to appear neither nonchalant nor overly eager. It's a fine balancing act, keeping him interested. Scaring him off is the last thing I want to do. I've worked too hard to catch his eye to then blow it at this stage by appearing too brashy and needy. Easy does it.

'It sounds just perfect.'

We sit in companionable silence for a few minutes, drinking, watching the world pass by outside the window before he breaks the stillness. 'I was thinking that maybe we could go out for a meal. Not now, I mean. I was thinking of an evening. There's a place in town that I know. They do the best lasagne.'

I am tempted to refuse, just to keep him dangling for that little bit longer, but know that it would be churlish and downright stupid. Who is it I'm trying to punish here? Peter or myself?

'Thank you, I would love to go. It feels like an age since I've been out for a meal.' I laugh and turn to look around the café. 'I mean a proper evening meal in a restaurant, that is.'

'I know what you mean. Apart from lunch with my daughter yesterday, I've not been anywhere either. Maybe it's time to start living again.'

'I think you're right. Those grieving session were the highlight of my week. They gave me something to look forward to but now I think perhaps it's time to find my own way back into the world. I was relying on them just a bit too much.' My hands are pressed against my knees as I speak, my knuckles taut, my nails digging into my flesh as embellishments and untruths pour forth from my mouth. I'm becoming quite the liar. And enjoying it too.

'I totally understand that. After losing Sophia, I thought the world had come to an end but now given time, I'm getting back on an even keel so I'm thinking that it's time to step away from the church and those sessions. There's a fine line between needing support and relying on that support, not standing on your own two feet.' He is nodding now, as if he has just confirmed his own innermost thoughts and approves of them.

I lean forward and stare into his eyes. 'Finish your coffee and let's take that walk, eh? The fresh air will do us both good.'

He nods, drains the last of his drink and stands up. 'Come on,' he says softly, 'before I succumb to my caffeine addiction and order us both another. Let's get out here and explore.'

10

PETER

It's such an easy feeling, he thinks, sitting here talking to her; like slipping into a comfortable old shoe. That's not how a relationship is supposed to begin but that's how it feels. She is attractive for sure, not in the same way Sophia was, but she has a quiet charm about her and exudes confidence which is exactly what he needs right now. He likes the way she lets him go at his own pace. Maybe that's because she knows what it's like to lose somebody. He thinks that perhaps they are like a pair of drowning souls, trying to resurface and breathe again, to look up at the sky and appreciate the warmth of the sun on their backs.

He is almost there, back into breathing mode once more. No more holding his breath, praying he doesn't get sucked under into a whirling vortex from which there is no escape. The whirling vortex that was his life while Sophia was alive. Her death was traumatic. Devastating. It was also a welcome reprieve.

'Right,' he says, trying to sound self-assured and affable when in fact, he feels incredibly and stupidly nervous. 'Let's get out there and explore.'

Even as he says it, his words feel awkward and silly. *He* feels awkward and silly, like an over-excited child filled with a need to run and play. It's been a long time since he relaxed, played, did anything that lightened the load he has been carrying around for the past year. He tells himself to rein it in, play down his eagerness. Nobody likes a man who displays unacceptable levels of immaturity. Time to act sedate. Be the person Alice wants him to be. The person he needs to be for this thing between them to work.

* * *

He doesn't know how they ended up holding hands, but it happened and it feels natural. As if it was always going to be. He is aware that he needs to get back to Lauren, to make sure she's up and about and hasn't choked on her own vomit after one drink too many last night, yet he doesn't want to leave too early, to break this moment and leave Alice here before they've had a chance to properly meld together.

'If you like, we could go back to mine. You could meet my daughter, Lauren. She's a good kid. Been through a lot but you'd never think it to meet her. None of the usual teenage tantrums and surly ways.' He didn't plan on saying that. It just came out. He doesn't regret it. Already, he can visualise Alice meeting the family, rubbing along perfectly with Lauren and his mum.

He takes a breath and stops himself. Too soon. It's all too soon. After Sophia and a series of subsequent disastrous hook-ups with other women, he needs to be careful, to slow down and not rush headlong into anything. Therein lies the road to failure. He's tired of losing, being seen as a victim in the wreckage of his life. Time to take back control, to start winning again.

Only a few weeks after Sophia died, he trawled the town, looking for solace. He found it in the bed of women he met in the pubs. That was his way back then, what he did to mask his misery – drink, chat, fuck. He didn't even get to know their names. He can no longer even recall their faces. Driven by loneliness and guilt, he did his best to obliterate the memory of Sophia from his mind by replacing her with anyone he could find.

It didn't work. He continued to wake nights with their last heated discussion still in the forefront of his mind. And then there were the lies. Not just hers, but his as well. So many of them. Lie after lie after lie, a multitude of them heaped on top of one another. Too many to count. And of course, there is the biggest lie of all. The one he told the police and the one he keeps telling himself. The one he can't bring himself to think about without breaking out in a sweat.

'Lauren sounds like a dream,' Alice replies as she smiles up at him. 'And yes, I would love to meet her.'

They walk for a short while, the snapping of twigs underfoot and the echoing cawing of birds in the treetops the only sounds to be heard as they tramp through the mulch and back out into the daylight, emerging from the foliage with a slight rustle. Just two ordinary people spending time together, that's all it is. An ordinary lady and a damaged man who is doing his best to get his life back on track.

'We can go in my car if you like? Or you can follow me?'

She smiles at him, her expression unreadable. 'I don't have a car, I'm afraid. I got the bus here.'

A stab of guilt forces him to inhale. 'Sorry. I just sort of assumed...' He raises his eyes in an act of self-deprecation. 'Right, I'll drop you off home after we've been to mine. Unless you're planning on going somewhere else afterwards? I mean, I can give you a lift to wherever you want to be. I don't mind.' He is rambling now and needs to stop it. He is aware that he sounds like an apprehensive child, too eager to please. Frightened of doing the wrong thing. Again. So many wrong things. So much guilt.

'If you could drop me off home afterwards, that would be much appreciated. Thank you.'

She reaches up and gently kisses him on the cheek. It's barely a touch at all: as light as the breeze passing over his skin. He has forgotten what it feels like to have somebody so close to him, to be shown true affection by another female. Not just skin against skin, carnal lust, but a true and soothing touch with more behind it than desire. A flame starts up under his face, spreading over his neck and down his chest. He swallows and lowers his gaze.

'Right, well my car's just parked over there on the road next to the café. And I live about a mile away so it won't take us long to get there.'

She nods, her hair bobbing around her face, her eyes crinkling up at the corners. 'This is really kind of you, Peter. I'm looking forward to meeting your daughter. I haven't got any children of my own.'

He's not sure how to answer this statement. It's an emotive subject, a sensitive topic. So many variables and possibilities. So much that can go wrong.

'And with me not having Stuart around any more, I suppose it's never going to happen, is it? Time is against me.'

They reach the car before he can reply which he thinks is probably for the best. He presses the key fob and opens the passenger door for her to climb inside, relieved that she's still smiling. Relieved that she hasn't turned around and fled. This is how grief works. So much unsaid. So much left undone. He thinks about her husband, his death and how little she has said about him. Soon he will ask, but not just yet. They have time enough to cover that area of her life. For now, he's content to just be with her.

'Right,' he murmurs, thankful the moment of awkwardness has passed, 'let's see if that daughter of mine is up out of bed, shall we?'

* * *

The journey takes just a few minutes. He breaks the silence by turning on the radio and humming along, a deep thud starting up under his sternum as the music fills the air around them.

They pull up outside the house and he can see that Lauren's curtains are pulled back, the window cracked open slightly. He wonders if she has a hangover and then thinks about how reckless he was at that age, drinking everything and anything just because he could. He likes to think that his daughter has a little more about her, a greater level of sensibility and decorum, and fewer bad influences driving her on, but isn't entirely sure.

'Well, it looks like she's out of bed,' he says, traces of optimism in his voice as they step out of the car.

He slips the key into the lock and opens the front door, the smell of fresh coffee wafting through as they head into the kitchen.

Lauren is sitting at the table, her hands clasped around a large mug, her eyes rimmed with smudged mascara, a haunted look carved into her expression.

'Good party?' He leans down and kisses the top of her head, something he hasn't done for a long time. There seem to be a lot of things they have forgotten how to do. Like being truthful and honest.

She doesn't reply, closing her eyes and taking another sip of the steaming liquid instead.

'Lauren, there's somebody I'd like you to meet. This is Alice. Remember I told you I was going out for coffee?'

He is relieved when she stands up and holds out her hand like the polite young woman that she is, even though she is clearly suffering from a mammoth hangover.

'Lovely to meet you, Alice. I'm Lauren.'

They shake hands like old friends and a small blossom of joy unfurls deep in his chest, green shoots of hope that this thing is going the way he wants it to. Every act of kindness and joy is a step closer to eradicating the badness, the festering darkness that sits at the base of his belly, clawing its way up, reminding him of the past. Of what he did.

'Right,' he says a little too loudly, clapping his hands together for added effect as if to scare away the demons that continually nudge their way into his brain. 'Who's for more coffee?'

11

ALICE

She's perfect. Everything I hoped for and more. Amenable, gracious, affable. I have a feeling this is all going to work out just fine. I have to remember keep my cool, not get too over excited at being welcomed into their little family unit. I don't want to reveal my hand too early in the game. Not when there is so much at stake. I have a lot to gain from this venture. I also have a lot to lose should it stray off course.

'Lauren, I love the way you've styled your hair. I wish mine would look like that. I've got dry, frizzy, split ends. I can't seem to do anything with it.'

She runs her fingers through her curls then reaches out and touches my hair, her fingers long and lean, her nails painted a pale shade of pink. 'It's lovely, your hair, but I could curl it for you one day, if you like? It's really easy to do.'

Out of the corner of my eye, I can see Peter smiling, a relief evident in his features. He is as happy about this little set-up as I am. Except my reasons are different to his. Very different indeed. If only he knew, then he might not be standing there grinning, his face soft and gentle, his eyes full of hope and wonderment.

'That would be great. I'd really love some kind of hair makeover. I'm useless with things like that.' My voice sounds disembodied. I've rehearsed this scenario in my head so many times and now it's happening, it feels surreal. It's like an out-of-body experience. I'm floating up above this, watching it all as it unfurls, my mouth saying the words while my brain is disengaged, busy observing it from afar.

'Well, next time you come around, I'll have my things ready. It's just that today, I'm a bit under the weather.'

'Under the weather?' Peter stands beside us, laughing. 'That's the best euphemism I've ever heard. Did a bottle of vodka do that to you, put you *under the weather*?'

Lauren blushes and dips her head away, sliding down into the chair again and groaning. 'Oh God, don't. I am my own worst enemy. Never again.'

'You're also underage, young lady,' he whispers and ruffles her hair playfully. 'Come on, Alice. Let's head into the living room and let Lauren recover in peace.'

I follow him out of the kitchen into an average-sized living room. In the centre is a small, oak coffee table. On either side are two cream, leather sofas. There are pictures on the wall. A shelf full of books. Pictures of Peter and Lauren. And Sophia. She is there, smiling down at me. I try not to look but my eyes are drawn to them, to her casual, effortless poses and charismatic smile. She's attractive. There's no denying that. But of course, I know the real Sophia, the one that maybe her husband doesn't know. I know all about her secrets and her alluring manner. I know all about her devilish, wily ways and how she tried to rip my family apart. I know her all right. And I wish I didn't.

'I did consider taking some of them down.' Peter is standing next to me, following my gaze as I pore over the collection of photographs. 'But it felt a bit disloyal. An insult to her memory.' An unfathomable look flits across his face, his eyes darkening as he tries to disguise it. 'So I kept them up and even added a few more.'

I don't know what to say. I want to question why he would do that, add more of that woman to this house. I remain silent for a few seconds before speaking. 'I think they're beautiful. She was obviously a very attractive lady. You must miss her so much.' I watch his eyes mist over, see his face colour up and wonder what he is thinking. So far, our conversations have been directed towards his family, his partner. I wonder when he will ask about mine – my absent partner who is now dead to me. My philandering shit of a husband.

'She was beautiful. Very photogenic. I see a lot of her in Lauren. Every single day, there is another look that I hadn't noticed before.' He turns and glances at me. 'But we have to move on with our lives, don't we? No point in continually harking back to the past.'

I take a step towards him and squeeze his hand. I can feel the heat from him as he moves even closer to me. 'We do need to move on,' I say, choosing my words carefully. 'But we need to get the equilibrium right, don't we? Carving out a new life for ourselves whilst making sure we still honour their memory.' I almost laugh out loud at myself. Listen to me. I sound like a grief counsellor. Anybody would think I had taken notice in those sessions, learnt how to comfort people who have suffered a bereavement. If only I could apply those strategies and wise words to my own losses. If only people would see the truth and know my suffering. I may not have actually experienced the death of a loved one but what I have suffered is far worse than that. It's an ongoing process with no end in sight. My life has been torn to shreds while here Peter is trying to get back on his feet, on the lookout for a new partner. He has a chance to start again. I am stuck on an endless, bumpy ride with no way of getting off.

'Anyway.' Peter nods then shakes his head as if to clear away all those memories. 'Enough of being surrounded by all these pictures. Why don't we sit in the garden instead? It's lovely and warm out there.'

I nod and follow him back out into the hallway where more pictures and photographs adorn the walls. I wonder how many he added after she died. Grief can do strange things to a person. A tumult of emotions rushing around their brain. This place is a shrine to Sophia. He is far from over her. I am going to have to work very hard here. Very hard indeed.

The garden is a spread of lush foliage and vegetation. The sun is making its ascent into the azure sky as we find a seat, Peter clearing cobwebs off the table and then pulling out a chair for me to sit down. Beside me is an array of pot plants in dire need of attention, their stems wilting, the soil desiccated.

'You're growing azaleas?' I point to a clump of pink flowers in the corner of one of the borders that surround the lawn.

Pete laughs and runs his fingers through his hair. 'Am I? To be honest, I wouldn't know an azalea from an African daisy.'

'Ah,' I say raising my finger and pointing it at him. 'But you do know that African daisies exist so that's a start.'

'You're a gardener then?' He leans back, raises his face to the sun and I see him relax, his body bending in the middle, a slight twinkle dancing in his eye as he looks back to me, watching me intently. I wonder what he sees when he glances at me? Does he see a grieving widow or is he able to view the real me – the spiteful, embittered me that can see only darkness ahead and will do anything, *anything*, to clamber back into the light?

'I try. I'm not an expert by any stretch of the imagination, but I do enjoy pottering about and doing a bit of planting whenever I can.' I'm lying. I'm not averse to gardening but neither am I well versed in the ways of horticulture. I know what I know from listening to my parents who loved their garden with a passion. I do have a garden but I do very little out there; it's a lawn with a few plants dotted about. I tended to it when I had something resembling a life. But now look at me. I have nothing. At least I used to have nothing. I now have Peter and Lauren. I say those names over and over in my head like a mantra, and smile, the sound of them, the *feel* of them, as they roll around my brain like warm syrup. I think he likes me. And I am almost certain he believes me too, isn't able to see the real me. The destructive, angry me. This is good.

For once, things are looking up.

'Maybe you could start helping me get to grips with this one? What I know about flowers and soil and planting can be written on the back of a postage stamp.' He shuts his eyes briefly and sighs. 'God, sorry. That was really presumptuous of me, wasn't it? What a bloody clown I am. We've only just started chatting and here I am ordering you about like some sort of hired help.'

I ball my hands into fists, flexing them beneath the table, and smile. 'I honestly don't mind at all. I love helping out and I love gardening so it's a win-win for me.'

Peter drags his chair closer to mine, his interest in me now a palpable force. 'How have I not noticed you before now? The only excuse I can give is that I was too mired in my own misery. But you're here now, and I have to say, I'm really glad about that. I'm just hoping you can forgive my clumsy mouth. It's been a while since I sat next to somebody as pretty as you. It's been a while since I was single and had to—'

I reach up and kiss him, his mouth warm against mine. Not too much pressure. I don't want to scare him off, send him running in the opposite direction. Not when I've come this far. Not when I've worked so hard to get him exactly where I want him.

'Sorry,' I say softly as I end the kiss and turn away, feigning shyness before turning back again to look at him. 'I don't know why I did that. It just felt right at the time.'

'Don't be sorry.' His eyes are shining, two small diamonds sparkling with such intensity, I find myself backing away a fraction. He leans across and takes my hand, resting it in his. His palm is cool and dry. He's not as nervous as I imagined him to be then. Neither am I. I've practised this for a long time, rehearsed it so many times, I wondered if it would ever come to fruition but here we are, our purported romance beginning to blossom.

We kiss again, his breath warm, traces of coffee still present. His cologne surrounds us in a misty, invisible haze. I wonder what he is thinking about? Is he falling head-over-heels in love with me or is he being cautious, finding his feet and thinking that we should take this thing one day at a time? I will follow his lead, walk in his shadow. I will take my cues from him and when the time is right, I will put my plan into action and I will strike. But not yet. The build-up is almost as appealing as the climax. Almost, but not quite.

'This,' I say, pulling back and sweeping my hand around the garden, 'is a work in progress.' I narrow my eyes and grin. 'So, when do you want me to start?'

12

LAUREN

'Dad, she seems lovely.' I am buttering more toast as he walks in the kitchen after Alice has left in a taxi despite Dad's insistence he would take her home. He stands next me and helps himself to a slice.

'Yes, she is, isn't she?' He bites into it, crumbs flying everywhere, sticking to the corners of his mouth and dropping on the floor at his feet.

'Plate,' I say, handing one over.

He raises his eyebrows and holds it underneath his chin.

'So, is she an avid churchgoer?' I place the butter back in the fridge and sit at the table, watching him, waiting for his reply, thinking she doesn't appear overly religious but then, how would I be able to tell? It's not as if she's going to walk about carrying a bible or making the sign of the cross on her chest, is it?

'I don't think so. She said she's just about done with the grieving sessions and probably won't be going back.'

'How did her husband die?' I don't know why I'm asking. It's not as if matters how a person dies; it's the heartache and devastation they leave behind once they're gone that's important. Or sometimes, it's the heartache and devastation they cause while they're still here. That leaves a lasting impression too.

'A car crash, apparently. She didn't go into too much detail and I didn't ask. Death isn't really the sort of thing you dwell on when you meet somebody new, is it? Maybe we said all there is to say when we were in the church.'

There is a heavy silence. It hits him like this sometimes, right in his solar plexus, a reminder of Mum. I see it in his face, the greyness in his eyes, the wrinkling of his brow. A stray word, an unexpected whiff of perfume, a flash of colour and she is back in the room standing next to us. Except she isn't and never will be. I swallow and wipe at my mouth, turning away from him, thinking that death is exactly what connected them and that they should talk at length about it, offload their burdens to one another, otherwise what was the point in all those sessions?

'You at least have some sort of chemistry, though?'

'I guess we do.' Dad is smiling at me. I'm glad about that. The last thing I want to do is upset him. He's been through enough – more than most – but more than that, he's also my mate. Not many fathers and daughters have a relationship like ours, I'm aware of that, and the last thing I want to do is destroy it with a careless word or an ill-thought-out question that cuts him to the quick. For a while, we drifted apart, two ships sailing on empty, rough seas, but things are settling down, our navigation paths synced once more. God, listen to me. I sound like one of those counsellors Dad visited every Sunday. He's right about one thing, though – I definitely need to get out more, stop talking like an old fart and not a teenager whose head is almost falling off after downing too much vodka.

'I've asked her out for a meal.'

'Have you now?' I suck in my cheeks and give him a playful punch on the arm. 'Well get you, Mr ageing Lothario. Where are you going to eat?'

Almost immediately, his face colours up, creeping up his neck and over his stubble covered cheeks. My mouth drops open. I close it and swallow hard.

'Really? You're taking her *there*?' I shrug and wipe down the kitchen surface with a cloth, sweeping the crumbs into my palm before throwing them in the bin. 'I guess it's time now though, isn't it? I'm sure you'll have a lovely evening.'

He reaches over and grips my hand. 'Thanks, sweetheart. I wasn't sure about it but I feel so comfortable there, and it seemed like the natural thing to do.'

He's right. It is the natural thing to do. This is a bold move for him, though. He needs to be on firm ground, somewhere he feels at ease and The Half Moon Inn is that place with its inglenook fireplace and lovely, familiar staff. I hope he has a great night. I really do. I try to visualise him as he makes small talk with Alice, drinking his wine and relaxing.

'I can drop you off and pick you up if you like?' I passed my test a few months ago and Dad keeps promising to let me drive his car. 'You might find it easier to chill out if you have a drink, you know, a couple of glasses of vino?' I am so desperate to get behind the wheel of his car.

He lowers his eyes, his hand still grasping mine. 'I'll think about it. Alice doesn't have a car so I can't really expect you to drop her off as well and I can't exactly just shove her into a taxi on her own.'

'I don't mind, honestly.' And I don't. He seems happy and is no longer pining after Mum. This is a positive step for him. It seemed like he thought more about Mum after she died than he did when she was alive. I may only be seventeen years old but I know a crumbling marriage when I see one. I also know deceit when I see it.

After Mum died, Dad put up even more photographs of her, as if we didn't have enough up to begin with. I don't know why he did it. Maybe it was his way of trying to make us feel as if she had never left, her face peering out at us, staring down as we ate and slept and watched television. It was eerie and unnerving. Still is. I wanted to take some of them down but knew what sort of a reaction that would provoke so instead, we just got on with our lives. Dad fell into a slump, going through his daily routine like a robot, not an ounce of happiness or spontaneity in his life. But perhaps all of that is about to change, or at least I hope so. Our dry, purposeless existence was wearing on us both. This house needs some life breathing back into it, like flowers coming into bloom on a fresh, spring day. It needs a third person to bind us back together. Mum is gone and Alice is here.

She may well be the best thing to happen to us in a long, long time.

13

ALICE

This place is special to him. I can tell. It's the way his eyes glaze over, the way his mouth sags ever so slightly whenever he looks around the room. The staff all know him, smiling as he passes, touching him lightly on the shoulder, giving him a subtle nod, a knowing look, a surreptitious glance when they think we're not looking. I'm guessing it was their favourite restaurant, he and his wife. Did the staff know about the fractures in their marriage? The damage Sophia was doing to both of them? The damage she was doing to people she had never even met? I'm guessing not. All they saw was the polished version of the Saunders family, the one they presented to the outside world – their carefully varnished veneer, all shine and gloss when all the while, underneath it all, cracks ran right through their little world, threatening to split them apart.

I dismiss those thoughts, pushing them away. It's the here and now that counts, the chance to even things up. He must think highly of me to bring me here so early in our relationship. I'm obviously doing something right.

A warm glow stirs deep inside me as he pours my wine, then fills his own glass and clinks it against mine, smiling and raising a toast.

'To a lovely evening.'

'To a lovely evening.' I sip at my drink, the heady aroma of the Pinot Noir wafting towards me, making me settled and comfortable.

'I take it you know this place?' I can't help myself. I had to ask, if only to see him twitch and shift in his seat, to see the cogs whirring in his brain as he tries to formulate a safe reply that won't make us both embarrassed and self-conscious. I look forward to his response, to his choice of words so as to not spoil the moment and possibly even ruin the rest of the evening. It's a strange thing, marriage, isn't it? Even in death, people still do their best to remain loyal to their spouses, to not denigrate them publicly. Even if they were being unfaithful. It's bad manners. A gross misdemeanour. Nobody ever speaks ill of the dead. To do so would be deemed unseemly and indecorous. What a strange world we live in, where the dead are forgiven, regardless of their sins and yet the living are continually belittled and insulted despite working hard to shake off the shackles of their past.

'Yes, I know this place pretty well. We used to come here, Sophia and me. It's not quite our local but everyone knows me well enough.'

I nod and take another sip of my wine. 'So I guess they'll all be wondering who I am?' My voice is gentle, unassuming. I've rehearsed it well, this particular tone, practised it over and over, making sure I complete the whole look with a furtive glance from under my carefully applied mascara before looking away and smiling wanly. I like this new look I have constructed. I think it suits me.

'Ah, I'm sure that's not the case at all. They know it's time for me to start having fun again, getting out and about and meeting people.'

I wonder if he too has rehearsed his lines carefully in his head, choosing each one with precision. He has as much to lose as I do. He has invested his emotions in me, opened himself up to possible hurt and rejection just six months after the man who killed his wife was sent to prison. I need to tread carefully around him, be both malleable and compliant whilst not losing sight of my dignity. Or my carefully constructed target.

We order and eat, the atmosphere softening and becoming more uncomplicated the more wine we consume. At the back of my mind is the question of what lies in store at the end of the evening. Will we part as friends, or will we take this thing one step further? I decide that I'll let Peter take the lead. He is the fragile one here. I will follow submissively, be the person he wants me to be. I will be his new partner, his substitute Sophia. Except unlike her, I am not currently sleeping with somebody else's husband, trampling all over their life and ruining it. Not yet anyway. Give it time. Who knows what the future holds for us? The world is my oyster. I plan to enjoy this little venture, regain some of my self-respect. God knows I deserve it.

By the time we order our dessert, we are on to our third bottle of wine. I can't decide if we have drunk so much because we are nervous or because we're relaxed in one another's company. I like to think it's the latter but everything has taken on a soft haze and I'm finding it more and more difficult to work out what he is thinking. Truth be told, I'm finding it hard to steer my way through my own muddled thoughts, never mind trying to climb inside Peter's head. I should drink less, remain sharp, incisive. It's important I don't lose focus. However, this man isn't the only one who's had a tough time of late. I've had more than my fair share of heartache and sorrow. I don't have anybody at home to help shoulder the burden of my own personal misery. At least Peter has his daughter, Lauren. I have nobody. I am truly alone in this world.

'Everything okay?' He is watching me. I go hot and cold at the same time, my blood sizzling then cooling. I stare at him and smile.

'Everything is fine. Better than fine. It's perfect.' I tap at my glass with my nail, my hand dropping into my lap as I let out a low sigh. 'Thank you for a wonderful night.'

He dabs at his mouth with his serviette and leans back, twisting to catch the eye of a waiter to indicate that we have finished and need to pay the bill.

'Let me pay my share,' I say, steel in my voice.

'Absolutely not. This is my treat. It was me who asked you to come here. This one is on me.'

'Thank you, Peter. That's really kind.' Is my voice gentle enough? Passive enough? Sophia was hardly the embodiment of selflessness and after drinking so much, I'm not entirely sure which way I should go with my character development. I decide to opt for soft and subservient. Soft and subservient seems to work well with him. I see the flames of desire in his eyes whenever I turn on my charms, the innocent glances and gentle sighs that I direct his way. He responds well to them.

He settles the bill and we stand. I am mildly giddy, the floor spongy beneath my feet. I can't remember the last time I drank so much. Tonight has been a shift from my usual stance of always being on my guard, never letting anybody get close to me. I made that mistake with Tom, somebody I allowed into my life a while back. It didn't end well. Tomorrow, I will return to that mode but for now, it feels rather pleasant to be carried along in the slipstream of Peter's happiness. I'm going to enjoy it while I can because it's not going to last. Not if I get my way.

He places my jacket around my shoulders and accompanies me outside. The air is still warm, summer peeking its head around the corner, nudging spring out of the way. A smattering of people pass by us, their chatter filling the silence of an otherwise deserted street. Peter catches me by surprise as he pulls me close to him and kisses me, his mouth soft and welcoming, a slight hint of garlic on his breath. There is real passion in his kiss. I reciprocate, pressing my body close to his. This man is an open book. He is making it so easy for me. So very, very easy. Does he have any idea what I am thinking? What dark thoughts are racing through my brain?

We part, warmed by the food and wine, warmed by each other. He's handsome, there's no denying that. And charming. It makes it all so much easier. I'm not sure I would find this task so appealing if he had a face like a pig and the manners of one too but as it is, he is affable, charismatic and good looking. Not what I expected. Or maybe I did. People like Peter and Sophia live charmed lives, taking everything for granted, never questioning the good things that come their way. Always expecting. Always ready to lap it all up while the likes of me sit by in the shadows, watching. Waiting for my time to step into the sunlight and bask in its warmth. Except of course, Sophia spoiled the good life that they had by deciding to sleep with another man, by cheating on her husband and then dying unexpectedly. Their good thing came to an end, as did mine. At least that's something we have in common.

But now after a long wait, I'm here, taking part, and I plan on enjoying every minute of it for as long as it lasts. For as long as I decide it will last. I'm the one in control here, the puppet master. Peter and Lauren are marionettes, dancing to my tune.

I take his hand and we stroll along the pavement together, my heart battering in my chest while Peter scans the street for a taxi. When none arrive, he reaches for his phone and makes a call. Within minutes, a sleek, black vehicle pulls up alongside us and we slip inside, our bodies huddled together on the vinyl seat like a pair of lovestruck teenagers.

I tell the taxi driver where to drop me off. By the time we arrive, I have my question ready, my voice honed to perfection.

'Would you like to come in, you know, for a nightcap?' It's almost a purr, my timbre deep and resonant.

There is a delay, a moment of hesitation and then his voice, a trickle of despair as he shakes his head and clasps my hand, stroking it with his thumb and forefinger. 'I'd love to but I've got to get back for Lauren.'

Relief floods through me. 'I understand.' I do understand. I've waited a long time to get this far. I'm not sure what I would have done if he had taken me up on my offer because this isn't my house. It's not even my street.

I slide out of the cab and stand in the darkness, waving until the taxi vanishes into the night, and then make my way home.

14

PETER

'So how did it go last night?' Lauren watches him closely, a smile twitching at the corners of her mouth. 'I mean, I take it by your flushed complexion and smirk that you had a good time, yeah?'

Peter turns on the television and scrolls through the channels looking for inspiration. 'Okay, smart arse. The flushed complexion is because I've just stepped out of the shower and my smirk is because you keep asking me ridiculous questions.'

She laughs. 'Yeah right. Whatever you say, Dad.'

They sit for a few seconds, the television blaring out a stream of inane sounds until Lauren breaks in, her mood more sombre, the smile fading from her face. 'Can I ask you something?'

He takes a deep breath and braces himself for whatever it is she is about to say. Sometimes, Lauren likes to throw him a curveball. She catches him unawares, knocking him off balance. He doesn't like feeling off balance, defenceless. 'Go ahead. As long you don't want money, that is.' He laughs and his stomach clenches as she sits, her face like stone, her eyes downcast.

'Do you think you and Mum would have stayed together if she'd lived?'

Her question knocks every last bit of air out of his lungs. Somewhere in his chest, a rhythm takes hold, the pulsing of his heart that thrums beneath his sweater like a metronome. He wasn't prepared for this, expecting instead questions about Alice or Lauren going off to university but definitely not this. It takes him a few seconds to prepare his answer.

'Well,' he says quietly, moving closer to her, slowly shifting along until they are almost side by side, 'I'd like to say I have no idea why you've asked such a question but of course, we both know things weren't easy between us, don't we?' Sweat blooms under his armpits, trickles down his back. He would rather not answer this. He would rather be elsewhere right now, afraid that whatever he says will betray his innermost thoughts. Afraid his secrets will come spilling out. He's been good at staying silent in the past year. Good at keeping everything concealed. The perfect liar.

She sighs and turns away. 'I don't want to spoil your good mood. I mean, you obviously had a great time last night and that's totally brilliant. It really is, and I suppose that's why I feel it's like y'know, okay to bring it up because I know you won't get as upset with me speaking about Mum and everything.' She stops and he nods, remaining silent while he gathers his thoughts and tries to prepare an answer. 'Thing is,' she says, continuing. 'I found something shortly before she died.'

He nods again, waiting for the next part, still unwilling to speak. Not wanting to hear what's coming next.

She looks at him, waiting for some sort of recognition at her words. He can't bring himself to say anything. Even a slight head movement feels laboured and arduous. He thinks he knows what's coming next, can feel it in the air – the apprehension. The unspoken knowledge she has stored away.

'You knew, didn't you? About what was going on with her?'

He can't seem to breathe properly. The room tilts and blurs, the happiness from last night draining away like water swirling and gurgling down a plughole.

Lauren stands. She's going to get this thing that she found. He knows it, doesn't want to see it, whatever it is. He's seen enough, experienced enough. Time to put this all to bed.

Sophia stares down at him from the wall as Lauren heads upstairs, leaving him on his own with only his thoughts for company. Her stare is accusatory. Lauren is right. He knew about her affair. Of course he bloody well did. He always feared he was punching well above his weight with

Sophia and although he didn't brood over it or think about it every day, the nagging doubt was always there that there was somebody better out there who would snatch her away from him. Somebody wealthier, better looking. Somebody with more to offer than he could ever give her. And that is exactly what happened. Except she died before she made any decision to leave him. His head aches at the thought of it. The thought that he wasn't enough. Then comes the anger: the all-consuming anger that he has tried to suppress. It burns inside him, white-hot flames of fury that scorch his insides.

He listens as Lauren comes back downstairs, her movements clumsy and awkward, her noisiness dragging him out of his reverie. She'll be trying work out how to show him this thing that she found, how to produce it with enough sensitivity so he doesn't become over emotional, break down, cry, do anything that any normal, grieving husband would do. But he won't do any of those things because he's become adept at covering up, at masking his true feelings. He's become a proficient liar.

'Here.' She holds it out for him to take. He can see the slight tremble in her fingers, observes how her skin is pale and waxy as she clutches a crumpled piece of paper in front of him.

He opens it, straightening out the creases, staring at the message, at the words no man should ever write to another man's wife. Words no husband should ever have to read.

> *My darling Sophia. This cannot be over. I refuse to believe it. I need to see you one last time. Please say you will give me one last chance.*
>   *Love Phillip xx*

'Well,' he murmurs, his heart pounding in his chest. 'I'm not sure what to say, except why is this written in your handwriting?'

Lauren sighs, stares down at the floor then back up at her father. 'It was a text on her phone. I found it and copied it down word for word and then deleted it off her phone. I should have shown it to the police, shouldn't I?' Lauren looks away, her voice a whisper. 'But after Mum died, everything went to pot and I forgot all about it.' She blinks, bats away a rogue eyelash. 'Actually, that's not entirely true. I didn't forget about it at all. How could I forget about something like this? I didn't want to anybody to see it. I was so fucking embarrassed. I had snooped on her. My mum was clearly having an affair. It's not exactly family of the year stuff, is it? Still,' she says softly, 'I guess it only confirms what we now know, doesn't it? That he was angry with her and had every reason to kill her. He denied the affair, said he was just a friend, a colleague. But he wasn't, was he?'

Peter places an arm around her shoulders, doing his utmost to keep his voice steady as he speaks. 'What I think we should do now is get rid of this piece of trash. Throw it away and never look at it again.' Peter had no idea that Lauren knew about Sophia's affair before she died. He presumed she had only become aware of it after her death when the evidence was presented in court. Not that they attended on a regular basis. It was all too distressing, draining and humiliating, having their marital problems played out in front of everybody. Despite the arguments and acrimony between them, he had hoped that prior to her death, they had managed to keep it secret from their daughter – their issues. Sophia's affair. She knew. All this time, Lauren knew and kept it to herself. Shame burrows under his flesh. His daughter bore the weight of Sophia's deceit and said nothing.

Lauren nods, a lone tear travelling down her face, gathering in a thin stream on her jawline and dripping onto her beige T-shirt.

'There's nothing to be gained from going over old ground, is there? All that will do is make us feel upset and miserable. And I don't know about you, but I've had a gutful of feeling upset and miserable. I want to be happy for a change. I want *us* to be happy.' He sits down, pulling Lauren down with him. 'What happened is in the past. Your mother and I had our problems but that doesn't mean we have to go on brooding over it.'

'I agree,' she says hastily, crumpling the letter up in her hand.

He takes it from her, the paper sharp and cold against his skin. 'So, can we get rid of it now please?'

Lauren watches as he throws it in the bin behind them where it lands in a heap.

'Good riddance to bad rubbish, eh? Now, can we have a relaxing day with no more unpleasant memories to rake through?' He smiles at her, relieved that that particular conversation is over with. *Togetherness*, he thinks fondly. That's what they need more of in this house. A bond that draws the two of them together. No more talk of Sophia's murder. No more reminders of his wife's lover. Just him and his daughter. And Alice. He doesn't want to forget about Alice.

'Tell you what,' Lauren says wistfully. 'Why don't we watch an old film, get some crisps and chocolate and just pig out like a pair of old slobs?'

He rests his head back on the sofa, surprisingly enamoured by the idea. He's tired, every nerve, every muscle and sinew in his body crying out for respite. He's ready to do nothing except lie back and be entertained by some mind-numbing movie that will glide over him and not force him to think too hard about Sophia and Phillip, about his own actions. About what he did. 'You're on. What you got?' His voice echoes in his head, incorporeal and eerie, memories of that day still present, nagging at him, refusing to leave him be.

He had followed Sophia the night she was murdered, salting himself away behind trees and shrubbery as she headed along the path that ran parallel to the riverbank. She had told him she was going to meet up with some colleagues for a drink. He knew different. She was going to meet him – Kennedy. It was obvious in her body language, her tone, the way she put on another coat of lipstick and fluffed up her hair. This was no ordinary walk. It was a clandestine meeting.

Still dressed in her work clothes, she left the house, hands slung in the pockets of her coat, head dipped against the gathering breeze.

Knowing that Lauren was upstairs studying, her head buried in a book, Peter took the opportunity and slipped out into the night after his wife, his heart battering beneath his ribcage like a trapped bird, its wings fluttering wildly in a frantic bid for freedom.

'How about this one, Dad?' Lauren is standing in front of him holding up one of her firm favourites – *Dirty Dancing*.

He groans, shuts his eyes and listens to her laughter and she slips the disc into the machine and turns up the volume. Peter allows himself to be carried away by the noise, the music, the distant crackle of chattering voices. Anything is better than the continual whispering that storms through his head day after day after day, telling him that he is the guilty one, that he is the one who is responsible. That he is actually the one who killed his own wife.

15

ALICE

'Alice, I don't suppose you've come across an old receipt, have you? I seem to have mislaid it.' Jack is standing next to me, his face flushed, perspiration standing out on his top lip. He is wringing his hands, his knuckles making a sharp, cracking sound.

'No, not that I recall,' I say, keeping my expression neutral. 'What sort of receipt?'

He hops from foot to foot, his usual cool demeanour absent. 'Oh, nothing too important. It's just for a meal I paid for recently for some clients at work. If you stumble across it, could you pass it onto me, please.' He smiles at me and winks conspiratorially. 'And it would be really helpful if we could keep this little mistake of mine between the two of us. Elizabeth gets rather riled at the amount of money I spend on some of my customers, so if you wouldn't mind…?'

I give him a smile, indicating that I will keep our little secret between just the two of us, nodding and lowering my gaze away from his. Doing my best to look discreet, humble, unassuming. 'Of course. No problem at all.'

He heads off in a different direction, his shoulders ever so slightly slumped. He's definitely nervous and agitated. Jack is a cool customer, playing everything to perfection. Always the consummate professional, his behaviour is often difficult to decipher. But not today. Today, he is off balance, his usual reserved composure absent. It doesn't trouble me too much. I have the receipt. I hold all the cards. I think about that small piece of paper that is laid out on my kitchen table at home, all the secrets it holds. And now it's mine. For all the locked doors in this place and immaculately placed objects, I have finally managed to procure a piece of evidence that could damage their perfect little lives, perhaps irrevocably.

I spend the remainder of the afternoon vacuuming the children's bedrooms, wondering who the woman is that he took out to that restaurant, what she looks like, where she lives. Not that it matters. I know about her and that's enough. And I'm almost certain he knows that I know. I hum as I shake the rug and run the vacuum over it. It feels good to wield some power. For so long now, I have been scrambling around in the dirt, trying to make ends meet, wondering where the next nasty surprise is coming from and now, I have a way out of it. A way of making sure Jack Downey gives me what I want to keep his tawdry little secret away from his unsuspecting wife.

'Alice, if you wouldn't mind giving the surfaces a dust down before you go, that would be marvellous.' Elizabeth is striding along the wide landing, her attention already fixated on something else. Her long skirt swishes along the rug as she glides down the stairs and click-clacks her way across the parquet flooring of the large hallway. I wonder what she does with her time, how she manages to appear so busy whilst doing absolutely nothing at all. I cannot remember the last time I saw her do any household chores, if indeed I've ever seen her do any at all.

Perhaps she has a secret lover as well. Maybe this is how the Downeys live their lives, with clandestine flirtations and liaisons and my hanging on to that receipt is a pointless exercise. Except I don't think that's the case at all. I think Jack Downey appeared very nervous and is desperate to get it back.

I pick up a duster and bite at my lip to suppress my excitement. It might be worth my while to snoop a little more. Not too much. Things suddenly going missing would look suspicious. For now, I have a piece of incriminating evidence, something he is keen to retrieve. I wonder how much he will part with to keep me quiet? I need to make it worth my while, perhaps find something else to raise the price of my silence because afterwards, he will find a way to fire me. If he dares, that is. I'm not so stupid as to hand it over without taking a photograph of it first. A photograph I could pass on to his wife. This all rather outlandish, and so very delicious. Elizabeth often goes out shopping leaving her husband alone in the house while I clean and look after her children. I could approach him then, let him know I have the evidence of his infidelity.

A frisson of excitement runs through me, firing up my senses. This and Peter, all within my grasp. And not before time. My downward-plummeting life appears to be taking an upturn. Perhaps my visits to church have paid off and God is finally smiling down on me.

None of the surfaces need dusting. They gleam and shine like cut glass but I dust them anyway. Fionn and Yasmin are at school and I'm not due to collect them for another half hour. There is little else for me to do around here. I have scrubbed surfaces, ironed, washed windows and swept floors Cinderella-style until my back aches and my temper frays. This house couldn't be any cleaner if I tried.

It's as I'm moving a pile of books in the library to dust behind them that I see it – a small, clear packet, sealed and full of white powder.

My heart thumps, a slight sheen of sweat breaking out under my armpits. A thousand thoughts run through my head – if I pick this thing up, my prints will be on it. What evidence do I have that it belongs to either of these two people and not to me? If I were to produce it and show it to them, they could claim that I brought it in the house and planted it there. My palms are slick with sweat as I pull out my phone and take a photograph of it without even touching the packet. I push the books back in place and head into the kitchen where I snap on a pair of latex gloves then make my way back to the library, stopping first to check for any signs or sounds of movement. There is nothing. This is a dead house, no love in it, no vibrancy. A house full of emptiness. Aside from the pristine furniture and expensive-looking trinkets, there is nothing at all to indicate that anybody even lives here. It's as if spirits and ghosts roam the place, sailing past in a cold, invisible haze. They have everything anybody could ever want, these people, except the one thing that matters – love.

I check over my shoulder before moving everything again, picking up the packet and slipping it into my pocket. It weighs next to nothing yet feels as heavy as a brick as I carefully put the books back in place. I need to put this somewhere safe while I pick up the children from school. The thought of having it on me while I am standing there outside the gates, waiting for them to come out sends a shiver down my spine. Too risky by far.

My leather handbag is filled with detritus – old tissues, discarded lipsticks, loose coins that have fallen out of my purse. I open a side pocket inside and place the packet in there, zipping it up. Then I put the bag in a locker in the utility room that the Downeys provided for my belongings. I lock everything away, satisfied that it will be secure while I'm out of the house for the next half hour. I could present the picture and the evidence to Jack right now but time is against me. This type of thing shouldn't be hurried. It takes careful planning. Just like the receipt, I have already decided that I will wait until one of them approaches me and asks if I have seen it, and then I will strike. I will produce the photograph and ask them to name their price so that their secret stays with me and doesn't make it to the police or the school or social services. The Downeys are proud people. Prestige and wealth mean a lot to them, as does how they are perceived by others. Such a scandal would break them.

'I'm going to pick the children up from school!' Neither of them responds. They rarely do. They will have heard me for sure but in this house, my words carry no weight, sailing over their heads, unwanted and unacknowledged. But soon, they will take notice of what I have to say. They will be very interested when I speak, jumping to attention, desperate to quieten me down and supress any possible shame that may come their way.

I leave the house with a spring in my step, my body lighter than air. It was only a matter of time. The Downeys of the world are too complacent, too damn arrogant to think they are incapable of ever making mistakes. I smile as the sun hits my face, its rays beating down on my cold flesh. If this is what they leave lying around the rooms that I am allowed to enter, what the hell are they hiding in those locked rooms? That bedroom and study must be a minefield of secrets. The thought of getting in them makes my skin tingle with excitement. But of course, I don't need to get inside them. I have enough to be going on with. A small packet of cocaine and a rogue receipt from a tryst with a lover is more than enough to get me what I want.

The sky is a little bit bluer, the clouds whiter, the sun that little bit brighter as I turn the corner and make my way towards the school, slipping among the crowds of parents standing outside the high, wrought-iron gates where I wait in silence.

16

LAUREN

It's been a long year and I was tired of feeling miserable, tired of seeing Dad so miserable. With Alice coming on the scene, maybe I can now look forward instead of continually looking backwards over my shoulder, analysing, questioning everything. I can think about university and there will be no guilt about leaving Dad on his own. I can see now that he'll manage just fine without me.

The beep of my phone cuts into my thoughts, dragging me back to the here and now. A message flashes up from Josh. My face grows hot and my stomach goes into a spasm. Twice he has contacted me now. Twice since we got talking at the party he has asked if he can see me again. I thought it was the alcohol talking, his beer goggles skewing his judgement, but it appears he does actually like me and wants us to meet up.

A pulse throbs in my neck as I read his message, asking if I want to go for a drink in The Grapes next week. I would *love* to go to The Grapes but decide to play it cool and leave it for another hour before I reply, finishing an essay and tidying my room first to pass the time. If he's as keen as he appears then he won't mind waiting, will he? My heart thuds as I type up my reply, my fingers clammy with anticipation.

> That sounds really cool. What time?

I click send and refrain from putting a kiss at the end of my message. Too familiar. Too soon. Don't want to scare him off, make him think I'm a bunny boiler. There's a fine line between keeping somebody interested and making them think you're some sort of unhinged individual. The type of person who puts kisses at the end of a text for fuck's sake or stalks people.

Somebody like Phillip Kennedy.

I sigh and close my eyes: despair, anxiety, that *man* never far from the fringes of my mind. He's always there – waiting, ready to jump into my head even though every fibre of my being doesn't want him in my thoughts. I don't want to think about him and Mum together. I'm almost certain they both thought they had kept it from me – Dad and Mum – but I'm not an idiot. I could see what was going on. As much as they tried to mask their troubles, there was no way to stop the truth from leaking out. And then of course, I saw that text. There was no escaping from the reality of the situation once I saw those words. The intensity of them. The intent.

It's as I'm sitting waiting for a reply from Josh that it happens. The sound almost sends me into a meltdown. I'm already on edge. Jittery. Dad is at work and I'm in the house on my own. I have no idea what's happened and am too scared to go downstairs and look. It was a loud bang, something smashing or breaking. My head is pounding, my heart pummelling against my ribcage, making me woozy and slightly sick. The thought that somebody could be down there, somebody who *knows*, and is wandering about, is enough to make me crumple, my body folding and becoming floppy with fear, my innards turning to liquid.

I sit for a few seconds, arms wrapped around my body, legs tucked under me on the bed, listening, waiting. Waiting for what? I should get up and investigate. I know this but am unable to move, my limbs solid as rocks, my entire body frozen.

The sound of my own breathing rattles around my head. I take a few gasps and tell myself to stop being so bloody ridiculous. The door is locked. Nobody can get in. I am the only one in this house. I *know* this for certain. So why do I feel so full of dread, as if something terrible is about to happen? I visualise a big hammer smashing down on me, fragmenting my skull, atonement for my sins.

Time ticks by as I sit, listening out, trying to regulate my breathing. I'm greeted by a long, drawn-out silence. Nothing to hear. Nothing to see. Nobody else around. I stand up and tiptoe across the landing, peeking into rooms as I pass, making sure they're empty and there isn't some skanky druggy waiting to smash my head in. Then I look down the stairs and let out an involuntary shriek.

Shards of coloured glass are spread over the mat, scattered over the tiled flooring and even sprinkled on the console table next to the front door. There is a hole in the top panel where the rock was thrown through it. It sits there, a large, jagged stone, incongruous and scary looking against the polished floor and recently vacuumed rug.

Adrenaline pulses through me, whistling through my veins as I thunder downstairs and pull at the handle with clammy fingers. I step outside, craning my neck to look up and down the road. It's empty. Nobody around. Nothing to see. Whoever did this could have strolled up and announced their presence on a loudspeaker and they wouldn't have been seen. Everyone's at work or school or out shopping. Nobody home to witness this shitty little act.

The pulse in my neck is so strong and rhythmic, it makes me feel as if I'm going to vomit or pass out. I step back inside the house and lock the door, bending down to pick up the lump of rough, serrated rock, clutching it, inspecting it as if it holds the answer as to who did this.

It sits close to my chest, pressing against my sternum, the sheer heft of it causing me to catch my breath. So many awful thoughts buzz around my brain – worrying thoughts, sickening images. Who did this? Am I being watched? Maybe this was meant for Dad but part of me thinks not. I have a horrible feeling it was definitely directed at me.

I tell myself to get a grip, not be so stupid, so paranoid, my tendency to over-react a physical force within me. I have no idea what to do next, how to deal with this thing. I don't want to ring Dad and worry him. He's just started to climb out of a deep, dark hole. No way do I want to drag him back in there before he has seen real daylight. Fucking stupid, rock-throwing bastard. Whoever it was that did this needs to get a bloody life.

Glass crunches under my feet. I get a brush and dustpan and sweep it all up, picking up the larger shards with my fingers and placing them in the bin. This door panel has been in place for decades, small pieces of stained glass set in individual panes. It's eye-catching, unique, expensive. I am immediately furious. How dare they? How fucking *dare* they try to scare us, whoever it was that did this. They have no right. My palms are hot, my skin flushes with anger and frustration. I thought it was over. It was all meant to be over and done with, our worries and unhappiness.

Grunting loudly, I finish cleaning up and go around checking all the windows and doors, making sure they're locked. I carry the rock through to the kitchen and place it on the table in the centre, trying to work out how to tell Dad about this. How to explain that I sat tight, did nothing for as long as I did, too fearful to move. Too fearful to do anything at all. He's been through enough. He doesn't need any more shit throwing his way and I don't want to have to show him this after he's had a long day at work. Life with Mum was difficult. Things are getting easier now. We don't need any more hatred or upset in this house. I hope that this is just a stupid, awful coincidence. I really hope so. I can't think what else it could be.

I'm still mulling it over when I hear his key in the door. A chunk of air sticks in my throat like a jagged pebble. My heart starts up its uncomfortable, erratic beat once again. I stand and wait for him to come in, for him to ask what the hell has gone on. There is the familiar shuffle of his feet on the mat, the clink of his keys as he places them on the console table and then his voice as he calls my name.

17

PETER

He stares at the gaping hole in the panel. What the hell has happened here? This door and the glass in it are as old as the house itself, each pane carefully set in individual pieces and held together by the leading. It's irreplaceable. Sickening.

Lauren stands beside him, both of them staring up at the large hole as if it will magically repair itself if they wait and watch it for long enough.

'I couldn't see anybody,' she says weakly, as if she is being blamed for this. 'I ran out into the street after it happened but it was empty.'

He puts his arm around her shoulder and cuddles her tightly, her sharp bones pressing into his thick chest. 'I'm glad you didn't. Whoever did this could quite as easily have turned around and done something to you. If anything like this ever happens again, promise me you'll call me, okay?'

She nods and sniffs. For all of her initial bravado, pretending that everything is fine, feigning bravery and telling him that she wasn't alarmed or frightened, he can tell by her quiet demeanour that this has shaken her up. She's fragile, easily startled and upset. She needs protecting.

'Well, my thinking is that this was done by kids,' he says with a sigh. It's the only rational explanation. That's what he tells himself. And it's partly true. Sophia's death evoked pity from neighbours and friends, not hatred. This definitely wasn't done by somebody local, somebody who knows their circumstances. His face still prickles with fear and apprehension: emotions he tries to conceal from Lauren. Did somebody see him that night? The night he trailed behind Sophia, dipping in and out of the bushes and shrubbery, anger and jealousy pushing him on, forcing him to do their bidding. Does somebody know that he was there, right behind her and this is their way of letting him know that they saw him? A sharp reminder that the past is never far behind him. Always ready and waiting to throw everything back in his face, the things he thought could be kept hidden, nicely secreted away. If he is being honest with himself, Peter knows that there is no such place as away. Everything is visible. Known. Nowhere to hide.

'You reckon?' Lauren is looking up at him, a glimmer of hope in her eyes.

'I do reckon. There's no other explanation for it.' He swallows down his fears, tells himself this is a coincidence. He won't think about the other possibilities. He can't. It's over and done with. No going back.

He makes a call to a glazier and after cleaning up the mess, they sit and eat, talking about their day, avoiding the subject entirely. Easier. Less troublesome than raking up the past, delving into the trauma of the past year, the guilt and regret, thick like tar, coating his insides.

'I was thinking about going to university. I'm definitely going to do it.' Lauren is watching him, waiting for his reaction. Her plans for further education were put on the back burner after Sophia died, all discussions about it grinding to a halt.

It's about time, he thinks, *that she put it back in her sights.* Having a goal to work towards will help her focus. Keep her grounded. Not that she isn't already. His daughter is a marvel. One of the best. The sensible parts of him and Sophia combined minus the bitterness and spite. The best of both worlds.

'Sweetheart, I think that's a great idea.' He reaches across her and scoops up lumps of fluffy, white mash with a large spoon, piling it on his plate before smothering it in gravy. Lunch was a prawn sandwich and his stomach feels hollow, as if it has been deprived of food for an age.

'Really? You're not upset about it?'

'Why would I be upset? You've always wanted to go. I think it's a fantastic opportunity. You'll broaden your horizons, meet new friends.

Drink lots of alcohol and party like a demon.' He narrows his eyes and winks at her.

She laughs, a deep, throaty chuckle that helps soothe his nerves and warm his heart. 'Dad, I am never drinking again after that party.'

'Oh, we've all said that,' he replies, chewing on his food. 'I still do after too many glasses of whisky.'

'No, really. I honestly thought my head was going to fall off the next morning. No more vodka for me.'

'Whatever you say,' he murmurs, eyeing her carefully. 'Until next time, that is, eh?'

They chat like a family that doesn't have a care in the world as they eat their evening meal. *Maybe we don't*, he thinks. *Maybe at long last, all our troubles and worries are behind us.*

Maybe the rock was a horrible coincidence, thrown by the little shits that regularly parade around the street with nothing else to do; young lads with nowhere to go and nobody to monitor them. He daren't be too optimistic and he daren't pin his hopes on this relationship with Alice working out and Lauren getting a place at university and all the things that many people take for granted happening to them. He just daren't hope.

Before Sophia died, before their marriage crumbled and she turned to another man for comfort and solace, he didn't give such things a second thought. Life rolled along in a linear fashion and not once did he think that things could go so badly awry. But they did. And they can again. He needs to be vigilant at all times, never letting his guard down. Be mindful of everything he says and does, sticking to the story he told the police about that night, that he was ill in bed. A phone call he had made to the doctors earlier in the day gave his story a little more credence.

Lauren was out with friends. He had no alibi but then neither did Phillip Kennedy. Apparently, his wife was unable to vouch for his whereabouts that night. He too, was out walking the streets, clearing his head, no doubt trying to push all thoughts of Sophia out of his mind. At least that's something they have in common.

He stops, takes a shaky breath, recalibrates his thought patterns. Phillip Kennedy is in prison. Sophia is dead. He and Lauren are here. That's what he needs to concentrate on, not the negative images that penetrate his waking moments, the black and charred thoughts that jostle for space in his head, day after day after day.

'When are you seeing Alice next?' Lauren's voice is light, breezy and full of optimism, back to the girl that he once knew. Back to the girl who waltzed through life without a care in the world. It's good to see her emerge once again, tentatively peeking out from the shadows, eyes gleaming, features lit up with something resembling happiness.

Peter closes his eyes and sighs the briefest of sighs before snapping them open again. He can do this. He can live the rest of his life with his daughter and perhaps Alice by his side. No more Sophia. No more arguments. No more worrying, his anxiety levels sky-high, wondering if somebody was close behind him the night Sophia died.

'Tomorrow evening. I was going to speak to you about it, actually. I've asked her round for a meal. You don't mind, do you? I was thinking it would be a good chance for us all to sit down together and eat and chat, you know, get to know each other?'

'All?' Lauren has put down her fork and is staring at him as if he has just announced that he is going to strip naked and run down the high street with his underwear on his head.

'Well, yeah, if that's okay with you?' He wonders what is coming next, what pearl of wisdom she is about to come out with, what nugget of information she has stored away that he wasn't aware she possessed. 'Better than trawling through Tinder, don't you think? More age appropriate and a damn sight more dignified.'

Lauren manages a smile, shakes her head despondently. 'Dad! You've got to have some time with her on your own. You don't want me hanging around.' Her mouth is gaping, her perfectly straight, white teeth just visible as she stares at him, incredulity tattooed into her features.

'Why not? It's not as if we're a pair of lovestruck teenagers.' He relaxes again and holds up his hand, taking a deep sigh, aware of Lauren's tender age and inexperience. 'I mean, no insult intended, but we're both grown-ups and don't feel the need to spend the evening staring into one another's eyes.' *I'm not you,* he wants to say. *Young and tender and free of the troubles that love can throw your way, unaware of just how painful it can all be, this falling head-over-heels in love business.*

It worries him, how easily lives can diverge and change, souring beyond recognition. It concerns him that his daughter may have to experience it all, be subject to somebody else's moods and wants and needs and eventually discarded and cast aside like a piece of rubbish if she doesn't quite measure up.

She clicks her tongue at him and continues eating, unaware of his thoughts, his deepest fears for her future. For both of their futures. 'Well, whatever, but I'm going out anyway. We're going to have a study night round Jessie's house. You can save me some cake, though. The pudding is the best bit of any meal.'

Part of him is grateful that she is going out and another part feels nervous anticipation at spending the entire evening alone with Alice. He is attracted to her for sure and yet there is a small part of that woman that puts him on edge, questioning her sudden appearance in his life. She's too good to be true. Maybe that's it, he thinks. Maybe he's become so accustomed to being shat upon from a great height that an easy life feels out of his reach, as if he doesn't deserve it. Or maybe his previous encounters with females who like him, were looking for nothing more than physical comfort and pleasure, have coloured his judgement, skewing his expectations of what a proper relationship should look like. He can hardly use his marriage as a benchmark for happiness. Now he has to rely on instinct and his own gut feeling. But what if he's wrong? What if he throws himself into this thing with Alice and it all goes tits up, leaving him bereft once again?

'Make sure you keep your mouth shut when you eat and no burping or farting until after Alice has left.' Lauren stands up and clears away the plates, her laughter dragging him out of his thoughts and lifting his spirits. It's good to have his girl back, the light-hearted, witty Lauren that injects levity into his life. He needs her humour and smiles to keep him going. He thought that life without all the acrimony between him and Sophia would be at least easier if not easy, full of lightness. So why at times like this does it still feel so fucking difficult?

18

ALICE

It's been a full twenty-four hours and neither Elizabeth nor Jack have made any mention of the missing packet of powder. I am both irritated and disappointed in equal measure. There was no point in taking it if its absence isn't going to provoke an adverse reaction. Perhaps it's a weekend thing, something they take to wind down at the end of their hectic working week.

I grimace and pick up a cleaning cloth, dabbing it across already gleaming surfaces, resentment seeping out of every pore. Neither of them knows what it's like to sweat and toil, to have to get their hands dirty to earn a meagre crust. They don't even do their own cleaning, let alone anybody else's. They are both unbelievably privileged and have no reason to need any sort of recreational drug to relax and ease their stress levels. Perhaps they won't miss it. I hope they do. I hope one of them approaches me and asks the question while I attempt to suppress a smile as they blush and flounder and dance around the subject, throwing out twee euphemisms, trying to pretend that it is a harmless substance and not a class-A drug that they have mislaid the way other people lose their phones or car keys.

I detest them both with a passion. I detest their aloof, detached manner. I detest the way they ignore their children, foisting them off on me at every available opportunity, but most of all, I detest them because of how easy their lives are. They squander money on pointless items such as the outrageously expensive and totally unnecessary antique rocking chair that sits idly in the corner of the dining room, and the hideously ostentatious new Jaguar that is parked outside the house. They don't need these things. Nobody needs such vulgar items that serve only to show off their wealth to friends and neighbours. Except it would appear that they do. The Downeys thrive on them, talking about them endlessly, going out and buying more and more when this house is already crammed full of objects that collectively must be worth as much as the house itself. There are days when I feel as if they buy these things to get back at me, an aggressive display of their financial standing, a way of letting me know how deep their pockets are. But all of these things come at a price. Nobody can live their lives in such a fashion without something going terribly wrong. A crash and burn is just around the corner for this family. I can sense it. And now I have the power to bring it all about.

I yearn to ask them if they have lost anything, to confront Elizabeth with evidence of her husband's philandering and then produce the small packet, telling them that I plan on going public with what I have unless they pay me a handsome sum of money. Even then, once I get the cash, I may still report them to the police and social services, just for fun. Just because I can. Or maybe it's to let them get a glimpse into my life, let them know how things are on the darker side of the divide, to let them see how the poorer half live. But I won't do any of those things. Not just yet. It's all about the timing, getting it right, that delicate balance. Tip too hard one way and everything will slip and fall. I'll keep my secrets secret for the time being. Cling onto them and savour them, like fine wine or a particularly expensive serving of caviar. I will bide my time and enjoy the build-up. That's the best part, don't you think? The waiting, the almost sexual release when everything becomes apparent and unspools in spectacular fashion.

Tonight, I've been invited to Peter's house where we will eat and drink and get to know one another a little more. He may even have bought me some flowers, perhaps my favourite wine, the one we spoke about in the restaurant. God knows I dropped enough hints. I hope he was taking notice. In the next few weeks, he will have to pay very close attention to what I'm saying. Let's see if he manages to put all the pieces together, the hints, the subtle narratives I throw his way. He's obviously a bright man, albeit damaged and blinded by grief.

What he needs to realise is that losing somebody close to you isn't solely reserved for him. We've all lost somebody at some stage, it's just that some of us manage it better than others – the searing pain, the never-ending stab of separation and loss. We all suffer it at some point in our lives. Peter Saunders doesn't have the monopoly on sorrow and suffering. He needs to know that. Besides, what does he have to feel aggrieved about? His wife was a thoughtless liar, a cheating, callous bitch of a woman. He's better off without her. We all are.

Outside, the weather changes, a shifting mist swirling and swaying, obscuring the houses and cars. It suits my mood, the overwhelming darkness that grows within me exponentially, obliterating everything.

I'm lost in my thoughts, my mood down in the dirt when I hear something behind me. A shuffle of feet, a whisper of breath on my neck. I turn to see Jack standing close by, his expression dour, a restlessness about him as he moves closer to me, so close I can feel the heat of his body against my own skin, am able to smell his aftershave – a fresh, lemon scent with undertones of something musky. Something expensive. Always that, the money and the sense of distance that it brings between those who have it and those who don't.

I take a step back, readying myself for what he is about to say, wondering whether it will be a calm and restrained approach or whether he will fly into a rage, making accusations about me stealing. I suspect it will be the former, but of course I don't know this man. Not really. I wash and iron his clothes, clean up after him and care for his children day in, day out, but in reality, he is a stranger to me. I know nothing about him except that he is an immensely wealthy property developer who plays away from home and snorts cocaine in his spare time. That's enough for me to be able to have a stranglehold over him. Enough to make me think that he's wealthy enough to make sure I keep our little secret between us and not smear his good name. It's a perfect match. He needs to keep his reputation intact and I need the money.

'Alice?' He cocks his head to one side, his fingers flexing madly by his sides.

I hear the cracking of bone and cartilage as he brings his hands together and bends his fingers back and forth.

'Yes? Is there something wrong? I've finished ironing those shirts that Elizabeth asked me to do and I bleached the bathroom as requested.' I stifle laughter, thinking that I may as well curtsey and be done with it, all this subservience and kowtowing caper. Were it not for the fact there is some remuneration at the end of this little game, I would be tempted to spit in his face, to tell him how rotten he and his wife are with their superior attitudes and the knack they have of making me feel as if I am not worthy of their time or attention. An irritant, that's all I am: a fly to be swatted away. At least that is something the children and I have in common, all of us regularly cast aside for something or somebody better.

'No, no. Everything in the house looks perfect. I don't suppose you stumbled across that receipt, did you?'

I shake my head and narrow my eyes as if deep in thought. 'Not seen it. I'm really sorry. I'm guessing it was important?'

'No, honestly, it's fine. I can manage without it. Also, I don't suppose you've come across some of my medication? I think I left it in the library, which was really careless of me.'

I almost choke on my own saliva, a pulse throbbing in my neck as I blink rapidly and look into his eyes for some indication that he is being sardonic, but see only complete innocence. He is almost as good at this little game as I am. Almost. But not quite.

'Oh gosh. No, I've not seen anything like that. What did it look like? I can empty everything out of there and have a good search if you like?'

He doesn't like, shaking his head furiously, his eyes now glazing over at my suggestion. 'No, no. It's absolutely fine. I'm sure it will turn up.'

I am tempted to ask what the medication is for but stop short, knowing I have humiliated him enough for one day. 'Okay, well I don't mind searching. If you need any help, don't hesitate to ask me.'

'Yes, of course, and thank you. I think perhaps I'm ready for a break, losing so many items lately. I'm being rather scatter-brained which isn't like me at all. I'm usually very methodical and careful.' He moves away and stops, turning to glance at me, words formed on his lips that remain there, unspoken, held tightly before he squeezes shut his eyes and shakes his head, an imperceptible movement that I detect because I'm assessing him closely to see if he suspects me. To see if he knows what has really happened. He stops awhile then heads away, his shoes clicking on the wooden floor, echoing throughout the house like rapid gunfire.

My breath is hot and erratic, threads of anticipation that border on excitement running through me, darting through my veins. He is making this so easy. These people are rigid, uptight. Unable to allow their true emotions to run free. Imagine what damage I could do in a house full of lackadaisical folk who live in a haze of chaos and confusion. Perhaps Jack Downey has overreached his capabilities with too many balls up in the air and is losing focus, turning into one of those muddled people, his grip on his tightly reined little world slowly loosening and coming undone. I won't take advantage if that is indeed the case. Two items going astray is careless; three going missing is suspicious. Three would point the finger at me and I cannot let that happen. Besides, I have enough for now. Enough to cause him a few sleepless nights and make him edgy and anxious, his thinking scrambled and compromised. Then I will approach him, give him my price and watch as realisation dawns, crashing into his brain and shattering his perfect little world into tiny little pieces.

19

PETER

The sauce is bubbling up as the doorbell rings. He turns down the gas, wipes his hands on a cloth, aware that he hasn't yet changed his clothes, and heads into the hallway, the broken glass on the door panel still an ugly unwelcome sight to him. A silent reminder of who might be out there, watching, waiting. Letting him know that they know. He swallows and takes a deep breath.

He had forgotten how pretty Alice is as he pulls open the door, his eyes sweeping over her powder-blue dress and blonde hair that is swirled up in a loose bun, small, loose ringlets framing her petite, smiling face.

'Alice, you look amazing.' He leans forward on impulse and kisses her cheek. Her skin is as light and as soft as air and just as welcoming. He wants to breathe her in until she becomes a part of him. 'Come in, come in,' he says, his voice brisk but welcoming. 'It's lovely to see you.'

She steps forward, a waft of lilies and something musky flowing in her wake. His senses are heightened as she passes him and stands close by, his every nerve ending jumping and jolting in her presence. Taking her jacket, he hangs it next to the door, thinking how slovenly he looks in comparison to her immaculate appearance, with her soft, flowing dress and carefully coiffured hair. A new shirt wouldn't have gone amiss. Perhaps a haircut and maybe even a pair of new shoes. He needs to do better. To be better.

'I'll take you into the living room and then quickly get changed if that's okay?'

'What happened to your door?' Her eyes are fixed on the wooden board that Peter nailed into place: a makeshift covering until the glazier arrives.

'Ah,' he says, a slight hesitance to his voice. 'I think it was local kids. Lauren was home on her own when a large stone was thrown through it. Still,' he continues, keen to keep the mood light, 'at least nobody was hurt. That's the main thing, isn't it?'

She nods and smiles, her eyes the deepest blue. He could dive right into them, swim straight to her heart if she would let him.

'Right, come on. I'll get you a drink then I'll go and freshen up, try to get rid of the cooking smells that are hanging around me.'

'Oh, this is so kind. You remembered!' She takes the glass of wine from him, commenting about how it's her favourite and how clever of him it is to remember such a thing.

'Right. I'll be back in a couple of minutes.' He hands her the remote for the sound system, placing it in her palm. 'Feel free to change it if the music isn't to your taste. Lauren keeps telling me I have the musical preferences of an eighty-year-old.'

She laughs as he heads upstairs, mildly giddy, ready to embrace whatever lies ahead. Tonight, Sophia will become a dim and distant memory and if it's only for tonight, then that is enough. Small steps.

She's standing, leafing through one of the books on the shelves that's set on the back wall of the room when he goes back into the living room ten minutes later. 'You're a fan of the classics?' In her hand is a copy of *Great Expectations*.

She smiles, raises it higher, brandishing it close to her face. 'This particular one is one of my favourites.'

Peter's stomach tightens, his skin flashes hot. He silently chastises himself for not being more ruthless with Sophia's belongings prior to Alice arriving. He should have got rid of them long ago and inwardly questions his motives for keeping them. He has his reasons, skewed and irrational that they are. He didn't keep them for him. He did it for his daughter. His guilt would become an outward, obvious thing if he were to throw them away. Keeping this place like a shrine has alleviated his culpability, helping him to shrug off the heavy shroud of blame that settles on him every single day.

'Ah, no. It was Sophia who was the classics buff. I'm more action thriller.' He smiles, trying to deflect from his clumsiness. Perhaps he should have removed them, thrown everything away, but then what would everyone think? It would definitely look as if he was trying to erase Sophia's memory, the fact she ever lived here. He swallows, telling himself that he kept them out for Lauren – the photographs, the books, the wardrobe that is still filled with Sophia's clothes – it's all for Lauren. He is being too hard on himself. It isn't all to lessen his guilt. 'If there isn't a car chase or a shootout in it,' he says, a dull thud starting up in his neck, 'then I'm not interested.'

She places it back, seemingly unperturbed by his admission, and picks up a Lee Child paperback. 'I think I've read some of his. More things that we have in common, eh?'

Relief swells in his chest, a large, blossoming thing that is both warm and cooling at the same time. She's making this easy for him, swerving around his mistakes, purposely ignoring his clumsy faux pas. This woman may well be the best thing that has happened to him in a long time. He considers himself a lucky man. If only it hadn't taken him so long to notice her. If he had left church and not decided to go for an amble around the graveyard, Alice might not be here today. But she is, and he is grateful for it, for this woman who warms his blood and will freshen his outlook, smoothing out the wrinkles of his undulating life.

It was so peaceful, that day in the graveyard; it felt good to be outside in the silence where the ambience was gentler, its edges softer and less defined. He hadn't realised that Alice was there. He had spotted her bent over a grave as he made his way down to the bottom of the yard where the large oak tree, gnarled and twisted with age, provided some shade and a view of the hills beyond. The vista helped him to think, to dampen his negative thoughts, keep his demons at bay. It was pure chance that he was there at that time. Their paths could so easily have gone in opposite directions, yet they didn't. And now here they are, two lost souls, finding their way through this time in their lives, bonded by the death of their spouses.

'Can I refill your glass?'

She passes it over, her hands small and pale. A thought nudges its way into his brain; those small fingers deftly unfastening his shirt, running down his chest and over his stomach, her nails gently tracing their way lower and lower, his breath coming in short, hot gasps, Alice moaning softly, her lips parted in an act of desire... He snaps himself out of it and heads into the kitchen where he pours them both a large goblet of wine. He's taken three long slugs by the time he arrives back to where she is sitting, her skirt riding up her leg, exposing an expanse of a slim thigh. He wonders what time Lauren will be arriving back, whether it will be another 2 a.m. show like last week or whether she'll saunter back in at 10 p.m. prompt, shattering any ideas he has of coaxing Alice upstairs and into his bed.

'Thank you, Peter.' She takes the glass and glances around the room. 'It's a lovely house you have here. Very tasteful. Really elegant.'

'I'm afraid not much of it is my doing. And Lauren is superb at cleaning and keeping the place spick and span.' He glosses over the fact that Sophia decorated this house, turning it into the place it is today. This poor woman must feel as if she is constantly treading in Sophia's shadow, picking her way through the belongings of a dead woman. The detritus of Sophia Saunders. He should have changed things, nudged his deceased wife out of the way, and yet all the while, he felt sure he was being watched, scrutinised. People judging, ready to pull apart anything he did and point the finger at him. Or maybe that was his conscience speaking, reminding him to be a good, grieving husband, to do all the right things and look suitably bereft. Like attending the grieving sessions. That was definitely the right thing to do. It also helped him rid himself of the feelings that have been biting at him. What is the right length of time to leave before disposing of your dead wife's belongings and getting on with your life without arousing suspicion? A week? A month? A year?

'Anyway,' he adds quickly, keen to change the subject, 'why don't we take a seat in the dining room? Everything is almost ready. I hope you like seafood. I took a punt and made us a squid and chorizo salad for starters followed by tuna and lemon pasta.'

'It sounds perfect. You're obviously a very talented cook.' She gives him a sly grin and he almost melts.

They eat and drink and the more alcohol he consumes, the more relaxed and natural he becomes, everything blurred with an alcoholic haze, softened and smudged into a delicate state of tranquillity.

'Vanilla and chocolate parfait to finish,' he says as he places Alice's dish down in front of her, the temptation to lean in and kiss her so strong, it almost roots him to the spot.

'Chocolate,' she replies with a sigh. 'What's not to like?'

She's right. It may well be shop bought, saving him a lot of hard work and time, but it tastes as good as it looks, filling that last, tiny hole in their bellies. Insisting that they leave the dishes for him to sort later, they retire to the living room, where Alice slips onto the sofa, kicks off her shoes and tucks her feet under her legs, looking as if she has lived in this house all of her life.

Right on cue, Peter's phone beeps. He wants to ignore it, fearful of breaking the moment, but glances at it, curiosity getting the better of him. He smiles, glad he went with his instincts. It's Lauren telling him that she's staying out, spending the night at Jessie's house. There is a creeping sensation under his skin as his blood pressure soars, a quickening deep inside his veins that pulses through his body and snakes and coils itself deep in his abdomen.

He refills their glasses and slides in next to Alice on the sofa. 'That was Lauren. She's spending the night at her friend's house.' He keeps his tone light and casual as if they're discussing what to watch on TV. Just idle chit-chat, that's all it is. Nothing more. He inhales, is able to smell Alice's floral perfume, to feel the heat of her body close to his as he edges nearer.

It happens rapidly, naturally, quickly and without preamble or planning, their lips meeting, their bodies practically suctioned together with desire. No disruptions, no teenagers stumbling in and interrupting their time together. Just Peter and Alice. Alice and Peter. Together as one.

***

Later, they lie in bed, him playing with her hair, wondering if she is as enamoured with him as he is with her.

'I should go.' Her voice is like warm honey, coating his skin, healing him, her medicinal qualities reaching deep inside his chest and turning him back into the person he used to be. The man he once was before everything fractured and fell apart around him. Before Sophia broke him and he in turn, broke her.

'Don't go,' he whispers as he kisses her neck, his mouth moving over her throat and down towards her collarbone. Lower and lower he travels, unable to stop himself.

'I have to, I'm afraid. I'm at work in the morning.' She is up and getting dressed before he has another chance to protest.

'I'll book you a cab.' He throws on some clothes and grabs at his phone, disappointment rippling through him.

'Thank you. I've had a lovely evening, I really have, and I'm sorry to be leaving but I've got an early start in the morning. I wish I didn't but I do.' She slips into her shoes and heads downstairs, flashing him a conciliatory smile that helps to lessen his fears that he has scared her off and she won't be back. 'Maybe we can see each other again soon?'

He is like an over-excited schoolboy, his head buzzing with eagerness, a thousand bees in there flying about in an enthusiastic frenzy. He has to stop this, to calm down and act rationally, not let his heart take over his head. He's a grown man, not a teenager with a crush. A man with a past. Heavy baggage. He needs to be careful, controlled.

The taxi arrives in a matter of minutes. He stands on the doorstep, a longing to see her again already growing within him, twisting its way under his flesh, heating up his blood. Her face, the soft skin – it's all he can think about, filling his mind, arousing him in ways he didn't think possible.

'You really need to get that fixed,' she says, pointing up at the rough piece of timber covering the broken glass panel. 'Anybody could break in through that bit of wood.'

They hug and a little bit of him leaves with her. A void in him until the next time they meet. He waits until the car disappears around the corner and then closes the door, his skin still burning with desire, his heart doing somersaults in his chest.

Alice, Alice, Alice. Where have you been for the last year of my life?

He climbs into bed and lies back, the weight that has been pressing down on him for what feels like a hundred years lifting. Life is brighter, the path easier to navigate, all thoughts of Sophia and the night she died, all those dark memories pushed to the back of his mind. He sleeps soundly, dreaming only of Alice.

20

ALICE

Sleep cannot come fast enough. I shower, turning the water up as hot as I can stand it, and scrub every inch of my skin before climbing inside the cool sheets and closing my eyes, longing for the blackness to descend. His mouth, his hands all over me – that's all I can think about. It makes my skin go hot and cold, a clammy sensation shifting over my flesh as I visualise his face, his soft groans as he pawed at me. Even his unarguably handsome face and sweet-smelling body cannot help me come to terms with what I have had to do tonight: getting inside his bed, allowing him inside of *me*. It's a means to an end, something I had to do to get close to him. I always knew it was going to happen. I've prepared for it. It doesn't make it any easier, however. It doesn't make me want him. Not in the same way he wants me. Ours is an asymmetrical relationship, his needs quite different to mine. His needs overshadowing everything, like the grasping hands of a spoilt, petulant child, desperate for attention.

Smashing the door panel inconvenienced them and gave me a warm glow inside. It was my starting point. A little bit of external damage, just for fun. Just because I can. They have no idea what lies ahead. No clue at all. I should pity them, being blind to the subterfuge and deception taking place right in front of them. Their minds are too idle to notice it: stuck in a rut, bogged down with grief and a desperate need to get their old life back. They don't see me. The real me. I am invisible to them. Just as well, really.

I clear my thoughts and concentrate on slowing down my breathing until at last, the darkness settles behind my eyes and I drift into a place of shadows and weightlessness where my life is full of meaning again and I'm at the helm, steering it in the right direction.

* * *

The light streaming in through the window wakes me the following morning. I was too tired, just too damn sick and repulsed to bother closing them. I look at the clock – 6.30 a.m. Time to get up anyway. The Downeys prefer it if I take the children to school even though it's only a ten-minute walk for them. They're busy people, they tell me. I rub at my eyes feverishly. Too busy for their own children, even.

I get up, eat breakfast and get ready, wondering what Peter will be up to this morning. Hopefully, he will call later or send a message. I've got him. That's the main thing. He is dangling on the end of my line. Today, regardless of what happens, regardless of how many demeaning chores Jack and Elizabeth throw my way, whether it be cleaning windows and scrubbing floors that haven't even been stepped upon, I will smile and walk on air.

Everything feels effortless, fluid and requiring minimal exertion as I head to the Downeys' house, ready for the day ahead.

I'm greeted with a deathly silence as I open the door and step inside. This isn't unusual. The people in this house are ghosts, a family of corpses floating from one room to another with no regular interaction or true purpose. They may as well be dead.

'Morning, Alice. Elizabeth left early this morning for a spa day in Durham. I was wondering if you could take the children to school? I'm working from home today but have a virtual meeting in half an hour.' Jack appears bright, his manner sprightly. No signs that he is nervous about his missing items. Just like me, he is the perfect liar.

'Of course. I'll go and get their things ready.'

I start to head towards their playroom but he calls after me. 'I was wondering if I could have a chat with you about something when you get back. Nothing to worry about. Just a few things I want to clear up.'

A frisson rushes through me. I turn and flash him a wide smile, doing my best to appear cool and unruffled. Which of course, I am. I've no reason to be nervous or afraid. I hold all the cards and have the power to crush this man. 'Absolutely. I'll be back in just over half an hour. I'll set to cleaning the children's bedrooms once I return. Feel free to come and see me when you've finished your meeting.'

* * *

The air is warm, the path thick with people hurrying to various destinations as we make our way to school, Fionn complaining that I'm walking too quickly and Yasmin focused on her phone.

'You'll need to hand that over to me once we get to the gates. You know the rules about phones in school.'

'Whatever,' she says curtly. 'You're not my mum anyway. You can't tell me what to do.'

I stare down at little Fionn who is busy waving to his friends and rummaging in his schoolbag for his small football, and then turn to Yasmin, my fingers clutched tightly around the top of her arm, my mouth close to her ear. 'Watch your mouth, missy. You don't want me telling your parents about the messages you've been sending to people on social media now, do you?' My voice is a hiss, tiny flecks of spittle escaping from between my pursed lips.

She stops walking, her eyes wide, her mouth slack with shock as I continue with my little hissed tirade. 'This stays between us, okay? One word to your parents and every text and nasty, pissy little message you have ever sent will get printed off and handed over to your mum and dad. Now change your attitude and start treating me with a bit of fucking respect, yes?'

She is nodding now, her eyes brimming with tears, her cheeks crimson with fear. Good. I have had enough of her shitty little attitude. Nine going on nineteen. She is a child. Enough is enough.

'Bye, Alice.' Fionn gives me a fist bump as we reach the school before running off to greet his little pals. He's a cute kid really – privileged and isolated but unlike his sister, hasn't yet developed an icy attitude. The attitude of a privileged child who is cocksure yet has been nowhere and experienced nothing of note.

'Phone.' I hold out my upturned palm and watch with satisfaction as Yasmin hands it over without question, her slightly freckled skin still red with shock and fear. 'Always remember,' I say icily, 'I'm the grown-up around here. What I say goes.'

She is nodding now, her brain possibly trying to work out which of her messages I've read. The truth is, I haven't seen any of them but I've met many girls like Yasmin before – feisty, aloof creatures, so firm in their belief that they are deserving of only the best that life can offer them, brimming to full with entitlement that I took a stab at the kind of texts and missives she sends to friends and enemies alike and hit gold. It didn't take a rocket scientist to work it out. I've seen the way she greets her friends, heard the way she speaks to them and about them. Yasmin is an Elizabeth Downey in the making. Like mother, like daughter. Spoilt, spiteful creatures interested only in themselves.

'I'm sorry,' she squeaks, her body seeming to shrink before my eyes.

'It's fine,' I say coolly. 'And as I say, if we keep this between ourselves, then there's no reason for your parents to be told, is there?'

More nodding. She bites at her lip and makes an attempt at linking her arm through mine. I give her a brief tap of acknowledgement and shrug her off. 'Right. Off you go. I'll see you later.'

And then she is gone, her small, lithe body swallowed up by the crowd of youngsters heading through the gates, all decked out in their silly straw boaters and bottle-green blazers. This place is so far removed from the school I attended, an alien environment full of rich children, their path in life already mapped out with a large pot of gold at the end of it, that it may as well be another planet, another universe even. My school was the local comprehensive full of disadvantaged, disaffected youngsters with no real aim or aspirations in life. Just getting through the day was a challenge for them. As a child, I came from an average, working-class family and we lived in a fairly average house. I went to university despite my humble beginnings, and that was where I met my husband. I thought

I had it all sorted. I thought we would grow old together. How wrong I was.

I turn and walk back to the house, a jumble of thoughts crowding my head, jockeying for position in my brain. I force them out of my mind and focus on the Downey family. If Jack has a study, why did he choose to leave his packet in the library? And then I realise that Elizabeth spends time in the study but rarely visits the library. Perhaps Jack has done this type of thing before and she is aware of it. Who knows how these people operate? I cannot begin to fathom their thinking. We are very different beasts, the Downeys and me. They think of me as the servant and nanny, and until discovering Jack's tawdry little secrets, I didn't think of them at all. They pay my wages and that's where my allegiance to them starts and ends.

Jack's Jaguar is the cleanest vehicle I have ever seen; those are my thoughts as I arrive back at the house and make my way up the driveway. Fitted with all the top-of-the range gadgets, it is a target for criminal damage. Even areas such as this one, a leafy suburb on the outskirts of York, can be susceptible to bouts of crime. It would be such a pity if one day, he were to come out and find that somebody had gouged the paintwork or slashed the tyres. A terrible, terrible shame.

He's standing with his back to me in the hallway as I enter and take off my jacket, hanging it up on the coat peg in the small vestibule tucked away next to the stairwell. He turns, his face half hidden, his phone clamped to his ear. He holds up his hand for me to wait, turns back again, mumbling into the mobile, telling whoever it is that he will speak to them later, and ends the call.

'Alice. Thank you for taking the children to school.'

I want to tell him that I do it every morning and pick them up again every evening and although it pains me to say it, that it is part of my job, unlike the cleaning tasks they put my way which is a different remit altogether, but remain silent, nodding instead and lowering my eyes obediently.

'Not a problem. They're lovely children. You must be very proud of them.'

This catches him unawares. I don't imagine he spends a great deal of time thinking about his children and how they present themselves to the outside world. Why would he? Jack Downey is a busy man, an important man in the world of commerce. They are, after all, just children. His children. Children I will probably never be able to have. I have no partner and up until recently, no hope either.

'Well, yes. Quite,' he says, his eyes slightly glassy as he attempts to put the conversation back on course with him controlling the direction it takes. He puts his phone in his pocket and steps closer to me. 'Anyway, I just wanted to chat to you about that missing medication again. And the receipt.' His tone has changed. Less bluster, a more direct and authoritative inflection in his voice. It carries across the empty hallway, imposing and confident.

I brace myself, the words I plan on saying already formulated in my head.

'You see, the thing is, Alice, what you may not realise is that we have cameras in this house.' He takes another step closer to me, steel in his glare, his body straight, his face chiselled and harsh. 'We have cameras in the hallway and in the library. And I checked those cameras last night, so I don't think I need to spell it out to you, do I?' His hands are balled into fists, his jaw pulsing as he clamps his mouth together tightly and chews at his bottom lip.

I guessed about the cameras. I didn't know it for sure but people like the Downeys living in a house like this are bound to be serious when it comes to security. His words don't faze me and neither does his aggressive stance. Whichever way this situation is viewed, I still have the upper hand.

'Well, maybe you do. You see,' I murmur, moving back from the heat of his body, the slightly rancid odour of his breath, 'whichever way you look at this, I'm not the one stashing class-A drugs in a house where children are present. Nor am I the one conducting an illicit affair behind my spouse's back.'

The colour leaches from his face. This, he didn't expect. I presume he was prepared for a weeping, apologetic, subservient nanny who begs to keep her job, promising she will never do such a thing again, asking if they can they keep it a secret between the pair of them because she needs this money and to lose her position would be the ruin of her. Blah blah blah...

I don't do any of those things. My pride is as important as Jack

Downey's pride, my needs just as important as his. I will not bow or scrape before him. Instead, I push back my shoulders and give him a wide smile, cocking my head to one side sympathetically. 'So perhaps we can come to some kind of agreement so that this thing stays between the two of us and Elizabeth doesn't get to hear of it.' I stare down at my nails, assessing them carefully as I speak again. 'Or the school. We wouldn't want the school getting wind of the fact there are drugs stashed in this house, would we? I should imagine poor Elizabeth would fall into a swoon if social services or, God forbid, the police should hear of this terrible misdemeanour. Imagine the scandal, all those wagging tongues...'

I don't need to say any more. My threats appear to have hit the spot. He will come back with some weak defence, no doubt, or a get-out clause making me look like the perpetrator but I'm prepared for that as well. I've thought this thing through.

'And what if I were to tell the police that it was you who brought the drugs into the house and stashed them? What then?' he says through gritted teeth.

'And what if I were to show that receipt to your dear wife? What then?' I delve into my pocket and retrieve my phone, scrolling through until I find the image that I need and hold it out for him to see. 'I made sure to take a photograph of the offending article. I also wore gloves so the only fingerprints on the packet of drugs are yours. Now what was it you were saying about speaking to the police regarding me and your secret stash?'

21

LAUREN

The atmosphere in the house is electric. Dad is acting as if he is the cat who got the cream, his movements through the house fluid and supple, yet at the same time electric and fiery, like somebody who is both relaxed and keyed up at the same time. It's as if something momentous is about to happen. Something unforgettable.

I have no idea whether or not Alice stayed the night after I stopped at Jessie's house. Dad meeting her is like him being given a new lease of life. I hope she did, not that I ever want to think of my dad in that way, you know, him sleeping with somebody. Still, I do know that she's restored some equilibrium into his existence, given him something to look forward to. Maybe she did stay over which would explain his mood. He's probably charged with excitement and adrenaline, his body bouncing all over the place. I try to not think about it. He's my dad after all. We have boundaries and we definitely don't have in-depth discussions about sex. Him having to deal with my tampons in his bathroom cabinet is enough.

I think I perhaps feel the same way about meeting Josh at the weekend. I'm nervous but also eager. My stomach somersaults every time I think of him. He isn't conventionally handsome but there's something about him that makes me light up, like a meeting of minds. I make him laugh, apparently. And I'm clever. It gave me a warm glow to hear him say that. He also said I'm really pretty which made me feel good. It may come to something; it may not. Only time will tell. We all need a little normality after what we have been through. I want to get on with my life, make Dad proud of me. I owe it to him. I owe it to myself.

I wonder if that's how it was when Dad met Sophia, if there was a time when they got along and she didn't feel the need to spread her legs for another man. My face burns at the thought, fury pulsing beneath my skin. How could she? Her actions tore our family apart. I hated her for it. Still do. Dad thinks I idolised her. I didn't. Perhaps when I was younger, I looked up to her, thought of her as glamorous and somebody I could become one day but that all changed when I realised what sort of a person she was. I've never told Dad about my feelings towards her. He's happy to continue with his belief that Mum and I had the perfect mother/daughter relationship. He was too wrapped up in his own misery and confusion to see the truth.

Dad's working from home today. This is both a blessing and a curse. I'm back early from college and I can hear him speaking to customers on the phone. I feel as if I have to keep the noise level to a minimum and am never quite sure when the right time is to interject if I want to speak to him. Yet at the same time, it's good to have him here, to see him happy and relaxed, almost back to his old self. I knew he'd get there in the end. Losing Mum was always going to be a blip in his life. Theirs wasn't exactly the happiest of marriages. It was a car crash for many years before she died. I keep quiet about that aspect of my life to my friends. It's not a good look, slagging off the dead but it's true. The day before Mum died, Dad gave her an ultimatum – Kennedy or him. Neither of them knew that I was in the house while they were arguing. I had snuck in and was lying on my bed, listening to their raised voices. Mum had said she had broken it off with him but Dad didn't believe her. That's where she was going the night she was murdered – to meet Phillip Kennedy. I'm sure of it.

I open my wardrobe and lean inside, pulling out the bag that I keep stashed at the back. Inside is every photo I had of Sophia. I should throw them out. There's nothing to be gained from keeping them. I peer inside and all those old emotions come rushing back – the fear, the all-consuming dread that something terrible, something final was going to happen to our little family. And in the end, it did.

The bag is filled with shreds of the pictures I tore apart, ripping and screwing them up, gouging at her face until there was nothing left of her. Dad thinks I keep them in here to treasure them and keep them safe. If only he knew. Their wedding photographs are ruined too. He hasn't asked for them and I haven't offered. Photos of us as a family on picnics, at the park, visiting the zoo – all in pieces.

Next to this bag is the one where I store the clippings of my hair, the strands I tore at, cut and pulled out when things got to be too much. I lift it out and stare inside, a small pain screeching across my scalp as the memories come blazing back into my mind: the raised voices, the accusations, the screaming matches. They drove me to it, to cause myself some pain in the hope it would detract from the festering wound that was my home life. Nobody noticed my bald patches, the coin-sized areas of shiny scalp. I styled my hair to cover them up, backcombing and fluffing, strategically placing certain strands to cover up my weakness. Mum and Dad were too bogged down in their own issues to notice me anyway. I was on the periphery of their lives, just another person who co-existed in this house with them. I could have done whatever I liked and nobody would have noticed. Which is what I did in the end.

I swallow and place both bags back, stuffing them deep in the darkest corner of the cupboard, out of sight. One day, I'll dispose of them, but not at the moment. I need them here to remind me of how it used to be, to remind me of how bad it was and how in the end, it all worked out for the best.

It's exhausting keeping secrets. Every single day is an ordeal. But not for much longer. I have things to look forward to. I've got Josh and now Dad has Alice. She's going to change things around here. I can just feel it, like a welcome tension in my gut, not the throbbing, sickening tautness that has been sitting at the base of my belly for so long, I thought it would never leave me. This is a welcome sensation, something that ignites a spark inside of me. A spark that got extinguished when Mum and Dad's marriage began to fall apart. It's beginning to burn bright again and I have Alice to thank for that. I just hope she sticks around and injects some warmth back into our lives. God knows we deserve it. Or at least, Dad does. I'm not sure what I deserve.

22

ALICE

He made it so easy for me, it was almost painful. Almost but not completely. Like taking candy from a small child. I slip my hand in my pocket and finger the notes, enjoying the sensation of the smooth, plastic-like texture that is rolled into a thick tight wad, gangster style.

Five hundred pounds and that's just for starters. I told him that if he tried to sack me, I would produce the receipt and message it to his wife. I will get the remainder of the cash later in the week and then I will hand over his stash. Or so he thinks. A lot can happen in a week. I may just decide to up my demands. It all depends on how he treats me between now and then, how many windows he and his precious wife make me clean, how much laundry they expect me to do.

The sun is warm against my skin as I head towards the school to pick up the children. It almost killed him, letting me collect them but as he said, he is a busy and important man and has too much work on to find the time to collect them himself.

I cross the road and wait alongside the small collection of parents and childminders and nannies, wondering if any of them work in circumstances similar to mine or do they breeze through their day, doing very little to earn their money? Few of them look frazzled or stressed. I'm guessing they all have relatively easy lives, their existences limited to keeping a loose eye on children and putting the odd toy back in its rightful place.

There is tug on my arm and turn to see a woman in her thirties staring at me, a quizzical expression on her face. 'Sorry, I'm sure I know you from somewhere.' She smiles and I feel her intense gaze as she scrutinises me, assessing me closely, her eyes roving over my features, setting them to memory.

'No, sorry,' I say quickly, turning away. 'I don't think so.'

'Did you used to go to St Peter's School?'

I shake my head. The name means nothing to me. A pulse of annoyance and fear beats in my neck. 'Nope, sorry.'

She lets out a disgruntled squeak and continues observing me. As much as I try to remain cool and calm, my face heats up under her analytical gaze. I want her to go away, to leave me in peace. I visualise myself pushing her backwards, hearing the bash of her skull as it meets the pavement.

'I work in York Crown Court as an usher. Maybe I've seen you there?'

My fingers are trembling ever so slightly as I run them through my hair. I lower my hand and stare at my ragged nails then shake my head once more and push my glasses up my nose. 'No, definitely not. I've never ever been in the place. Sorry again.'

She shrugs and at last, turns away defeated. But not quite. 'Sorry, I didn't quite catch your name.'

'Alice,' I reply, my smile saccharine sweet, my voice soft and cloying. 'Alice Godwin.'

This seems to appease her, her eyes no longer narrowed with curiosity. No more attempting to probe into my innermost thoughts. She shrugs and moves away from me, mingling back into the waiting bodies. I continue to watch her. She glances my way and catches my eye, a sharp, unforgiving look that tells me she knows I'm lying, before she disappears altogether and gets swallowed up by the mass of parents and carers.

A crowd of youngsters spill out of the gates in a noisy throng. I spot Fionn as he rushes towards me, then Yasmin as she saunters up behind him, her head down before she looks my way and flashes me what appears to be a genuine smile. It's fear and an attempt to be cordial after our encounter this morning, I do realise that, but it's better than her usual surly manner and superior attitude. Those traits piss me off and I had just about had enough of them.

We walk back, Fionn chatting about the football match and his art lesson, and Yasmin making small talk about her love of tennis and how Miss Jackson is the best teacher ever. She seems enraptured by her. I visualise Miss Jackson with her fresh complexion and effervescent manner and wish her dead. I don't even know her but hearing her name spoken over and over in such a gushing manner sickens me. All of these people with easy lives, no troubles, no worries, just a flowing, carefree existence, they infuriate me more than I can ever say.

Fionn runs ahead, leaving me and Yasmin on our own. I wonder what she thinks of me – whether she hates me with a passion, whether fear of my capabilities will force her to respect me. I don't particularly care either way. Yasmin is a spoilt, sulky child and I am her nanny. That is as far as our relationship goes. She doesn't have to like me, nor me her. I wash her clothes, clean her room, escort her to and from school. I am her servant, paid to be at her beck and call. My jaw aches as I clench my teeth together, a tic taking hold under my eye.

Before we get to the house, I stop and grab her wrist, gripping it tightly as I hiss in her ear. 'Don't forget our little promise now, will you? I know your every move, madam, so let's make sure you say nothing to anybody, okay?' She nods furiously, tears glistening, her skin bloated and blotchy. 'Good. Now stop crying and grow the fuck up.'

She is good, I'll give her that. Practically a professional. By the time we reach the house, her mood has changed dramatically. She enters the hallway a bubbly, young girl, full of laughter and excitement at being home.

They head to their rooms and I slip off into the kitchen thinking about the woman at the school gates and her recognition of me. Every time I glance in a mirror, I see a different person to the woman I was a year ago. Different hair, glasses, weight loss. I have a completely different look. I am no longer me. Unless she has an uncanny knack of remembering every single person she comes into contact with, it is impossible for her to have placed me as that distraught woman who sat in court that day, hearing the grisly details of her husband's sordid little secrets. I have altered so much, there are days when I barely recognise myself. That woman outside the school gates is no more than a gutter gossip, one of the nosy rabble of carers who stand there every day, looking for somebody to shoot down with their vicious tongues and wicked minds.

'You can take yourself off home now, Alice.' Jack is standing over me as I lean down in the cupboard to retrieve two tumblers which I fill with milk and place on the kitchen table for Fionn and Yasmin.

I stand opposite him, refusing to break eye contact. 'Are you sure? I don't mind staying and looking after the children until Elizabeth comes back home.' My hands are on my hips, my legs slightly apart. I'm enjoying this. I can see that he is both nervous and furious, a tension of opposites swirling about in his mind – the way his jaw twitches, his terse expression, his clenched fists – they all show me how conflicted he is about this situation. He wants me out of the way. I wouldn't be surprised if he offered me more holiday time with full pay. The less he sees of me, the better. But that's not going to happen. I want to get under his skin, to needle him and have him watching his back, constantly looking over his shoulder, fearful that I'm about to spill out his secrets to his darling wife. I have the power to rupture his world, to bring it all crashing down around him. For all of his influence and his ostentatiousness, Jack Downey is no more than a gaudy little man who is driven by his greed and let down by his many vices. He will do exactly as I want until such time as I tire of my little game and then I will be out of here, and once I am gone, I will not give this place or this family another thought.

'Of course. You get yourself away. We can manage here.' His last sentence is laced with menace.

He wants me to know that he will only tolerate this situation for a certain amount of time. I'm fine with that. By the time I'm done with him, he'll wish he'd never met me.

'Right, well, I'll just get the children a snack and—'

He snatches the tumblers out of my hands. Our fingertips meet, our eyes locking together. There's a darkness there that tells me everything I need to know about what Jack Downey thinks of me.

'As I said,' he hisses, barely able to conceal his contempt for me, 'we can manage here just fine. Please leave.'

I step closer to him, lean in and place my lips against his ear. 'Don't worry, I'm leaving. But tomorrow, I'll be back. And then I'll be here the day after that and the day after that, ad nauseum. Don't forget our deal.' I am so close I could kiss his cheek and run my lips over his neck, my mouth brushing against the designer stubble on his chin.

'See you tomorrow, Jack.' I am sorely tempted to give him a wink but think better of it. Men like Jack Downey will only take so much before their egos get in the way and they do things they later regret. Besides, I need the rest of my money.

Instead, I drape my jacket over my shoulders, pick up my bag and head out of the door, closing it behind me with a soft click.

23

PETER

'I can pick you up from your place if you like?' He is leaning back in his chair, his desk littered with notes and bits of paper. He really needs to tidy it but as a tiresome, mundane job, it always seems to slip down to the bottom of his to-do list. Alice fills his mind these days: the scent of her hair, the twinkling in her eyes as she smiles at him. The softness of her naked skin. It's all he can think about, stirring up his blood, desire running through him like flickering flames, setting every nerve ending on fire until he feels as if he is about to combust.

'No, honestly it's fine. I don't mind getting a taxi. I'll meet you there, shall we say at 8 p.m.?' Her voice has a calming effect on him, like warm oil being gently massaged into his skin.

'8 p.m. sounds perfect. Are you sure you don't want picking up?'

'Absolutely certain. You get ready at your leisure and I'll see you at eight o'clock.'

He puts down his phone and barely has time to ruminate over how amazing it is that he and Alice have clicked together in such a short space of time before his emails start pouring in and his mobile rings, pushing all thoughts of his new relationship to the back of his mind.

The rest of the afternoon is spent reassuring customers that their machine parts are on delivery and that they have no reason to worry about the whole factory line grinding to a halt as he can promise faithfully that their actuator will arrive promptly next morning and yes, he will deliver it himself if need be.

Lauren is standing behind him as he turns around, her slim frame filling the doorway. 'Just wondering what you fancy eating tonight?'

'Ah,' he replies meekly, remembering that he hasn't told Lauren about his plans for tonight. 'Sorry, I should have said something. I'm meeting Alice tonight. We're eating in town. Really sorry. Completely slipped my mind to let you know.' He stares at his inbox, which piling higher by the minute, and sighs ruefully.

'Don't be sorry!' Her face lights up at the mention of Alice's name. 'I'm so glad you're seeing her again. Anyway, it means there's more food for me if you're not here to scoff it all.'

She walks into the room and places her arms around his shoulders, hugging him close to her. It's been a long time since they have done something like, this – joked, chatted about inconsequential things and laughed together. It's getting easier for them both. He can just feel it. They have Alice to thank for that. She has eased the burden of worry and sorrow that they had been carrying around, made their days that little bit brighter.

He shuts his eyes briefly, aware that he is trying to hold himself back with Alice, not come across as too eager or pushy when he's in her presence but it's so damn difficult. His heart is racing ahead of his logic, blotting out all rational thinking. Sometimes, love doesn't need rationalising. It is what it is and that's all he needs to know.

'I won't be late back. Got an early start in the morning.'

'Take as long as you like. Sod work. They did nothing to help you after Mum died, ringing you to ask when you were going back in and sending you emails when you should have been left alone to grieve.'

Peter knows that she's right. Steve, his manager took it upon himself to badger him every four or five days, asking how he was coping, throwing in the odd comment about how busy they were in the office and how stressful it was picking up the slack in his absence. Peter went back to work just three weeks after Sophia died. It was as if he had never been away. He didn't attend the court proceedings leading up to Kennedy being prosecuted and waited until the day of sentencing before he showed his face.

Both he and his daughter were too wrapped up in their misery to put themselves through any more trauma. They were both filled with relief when it was all over and they could stop reading about it in the local paper.

Afterwards, he mentally blocked it all out, wanting to forget Phillip Kennedy's name, what he looked like, who he really was. So, Lauren is correct. He owes work nothing. If anything, they are indebted to him for giving up his time and devoting it to them when he should have been allowed to be at home with his family. And yet, part of him didn't mind. It stopped him thinking, analysing. Feeling guilty every single day. It helped mask the memory of that evening. The one that a year on, he simply cannot forget.

'Have you got any plans for tonight?' He squeezes Lauren's hand and stands up, keen to clear his mind, to shelve his thoughts and erase all thoughts of Sophia from his mind.

'Me? Nah. A quiet night in with a soppy movie, I think. Where are you going for food?'

'Just to Metori's in town. Nothing too fancy and no drinking as I'm driving.'

'I can take you and pick you up, you know.'

He laughs and taps her hand. 'I promise you, the next time I go out anywhere, you can drive my car.'

'Well,' she says, raising her eyebrows and turning to leave, 'you know where I am if you want that lift.'

* * *

Alice, he thinks, is just Alice – her usual, relaxed, affable self, full of smiles and good cheer. She makes his heart sing. In a matter of a few weeks, he feels lighter than he has in an entire year.

They eat and chat. She drinks two glasses of wine then asks for juice. He sticks to the soft stuff all evening and before he knows it, time has passed and they're ready to leave. She insists on paying her fair share and he relents. The last thing he wants is a showdown over money in the middle of a restaurant. There is too much riding on this relationship, too much at stake. He doesn't want to lose her. He does, he abruptly thinks with a jolt, love her. The realisation washes over him in great, fluctuating waves. It's soon. Too soon, he supposes, but does love have a timeframe? Are there parameters that can be rigidly applied to it?

'Since you've paid your share of the bill, I insist on taking you home.'

She tries to argue but he holds up his hand and refuses to back down.

'No ifs or buts. There is no way I want you getting into a cab on your own when I can drop you off at your door.' He takes her hand and guides her towards his vehicle parked on the opposite side of the road, thinking how easy and effortless this all is. How he wishes he had met her before now.

The evening is warm, only the slightest of chills slipping over their skin as they cross and he opens the door for her to get in.

'Your carriage awaits.'

She lowers herself into the seat and he closes the door and slips into the driver's side. The conversation is stilted, Alice unusually reserved as they set off. He tries to glance in her direction, to work out why her mood has dipped and why she is now quiet and low-key but her thoughts appear to be elsewhere, her attention unobtainable.

'Just drop me off at the corner of Walworth Avenue. I can walk from there. Getting parked is a bit of a nightmare if I'm being honest, so the corner is just fine.' She relaxes and in his peripheral vision, he can see that she is smiling, her eyes fixed on his face as he concentrates on the road ahead. The fear he felt only seconds earlier dissolves. Everything is fine. *They* are fine. He has to stop this, constantly looking for flaws and negatives, waiting for the time when she ends their relationship.

'I'd rather drop you off at your door, make sure you get home safely.'

There is a second's silence before she replies. 'Honestly, getting down my road is like a slalom with so many parked cars and it's a really safe area so I don't mind the walk. I'm only twenty seconds from my house if you drop me there anyway.'

Sympathy and a responsibility for her welfare stabs at him. The last time the taxi dropped her off, he couldn't help but notice that she didn't live in a particularly upmarket area and although it wasn't rundown in the way some streets are, with old sofas stacked on the front garden and wheelie bins tipped sideways, it also wasn't the most salubrious of places.

'Okay. Not a problem, but only on one condition.'

'Which is?'

'You ring me as soon as you get home so I know you're safe.'

She laughs, her relaxed manner restored, her voice lighter. 'It's a deal.'

He pulls up at the end of Walworth Road as requested and she turns to him, her face a pale shade of grey, soft and unblemished, highlighted and silvered by the moon. 'Thank you, Peter, for yet another wonderful evening. And I promise to call you as soon as I get in.'

They kiss and he wraps his arms around her. It's not a long, lingering, passionate embrace but to feel her close to him, to smell her perfume and feel the softness of her skin is enough for him. For now. He doesn't need bolts of electricity and fireworks going off every time they're together to excite him. This isn't just about sex. It is so much more than that. Just having her sitting here next to him is enough to satisfy the yawning abyss that opened up inside of him after Sophia's death. Her murder brought relief, but it also brought with it fear, bitterness and loneliness.

She climbs out and he watches as she heads up Walworth Road, her silhouette becoming smaller and smaller until she disappears out of sight. He makes sure his phone is connected to his car and sets off at a lick, waiting for her call.

It seems to take forever for it to come through but as soon as he hears her voice telling him that she's home safe and sound, he relaxes. He heads home and climbs into bed, thoughts of Alice sifting through his brain, unknotting his muscles, loosening the months and months of tension that have built up inside him. He drifts off to sleep a contented man, safe in the knowledge that he and Alice are happy together. This relationship is beginning to feel real. Some things are just meant to be.

24

ALICE

My feet hit the pavement like lumps of lead as I pick up my pace, trying to evade his watchful eye while I weave my way through the parked cars. I slip around a corner and hide down an alleyway, my breath coming out in short gasps. I lean back against the wall, the cold bricks cooling my hot flesh through the fabric of my jacket.

    I don't know how long I am able to carry on keeping my real address a secret. Aside from the obvious connection, I also need some distance from Peter, a need for anonymity pushing me on. I want to keep at least a small part of me away from *him*. He's had enough of me already.

    I drank too much wine the last time we took a taxi together. I can barely to recall the road I directed the driver to. I need to remember or at least I need to hope that Peter too has forgotten, his memory, like mine, blurred and smudged by alcohol and exhaustion and a touch of excitement as he realised he was slowly falling in love with me. When I get home, I will look at Google Maps, try to work out which street it was, which house I chose so I can stick to my original story. I want my lies to at least be consistent.

    Only when I think enough time has lapsed do I ring him. I find myself a quiet street corner and huddle down against some signage close to a hedge to limit the echo of my voice.

    'I'm home safe and sound. No need to worry about me any more!' My voice is almost a squeak, like the chirrup of a small bird. This is how he likes me – fragile and coy, as if I'm a porcelain doll about to shatter into a thousand tiny pieces. I will perpetuate the mythical image he has of me for as long as I can. It has got me this far. Too early yet to ruin what I've worked hard to achieve. Too early to reveal my true hand.

'That's good. There are so many deviants around these days, it's frightening. We need to take care.'

I smile at the irony, all the while concurring with his words, cooing softly, assuring him I got home safely without anybody bothering me or following me along the way. We say our goodbyes, agreeing to call each other to arrange another date. I almost laugh out loud at the use of that word. We are both too old and too wise to talk about going out on dates and yet he insists on using that terminology as if we're a pair of teenagers with a crush. It's like dealing with a child. He really is making this easy for me. I expected more resistance, a greater level of loyalty towards his wife but it appears he is ready to move on. That's good. Because so am I.

The walk home takes me over half an hour. I live at the other end of town. My feet are aching by the time I get in, my heels not suited to such a distance. I step inside, kick off my shoes and slump down onto the sofa to catch my breath.

The room swims around me, exhaustion and a slight sensation of being overwhelmed taking over my senses. Tomorrow, I will speak to Jack Downey, ask him for another instalment of my money. I'm certain he has enough cash to pay me a lump sum, but he's being evasive, claiming he can only access a limited amount each day from the bank. I think it's bullshit and am certain he has a safe somewhere in the house with enough money in it to pay my salary for a full year but will go along with his excuses until I tire of them, at which point, I will up my demands. Finding those items was a bonus, a nice little addition to the plans I already have in place for Peter and Lauren.

Working for the Downey family was a way of keeping a roof over my head after losing my previous job at the kindergarten and being unable to find another one. I didn't set out to extort money out of them but I will gladly take it now it's on offer. Life has taught me that everyone has to get what they can from each and every situation, squeezing dry opportunities until there is nothing left. Life has spit in my face, insulted my intelligence and left me feeling worthless. Why shouldn't I claw something back from the debris of my existence? As far as I can see, it's every man for himself in this cruel, harsh world.

I fall into a deep and untroubled slumber almost immediately, and am up and out of the door after a brisk shower and a light breakfast the following morning. Every day brings a new and exciting endeavour. Things are now going my way. God knows I've waited long enough.

Elizabeth's car is still missing from outside the front of the house as I enter the driveway and let myself in the side door as silently as a tomcat on the prowl.

I'm greeted by a wail of protest and enter the hallway to see Fionn crying and kicking out at his father, who is bent down on one knee, trying to tie his son's shoelaces. A crimson hue covers Jack's face, spreading down to his neck. Even from this distance, I can see the small beads of perspiration that are standing out on his forehead as he struggles with the crying child. Fionn is a quiet, amenable boy, rarely given to bouts of anger or frustration. I wonder how it has come to this, how the person who is supposed to care for him has enraged his own son to such a point that the child is having a meltdown over something as simple as a shoe.

'Would you like me to do that?' I move towards them silently, kicking off my own shoes and shuffling over the tiled floor towards them.

Jack moves back, gratitude combined with resentment etched into his features as I slip seamlessly into his place, holding Fionn's shoe and placing it on my thigh while I tie the lace. 'There you go. All sorted. Have you got everything ready for school, little guy?'

He smiles down at me, his eyes still swimming with tears. A small smile curls up the corners of his mouth as he sniffs and wipes at his face with his little hands. 'I'm all sorted and ready. I'm just missing my mum.' The tears threaten to come again, his bottom lip trembling, his eyes pink and slick with more tears.

I raise my hand and wag my finger at him playfully. 'Now, now. No crying, young man. Mum will be back soon enough but for now, we're going to get you to school and you're going to see all your friends and have a lovely day.'

He nods and sniffs, his eyes wide as he listens to me before staring over at his dad who is standing, watching us. I can feel the burn of Jack's gaze in my back, flames of fury licking up and down my spine. I have usurped him, demeaned his status and nudged him aside to help his crying son. Another reason for him to hate me. But then, I would have to care about his sentiments for that fact to affect me, and I don't. I'm here to do a job and whether he likes it or not, I am better at this kind of thing than he is. He needs me and I am willing to bet that that undeniable fact is making him seethe, the very idea that he cannot manage without me swirling like hot lava somewhere deep in his gut.

I smile and place my arm around Fionn's shoulder. 'Right, young man. Go and get your sister. Tell her we're setting off in five minutes.'

He runs off, leaving me alone with Jack and his anger, a thick, tangible force that hangs in the air between us: a solid, insurmountable barrier keeping us apart. I can do nothing about it and neither can he. We have to accept that it is what it is and move on, going about our daily lives knowing the contempt we hold for one another is a brief phase in our lives. Soon, I will walk away from this place and Jack will replace me with somebody more subservient, less likely to snoop and steal and blackmail him. But for now, we need to learn how to rub along with each other with the minimum amount of conflict and ill-feeling.

'I'll take the children and then come back and get on with the laundry, unless there's anything else you want me to do?'

'The laundry is fine. Elizabeth has extended her stay at the spa as you've probably noticed.'

I don't reply, but nod to indicate that I've heard him. Where his wife goes and how long she stays is none of my business. I will continue with my daily chores and look after the children as I usually would. If anything, her absence makes it easier for me to communicate with Jack. He's more accessible. He works from home a lot of the time, although I do wonder if he will now find reasons to go into the office more often to avoid me. Or perhaps not. Perhaps he will stay here to keep an eye on my movements. I'll bet he scrutinises those cameras every single night, following every move I make while I am here, loitering in his house.

He is behind me now, having edged closer while we were speaking. I could hear the low shuffle of his footfall, detected his breath on my neck as he gained distance, closing the gap between us. For one awful second, I fear he is going to lean in and try to kiss me. I visualise his eyes full of fire, his breath hot and sour, his kiss, frantic and ugly, and quickly dismiss such thoughts.

'I'm not sure how long Elizabeth is going to be staying at the spa for, so Fionn is rather upset at the minute. He will learn to adjust, I'm sure.'

He moves away and I feel the absence of the warm air his presence provided, can smell the trail of expensive aftershave he leaves behind. He stops and speaks again, his words clipped. 'I appreciate your help earlier. I also have your envelope here for you. I'll pass it on to you when you return from taking the children to school.'

And then he is gone, disappearing into his study and closing the door behind him before I have a chance to reply. It's probably better this way. Our lack of contact and communication is the easiest way to get through this. It won't last for forever. Once I have everything I need and have enough money, I will leave this place, move onto somewhere else, changing once again back to the person I used to be before life forced me off track, nudging me into unfamiliar places full of unfamiliar people. I don't hanker after my old life but neither am I happy with the one I've got. It's a means to an end.

Who knows what life holds for me in the future? What I do know is that my current circumstances came about because of what Peter and his family did to me. What they did to my family. How they ripped it apart with their blithe, thoughtless ways, casting people aside and treating them with such contempt.

If only my other half hadn't approached Sophia, used her as his confidante, pouring out all his purported marital troubles, talking to her about his wife's mental health issues while they sat side by side with their cups of coffee in the staff room. Who knows where we would all be now? Our lives may have taken a different turn. We would all be at a different juncture. But we're not, and Peter must shoulder some of that blame. Our spouses were there, their paths crossing on a daily basis. The Downeys have simply been caught in the crossfire. Their only sin is to be wealthy and selfish and that is enough for me to shake off any guilt. They have no idea what it's like to suffer emotionally or to wonder where their next meal is coming from or how they will pay their bills. As far as I can see, they deserve everything that comes their way.

I gather up Yasmin and Fionn, aware that the young girl is watching me closely, evaluating my every move, wondering when I'm going to turn on her for being insolent or rude or for simply breathing too loudly.

'Right, come on then. Let's get going,' I say breezily as I slip my feet into my shoes, my voice as light as air. 'We don't want to be late, do we?'

25

LAUREN

I thought there would have been stricter rules when contacting a prisoner but it appears not. You simply write your letter, find out the address of the prison that your recipient is in, put a stamp on the envelope and post it. *Voilà*.

I finish writing and lean back, reading it over and over, wondering if I've said too much, thinking perhaps I've not said enough.

My back aches from sitting here, poring over every word, every single sentence. My handwriting looks like a childish scrawl; I'm more accustomed to using a keyboard and seem to have lost some of my fine motor skills when it comes to presentable cursive script but don't care enough about this man to try to change or improve it. Who cares what he thinks? He's a nobody.

I take a quick break, flexing my fingers and draining my glass of juice before starting again. I write up a final draft, making sure it's neat and legible and read it out loud, my voice echoing around the room, knowing before I even hear the words written there that they will mean nothing to him. Why would they? We both know the truth of the matter. Or at least I do. I need to write this letter, for people to know that I was and still am a good daughter. That I'm on my mum's side. That I am not a devious miscreant.

The Widower's Lie

Dear Mr Kennedy,

You may not wish to hear from me but I feel compelled to write to you. It's been a year since my mum died and only now have my dad and I begun to move on with our lives. Twelve whole months of getting up every day knowing we will never see her again.

I guess you're wondering why I'm writing to you. I found one of your texts, one of many that you sent to Mum. She had tried to break it off with you but you refused to accept it. I didn't show it to the police. There was no need. The evidence against you was damning enough. You were seen on CCTV footage heading in the direction to where Mum's body was found. They had other text messages showing how angry you were at her, how you threatened to tell my dad about your affair if she didn't agree to carry on seeing you.

I expect you will ignore this letter, throw it away and carry on with your delusional behaviour, blaming anybody but yourself for your cowardly actions. For breaking up our family. You're in jail now anyway so it's not as if an admission could make things any worse. You have nothing to lose by telling the truth, but we have plenty to gain.

When I first started writing this letter, I promised myself I would remain calm and not resort to insults but it's so difficult. I'll bet you understand that feeling, don't you? You know what it's like to want somebody in your life and not be able to have them there with you. You'll know how the anger can fester and take over in their absence. You have a lot of time on your hands now to recognise that sensation.

I don't expect a reply from you and doubt I will write any more letters. I just needed to send this one, to let you know that we are moving on from that period of our lives, leaving it far behind us. I wish you everything you wish for yourself and bear you no malice. Life has to carry on.

Lauren Saunders

My stomach is in knots as I put my letter in an envelope, seal it up and place a stamp on it. I leave the house with it clutched between my fingers and walk the short distance to the post-box. I know Dad wouldn't necessarily approve of what I'm doing but I'm seventeen years old and know my own mind. I have a right to do this. I *want* to do it. I have to do it. I've got my own reasons for writing it, a sort of insurance policy should things turn sour and everything comes undone. It's a way of making sure nobody can ever harm me or think badly of me if at some point, my own secrets come spilling out. I'm a good daughter. The best.

I feel lighter as I drop it in the post-box and head back home. It makes me feel one step closer to normality. One step closer to getting back to who I really am.

Alice is on my mind as I head back home. I'm glad she is here in our lives. Dad appears to have stopped going to church to take part in the grief sessions. Alice has stepped in and filled that void. I should be happy, I know that.

Perhaps it's my sixth sense, perhaps it's Dad's new and unexpected ability to fall in love again, or maybe it's what I find when I get back home that alters my thinking, pushing me in a different direction.

26

ALICE

Yasmin slips her phone away into her pocket. I catch her eye as she does it and watch her lower her gaze. 'I'll give it to you when we get there, I promise.' Her voice is expressionless – no nuance in her tone to indicate how she is feeling. Nothing for me to go on.

I nod and we walk, the sun at our backs, the roar of the passing traffic thunderous beside us.

Fionn is his usual self: a small, excitable boy who lives for the moment and wears his heart on his sleeve. He points out where his friends live, pats a passing dog and tells me about being chosen for the school cricket team. Yasmin speaks rarely, smiling at Fionn as he pets the Dachshund, commenting on its tiny legs and elongated body.

The usual crowd are there milling about outside the gates as we arrive. Expensive, sleek cars line the road. An array of immaculately dressed children wearing bottle-green uniforms spill out onto the pavement from the vehicles, armed with bags and violin cases and sports bags.

I turn to face Yasmin, who is already rummaging for her mobile, her eyes once again dipped away from mine.

'Bye, Alice. See you tonight.' Fionn hugs my midriff and skips off down the long path and into the courtyard, not waiting for his sister to go with him. I am delighted at his confidence and how he has warmed to me. It actually feels surprisingly good to be needed by somebody so small.

'Here you go.' Yasmin slaps her phone down onto my outstretched, awaiting palm, a frown creasing her forehead.

I lean down to her, aware she is forgetting, aware that she needs a stern reminder as to who is boss in this relationship. I turn and smile at a passing parent, who gives me a curt nod, and then hiss into Yasmin's ear. 'Remember your manners, young lady. And never forget who's in charge around here. Just think about those messages on Snapchat and TikTok and all those other social media sites you're not even supposed to be on. You wouldn't want your parents finding about them now, would you?'

She shakes her head but from her expression, the fear that I need to keep her under control appears to be waning. She flicks a sullen glance at me and walks away.

'Yasmin?'

She spins around, her eyes narrowed against the glare of the sun.

'I'll pick you up tonight. Have a good day, sweetheart.'

She stands and fiddles with the sleeve of her blazer, faltering and unsure how to respond to my sweeter-than-sweet tone. This is what happens when young girls get ideas above their station and start backchatting, thinking they can be on a level with the adults in their life. They get torn down and have to think very carefully before they speak. She'll learn how to deal with me soon enough. It may be the hard way but she will eventually get the message that I won't tolerate any of her nonsense. She is a child and I am an adult, the one tasked with looking after her. My remit, my rules and that's all there is to it.

'Right, okay. See you later.' There's a tremor in her voice, a slight difference to her usual poised self. I will need to keep chipping away at her to make sure she stays scared and biddable.

On the way back, I decide that I will rummage through Yasmin's belongings while she's at school, get some real background on her. I can only use the messages yarn for so long. A girl as savvy as Yasmin will have something else to hide; I am sure of it. She may only be nine years old but thinks of herself as much older. She will have access to things that most nine-year-olds can only dream of. I am certain that there is something locked away in her room she would rather remain hidden. All this could have been avoided if she had been more amenable, less voluble and disrespectful.

* * *

From the outside, the Downeys' property exudes privilege and tranquillity with its sweeping drive and Tudor-style beams flanking the huge, oak door. If only people had an idea of what goes on inside this house, how this family operates with their dysfunctional ways and illegal activities. The idea that it's only poorer households that run amok and damage their children emotionally is a myth. Jack and Elizabeth Downey have the life they deserve and young Yasmin is a product of her upbringing with her private schooling and a distinct lack of parental guidance over how she spends her free time, allowing the girl to frequent chatrooms and social media sites, many of which will lead her down a dangerous path.

I turn the handle of the side door that I use as my entrance and find it locked. I try my key which rotates as it should and push at the door, trying to nudge it forwards. It remains closed. The bolt has been slid across.

My breath gains in momentum. I see what is going on here. Jack has limited my access, forcing me to knock to get inside. This is a point-scoring exercise, a way of letting me know that he is in charge here and is calling all the shots. He isn't. This may well be his house but I'm the one with the secrets that could blow his little world apart.

I knock and wait, listening out for his footsteps across the hallway but hear nothing. Pins and needles start up in my fingertips, tiny pinpricks of fear and irritation stabbing at me. I flex my hands and a tic take hold in my jaw as I rap against the glass and wait.

'Here's the rest of your money.' Jack's voice behind me catches me by surprise. I spin around and see him standing there, a smirk on his face as he thrusts an envelope at me. 'Your services are no longer required. I've given you double the amount we agreed. Now do me a favour and fuck off.'

I return his smile and take the envelope from him, peering inside at the wad of cash there. 'Very kind of you, Jack. Looks like a healthy amount of money.' I stand up straight and look deep into his eyes. 'Except of course,

I'm not going anywhere. Unless you want me to march straight back to that school and show them the photos of your indiscretions? And after that, I will pay a visit to social services, although I think the school will probably have contacted them well before I do. Or I could just go straight to the local newspapers and tell them what you get up to in your spare time. You're a local property developer, a man of some standing. They would snap my hand off. They love to drag local wealthy people through the dirt, see their soft underbelly exposed, let everyone know that they're only human after all and not some sort of wondrous, God-like person.'

His gaze never wavers; I see a darkness in his eyes that is bottomless and vaguely threatening.

'Or I could just cut to the chase and call Elizabeth, tell her about that receipt. Completely up to you...'

My words hang there, shards of ice between us until he purses his lips and spits the words at me.

'From now on, you come around here and knock to get inside. I'll be working from home for the foreseeable future so I'll be here to let you in. Now if you wouldn't mind handing over your key?' He holds out his hand, his eyes never leaving mine.

I could easily refuse, but I'm prepared to go along with this new turn of events if it makes him feel powerful and restores some of his control. I can't push things too far. That would be foolhardy. I'm enjoying this extra bit of cash. My wages are all fine and well but this is something else, a way of injecting some excitement back into my life.

I place my key in his palm and we walk round to the front door together in silence, the atmosphere thick with his bubbling resentment and anger.

Once inside, he barks out a list of chores for me to do. Cleaning windows, washing floors, even disinfecting door handles. As long as he keeps paying me vast sums of money, I will do anything he asks. He thinks he is punishing me when in reality, he is doing me a favour, keeping me in a job and paying me large sums of cash for cleaning a house that doesn't need cleaning and keeping my mouth shut.

Jack Downey is a fool. He is a fool for getting caught out and he is a fool for allowing me to continue with this charade. It makes me wonder what it is he is really hiding. Many men would tell me to fuck off and slam the door in my face, ignoring my threats, refusing to cave in to my demands. There is definitely something else going on here. Something sinister. I'm certain of it. Perhaps he's a dealer? Somehow, I doubt it. It doesn't fit. So, what else is he hiding and is that why he no longer wants me in the house? Are there more secrets lurking? The thought of unearthing more of his dirty laundry fills me with glee.

The cash in my pocket is heavy, its weight giving me a warm glow somewhere deep in my abdomen. I head into the utility room, leaving Jack in the living room, and open the envelope, counting through the notes whilst flicking my gaze to the doorway in case he decides to follow me. The study door slams shut and I relax, kicking the utility room door closed and jamming a chair up against it.

The amount of cash he has given me makes me feel faint. Unless I've miscounted, it appears he has given me £5,000. No wonder he tried to give me my marching orders. I slump down onto the chair, wondering how long I can keep this little game going for. Jack is a businessman. He isn't about to carry on handing over vast sums of money. He will find another way to bring an end to this; I just know it.

I stuff the envelope in my bag and push it under the counter, hiding it behind a bucket and mop and an array of cleaning equipment and then think better of it and retrieve it, shoving it deep in my pocket, touching it lightly to make sure it isn't too bulky. The thought of Jack Downey sneaking in here and stealing back his cash while I'm on my hands and knees scrubbing the floors of his house makes me go cold. It's got to the point where we are both looking over our shoulders, watching and waiting for the next bit of conflict. Besides, the way the Downeys have treated me, forcing me to do tasks that are beneath them, makes me think I have earned this money a thousand times over.

It has a limited life, this racket I've got going. Soon he will tire of it, will start making threats, perhaps even become violent in an attempt to scare me away. I will have to think long and hard about my next move, be one step ahead of him.

The day passes quickly. I scrub and clean and rinse and wipe, smiling and thinking of the cash in my pocket and how far I can make it stretch.

After I collect Fionn and Yasmin, he tells me again that he can manage and gives me permission to leave.

'I don't want Alice to go!' Fionn rushes at me as we stand together in the hallway and wraps his arms around my legs, sobbing into the fabric of my trousers.

Jack steps forward and tries to extricate him from me, unpeeling his arms and pulling at his waist. Fionn holds firm, screaming and kicking, tears and snot smearing over my clothes. In my peripheral vision, I see Yasmin roll her eyes, her jaw stiff with annoyance. I flash her a smile and tighten my mouth to a grimace. Almost immediately, she changes her stance and drops her gaze to the floor, her flesh colouring up to a hot shade of pink. I found very little in her room. Either she is very good at hiding her secrets or she simply doesn't have any. I'll keep on looking. I'm not about to roll over and play dead.

'Tomorrow,' I say softly, reaching down to little Fionn and gently removing Jack's grasping hands from his son's small body. 'I'll be back tomorrow. Now be a good boy and go with Daddy.'

Jack hates me. Not just because of the money but also because he needs me to care for his children in his wife's absence. It must be eating away at him, having me here in his house, having his youngest child think more of me than he does of him. I suppress a smile and place my hand in the small of Fionn's back, propelling him towards his father, who is standing with his face set like stone, his spine rigid with barely concealed fury.

'I'll see you all in the morning. Fionn, you be a good boy for your daddy. And make sure you keep your room tidy.' And with that, I am gone, stepping outside into the late-afternoon sunshine, thinking that everything is as perfect as it can ever be.

27

PETER

He's driving home from Coventry when Lauren calls. It's been a pig of a week with demanding customers, late meetings and management breathing down his neck about sales figures and the constantly shifting targets that he has argued are unrealistic and unattainable. His neck is aching, his head stuffed with engineering problems about a particularly complex machine he has just seen and is supposed to solve by tomorrow morning. He is tired and in need of a strong coffee and a hot bath. And then a whiskey or two.

Peter presses the phone connection on the dashboard and does his best to not sound irritated and exasperated as an HGV overtakes him on the inside, splashing a wall of water up his side window.

'Hi, what's up?' Lauren rarely calls when he's on a long drive home. Coventry and back in a day is a five-hour round journey with a stream of snotty customers jammed in between.

'Hi, Dad. Are you okay to talk?'

He wants so much to say that no, he is not okay to talk, that a huge lorry has just nearly wiped him off the road, that he is travelling at 70 mph on the M1 in the pissing rain and that he is aching and exhausted, but he doesn't. Instead, he tries to sound light and cheery like he hasn't got a care in the world. Images of coffee and whiskey and a large plate of something stodgy that will fill his aching belly loom large in his mind.

'Yup, not a problem. Fire away.'

'Right. It's just that I'm doing some research and studying for my English exam.'

'Okay,' he says wearily, wondering where this is going. He is still over fifty miles from home, his stomach is now howling, crying out for sustenance, his eyes heavy.

'I thought I would use some of Mum's books to help me out. Have you read any of them recently or had them out for any reason?'

Peter suppresses a sigh. Why would he now choose to read any of Sophia's books? She was a fan of the classics – Dickens, Shakespeare, the Brontë sisters. Fine writers for sure, but not his cup of tea. 'No. They look good on a shelf but that's about as far as my interest in them goes. Why?'

He pictures a sickening, stomach-plummeting scenario – a note stashed in there from a secret lover – another one – and pictures of the two of them together on a sun-kissed beach. He thinks of the times he worked away in Ireland and Denmark and ruminates over how it could be a possibility, how there could have been a string of romances, too many to count, then shakes his head and runs his fingers through my hair, weariness gnawing at him. He has to stop this. She had *a* lover. There is no way he is about to turn this into something it isn't. Sophia was unfaithful the once. She wasn't a serial philanderer. Was she? She didn't have a store of secret men in her past, men she was deeply intimate with. One was enough to contend with. Thinking about any more would be more than he could handle.

'They're ruined, Dad. Pages torn out, some of them shredded into bits and then placed back inside. Others have been scribbled on, as if a child has got hold of a pen and gone crazy.' Lauren's voice dips.

He feels himself go soft and pliable, his grip loosening on the steering wheel, then straightens his back, a refusal to cave into this latest mini catastrophe forcing him upright. 'Right. I'm not sure what's gone on there, I'm afraid, sweetheart. I'll be home in just under an hour, weather permitting.' Right on cue, the downpour increases, water streaming down the windows, blanketing the car and limiting his vision. He clasps his fingers around the steering wheel again and leans forward, peering through the blur of water to the road ahead. 'Look,' he hisses through gritted teeth, 'I'll sort it when I get home. It's really bad driving conditions at the minute. The heavens have just opened and I'm struggling to see. If you fancy ringing up and getting a takeaway, that would be perfect.'

'A takeaway?' There's a slight edge to her voice.

'Yes, Lauren. A takeaway. I've had no lunch, driven almost 300 miles and the rain is so heavy, I can barely see. So if you wouldn't mind ordering our usual and using the credit card I keep in the box on the dresser in my bedroom, I would be very grateful.'

He ends the call, Lauren harrumphing at his words. He knows what this is. She wants him to be outraged at what has happened to the books but he refuses. He has enough to be going on with without her throwing some minor problems his way that he hasn't seen and cannot possibly control. Besides, maybe Sophia did it before she died. Anything is possible. He didn't check every item she owned after her death. Maybe he should have. Maybe he should have scooped it all up and chucked it into the nearest skip.

The rest of the journey takes longer than he hoped, with yet more rain falling like bullets onto the windscreen and slow-moving traffic hindering his progress. He arrives home, hungry, exhausted and all out of patience.

The takeaway sits on the kitchen table, still bagged up, cutlery positioned across the centre of the plate that is placed next to the bag. This is a message from Lauren that he is out of favour because of his reaction to her reports about her most recent finding. A small amount of anger builds in his chest. He will not kowtow to somebody who is upset over a couple of books and refuses to keep playing this game – the one where Sophia is portrayed as a perfect wife and mother and they don't speak about her many faults. Peter's job keeps this roof over their heads, puts food on the table and although they don't have a particularly lavish lifestyle, they do okay, and this is due to the hours he puts in. Lauren knows this. He has no idea what happened to the books and doesn't particularly care, but having a discussion about it while driving at breakneck speed on a busy dual carriageway in torrential rain with an empty stomach isn't the ideal time to do it.

Peter slumps into a chair and opens the bag of food, scooping it out onto the plate and heating it up in the microwave. Lauren appears in the doorway as he shovels forkfuls of it into his mouth like a man who hasn't eaten for a month, her shadow spilling over the floor like a portent of doom.

'Long journey?'

'The longest,' he replies, shaking his head in exasperation at the sheer amount of traffic on the roads. Sometimes, he is sure the whole of England will sink under the weight of the all the concrete roads and the vehicles that pass over them and everyone will disappear into the surrounding sea. There are days when it is all too much: work and its constant demands, the traffic, the crowds and the noise, and today is one of those days.

'Right. I'll let you get on with eating your food then. I'm going to have a shower. Maybe we can speak later?'

Uneasiness stirs within him. He is all at once racked with guilt but also infuriated at Lauren's lack of understanding at his position. Can she not see how tired he is? How long a day it's been for him? And yet she still wants to corner him about those fucking stupid books – a handful of old books that have probably fallen apart with age.

He lays down his cutlery and dabs at my mouth. 'No. I'm almost done here. I'd rather do this now and then I can relax for the rest of the evening.'

Lauren nods and raises her eyebrows as if to tell him to calm down and that he is being sharp and unreasonable with his gruff manner and voice, and then sits down opposite, her elbows resting on the table.

'So,' he murmurs, impatience rising within him. He thinks of a hot bath and visualises a pint of beer while formulating the next sentence in his head. He also thinks of Alice and pictures her naked in his bed. 'You wanted to chat about Sophia's damaged books?'

'They're ruined.' Lauren's words are sharp, cutting through the air like a knife being thrown his way. 'There is no way they can be salvaged or repaired. I didn't do it and I'm pretty sure you didn't do it. And it definitely wasn't Grandma on her last visit here. So how did they get like that?'

He tries to suppress his sigh, closing his eyes briefly while searching for the right words. 'Maybe they've been like that for ages? When was the last time you opened any of them?' He wants to tell her that maybe Sophia did it after one of their monumental rows, that in a rage, she took it upon herself to ruin her own belongings, just because she could. Just because she was Sophia, the killer of marriages. The destroyer of hearts.

'A month ago. I look at them on a regular basis. I'm reading one of them at the minute. It's on my bedside cabinet.'

Lauren is lying, doing her best to catch him out, to make him delve deeper into this less-than-catastrophic event, something that matters so little to him, it barely registers as an event at all.

He doesn't want an argument and doesn't know how to answer her statement so instead, shakes his head and stands up, the chair scraping across the floor. He is all out of words, all out of suggestions and all out of energy and patience. Here they go again, Lauren blind to the truth of what sort of person her mother really was. Blind to how difficult she made their lives with her callous behaviour and thoughtless endeavours. Peter knows he is no saint, not by any stretch of the imagination but Sophia took being cruel to a whole new level.

'I'm going to run a bath. I'm really tired, Lauren. I have no idea what happened to those books. No idea at all. As you say, neither of us did it. Maybe it will always be one of life's great mysteries.'

'You don't seem at all bothered.' She is glaring at him now, her eyes dark with undisguised annoyance.

'Look, sweetheart. Your mum bought these books mainly from second-hand shops. They're not valuable first editions. Some of them were well thumbed to begin with. Books get old, they fall apart. It happens. I really don't know what you want me to do.'

She pushes back her chair with force and storms out of the room, returning before he has a chance to say or do anything, her arms loaded up with paperbacks. They drop onto the table and she lifts them up one by one and opens them, showing Peter the damage. A patter takes hold in his chest as page after page drops out, some of them scrawled on with a black pen. Others have been torn into tiny scraps and placed back inside. The pieces float out and flutter onto the table in tiny, featherlike strips. He has no words, no idea what to say. A pulse starts up in his neck, thick and fast.

'So, you were saying?'

'I don't know, Lauren. I don't have a bloody clue what has happened here. What are your thoughts?'

She sucks at her teeth, screws up her eyes and narrows them, suspicion pulsating from her in great waves. 'I'd rather not say.'

A bolt of electricity soars through him. 'What do you mean, you'd rather not say? Why are we even having this conversation if you're not prepared to speak about it?' He is shouting now, unable to help himself, tiredness controlling his emotions. Things were looking up, they really were and now his daughter is throwing a hand grenade of unfathomable little problems at him, then stepping back and watching as it explodes, the shrapnel embedding itself in his skin. 'I mean, what the hell are you expecting me to do about it?'

She scoops up the books and paper, stuffing them back in with clumsy, trembling fingers. Her expression is dark, full of anger. He wants to close his eyes, make it all go away, the memory of the journey home still imprinted in his mind. This day cannot end soon enough.

'Look,' he murmurs, his weariness, his desperation to shut this thing down deepening with every passing second. It feels as if it is seeping out through his pores. 'Sit back down. I'm sorry I shouted. It's been a tough one today. I'm really tired. I'm not sure what it is you want me to do?'

Peter sighs, rubs at the stubble on his chin, the sharp, grating sound reverberating through his head. 'I'm not really sure what the point is, Lauren. We don't know how the books ended up like this, and to be perfectly honest, is it really that important an issue? We were doing really well, you and I. Let's not step backwards and ruin what we've achieved, eh?'

'First the rock getting thrown through the window and now this. Does it not strike you as strange?' She drums her fingers on the edge of the chair and glances away. He can see the throb of anxiety in her neck, the pink flush of her skin. Something is rattling her, something more than defaced books and broken glass. Peter swallows, uncertain of what is coming next.

'I didn't want to say this because I do really like her, so please don't fly off the handle, but what do you know about Alice? How well do you know her?'

Her question takes him by surprise. He struggles to make the connection between Alice and these books. Alice and the smashed window. A small hurricane whirls through Peter's head.

'I don't know what you mean?'

The noise Lauren makes as she drums her fingernails rattles his nerves, tearing at his sensibilities.

'I really like her, Dad, you know I do, but she is the only other person who has been in the house besides you and me. I'm not accusing her, not directly, but as you said, grief can do strange things to a person, and she lost her husband, didn't she? Maybe she is still struggling and has moments of uncontrollable misery and anger?' His daughter sits back, expectation on her face.

His thoughts travel at 100 mph while the world has slowed down around him, dulling his vision, blurring his logic. He simply cannot believe that Lauren is even considering this as a possibility. Rather than answer, Peter shakes his head and stands up, chest tight, flesh burning.

Without saying another word, he leaves the room, heads upstairs to the bedroom and slams the door hard behind him.

28

LAUREN

Oh God. I've done it now. I've opened my mouth and ruined everything. It's just that I don't know what else to do or say. The more I think about it, the more convinced I am that something is wrong in this house. I can't put my finger on it and I have nothing to link Alice to what has taken place here.

Maybe I shouldn't have blamed her. Or maybe it's about time we started speaking the truth around this place. I knew he wouldn't take it too well but didn't expect him to storm out of the room. Dad isn't by nature, a stormer. He endured a lot with Mum, tolerating more than many. Perhaps I'm not thinking straight. Perhaps this is the part when everything starts to unravel. Shame really. We were doing so well together, Dad and me, and now I've broken that spell. I'm going to have to work hard at getting that feeling back. I think maybe I should start with an apology. I'm going to wait until he's calmed down and then I'll grovel and scrape and tell him how sorry I am and just hope that he softens, sees it through clearer eyes. He's fallen for her big style, and to be honest, I did too.

But then things started happening. Weird things. Unexplainable things. And I don't like it. Not one little bit. It makes me jittery, out of sorts. I worry that she knows. We have so much buried in this house, so many secrets. Too much to lose should they ever emerge.

It occurred to me earlier, when I was thinking about all of this, after my grim find, that we don't even know Alice's last name. We know so little about her. That makes me uneasy. It certainly wasn't the glazier who damaged the books. He didn't leave the hallway or go anywhere else in the house. And as for Grandma – that's a laughable idea. Besides, she hasn't been round for a few weeks.

Which leaves only Alice. I didn't and don't want it to be her. She seems really nice. Genuine. I think. But appearances can be deceptive, can't they? I mean, look at Mum and Dad. Look at me.

Still, we've lightened a lot in this house since meeting Alice and now with my accusations and suppositions, I've dragged us back to where we were before she made an appearance. A horrible thought grows within me. What if it was Dad who did the damage? I've read about people who get really angry after the death of their spouse. Maybe he did this and sort of lost control and has since blocked it out of his mind? Or even worse, what if it was me? Who knows what we are all capable of? The past year has turned everything on its head, pushed us to our limits. Exposed our weaknesses. And our strengths. Sometimes, we need to tear things down to build them back up again, better and stronger than they were before.

My heart bashes around my chest as I stand up and shrug on my jacket. I tie my hair back and rub at my face. I'll think that perhaps a peace offering is in order – some chocolate or a cake. I can't stand it when there's an atmosphere in the house. Takes me back to before: the accusations and arguments. The awful lies.

I only wish I was old enough to buy him a bottle of wine. At this moment in time, fake ID seems like a good idea. Some people at college have it and now I wish I had one too. It's not the worst crime, is it? I visualise myself getting caught, being arrested, Dad having to come along to the local police station to take me home after I've been questioned and cautioned. A year ago, the very idea would be enough to make me laugh. But not now. Not after what has happened. Because it could be the turning point, the catalyst that shatters our lives. Other things could crop up. Dirty, nasty secrets I don't want anybody to know about. And once they were unearthed, there would be no going back.

I prop the large bar of chocolate up on the kitchen table and leave a note telling him how sorry I am. And I am. Not sorry that I thought it, but sorry that I upset the delicate balance of our relationship by speaking so openly about my suspicions. I head up into my room, padding quietly upstairs and then lie down on my bed, my head crammed with many thoughts. Thoughts about Alice. About who she really is. I need to know more. I need to know everything. We have much to preserve, Dad and I. Much to hide. More than he will ever know.

The knock on the door doesn't take long to come. I sit up, tension pulling at my chest. I hope he's in a better frame of mind and not still angry at me. Neither of us are particularly good at dealing with confrontation. It makes me nervous and restless and it I know it really takes it out of Dad, leaving him exhausted and frazzled too. Too many unpleasant memories of past arguments.

He peeks around the doorframe, eyes twinkling. Dad isn't by nature an angry and judgemental person. He gives me a cuddle, pressing me into his chest and then pushes me back and holds out a chunk of chocolate for me to take.

'Thanks,' I say with a smile, relief and euphoria coursing through me.

The chocolate melts on my tongue and swills around my mouth. I smack my lips together and savour the taste, letting it wash away the bitterness, the sour taste of guilt that had settled there.

We go downstairs and turn on the TV, me flopping on the sofa and Dad resting his head back in his favourite chair. He's asleep within a matter of minutes. I think of him today, driving those distances, sorting out customer's problems, and then think of how proud I am of him. And how sorry I am for upsetting him. I still have my reservations. Not that I will tell him that. This is something I will keep to myself. For now. It's all about timing, isn't it?

I spend the rest of the evening watching a horror movie that makes my skin crawl. I watch through my fingers, a combination of dread and joy running through me, the thrill of feeling scared whilst at the same time knowing I am perfectly safe making my senses soar, and all the while, Dad sleeps and snores, never once twitching or stirring.

I wonder what runs through his head when he's asleep. Is he tortured by nightmares, images of the past that are determined to spoil the present, or does he sleep soundly at night? I suspect that like me, it is the former, what we did firmly embedded in our minds, making sure we never forget.

29

ALICE

I drape the bracelet over my wrist, my face hot, my nerves sizzling and popping as the delicate, silver chain touches my flesh. I've earned this. This tiny piece of jewellery is the single most expensive item I have ever bought and it fills me with such elation, I almost cry out loud at the sight of it. I'm sure Jack would want me to use his money wisely. He is a capitalist after all, a man who values wise investments and this bracelet is the wisest thing I have ever purchased. The most expensive single item for sure. My own investment. A piece of jewellery that will never age or lose its appeal or value. I didn't use all of the money. I'm not a complete idiot, spending everything Downey handed to me in one fell swoop, but at £700, I just couldn't resist. I think this is the prettiest thing I have ever seen. It does sound like a lot of money for something so small. It *is* a lot of money but I happen to think I deserve this treat. It's gift to myself for all I've been through. A reward for my suffering and servitude. I've earned it.

The sun is still warm as I sit in the back garden. It's not a particularly large space, just an average-sized garden with a small lawn, all surrounded by a high brick wall, but I like it out here. It's my sanctuary. My own little piece of heaven. I can see nobody and no one can see me. Alone and yet not lonely. Not now I have my purchase. It is deeply satisfying to reward myself.

I've read about 'me time' and balked at such selfish idiocy and now here I am, partaking in it. Making everything about me.

I reach down to the edge of the grass and push it down with my hand, pressing and kneading until the small lump at the edge of the lawn is even and matches the rest of the grass. I haven't worked that hard in this garden over the past year but it still deserves to be kept neat and tidy, to be loved and cared for.

A banging comes from somewhere inside the house and I stand up, my hackles rising at being rudely disturbed. The thumping continues, coming again more loudly as I enter the kitchen and head into the hallway, to the source of the noise. I pull open the front door and am pushed aside by Sandra, who brushes past me, stalking into the house before grabbing my arm and pulling me with her.

'Hello, Sandra, lovely to see you. I take it you have a problem?' I keep my smile hidden, doing my utmost to not enrage her even more. She stands before me, a tall, willowy woman, her hair pulled back into a tight ponytail, giving her face the appearance of stretch nylon. I knew she would make an appearance at some point and now here she is, trying to conceal her shabby appearance with a bit of make-up and some expensive-looking clothes.

'Yes. You're the fucking problem.' Her face pushes into mine, her foul breath hot on my skin.

I recoil, glance down and remove her fingers from my upper arm then turn tail into the living room. 'You either come here and play nice, or you don't come here at all. Now what can I help you with?'

She scurries behind me, her heels clicking on the lino. 'Don't play games. You know fine well what I want. Now where the fuck is he?'

I sit and beckon for her to do the same. She flops down, her anger rapidly evaporating as she places her head in her hands and weeps.

'Sandra, we've already been through this, haven't we? Tom left here after an argument just over a month ago and I haven't seen him since.'

She continues to cry. I sit and wait for her to compose herself, a series of sentences running through my head. Sentences I will probably never say out loud. Not to her. Not here.

'I've contacted the police. They're going to treat him as a missing person case.' She says, raising her head and looking at me, all the fight gone out of her.

I reach over to the sideboard and pluck a handful of tissues from the box then pass them over. She takes them and smiles, rubbing at her eyes and wiping her face. 'I know that people argue and fall out at times but he's still my brother. I have to look out for him, don't I?'

'Of course you do,' I say, trying to sound sympathetic, my tone soft and reassuring. 'You know, he did say as he was leaving that he was going back up to Scotland, back to stay in his little lodge.'

'The police are going to search the place, although the last time I went, it was full of his fishing gear and not much else.' She blows her nose and shakes her head at me. 'I wish he'd contacted me, let me know he was upset. I would have flown home sooner. It was only when I tried to ring him and it kept going to voicemail that I knew something was wrong.'

'Look Sandra,' I say, my voice low and croaky, 'I did try to persuade him to calm down but he'd had a drink and he called me some pretty awful names.'

She stares at me, expressionless.

'You may think you knew your brother, but there was a side to him that could be very difficult. You've been living in Switzerland for the past four years. People change. He changed.'

'Why are you referring to him in the past tense?' The sharp edge to her voice has returned, her eyes full of fire again.

'Oh please! I'm not sure what you're alluding to here. You need to get a grip. I'm referring to him in that way because he is no longer a part of my life. Don't start getting all paranoid, throwing around thinly disguised accusations.'

'Right. Okay. I'm just really concerned, that's all. With no parents alive to look out for him, I'm all he's got.' She nibbles at her nails, her eyes glistening with tears.

'He's always been a drifter. You know that. I knew it when I met him. Didn't he once disappear and live off grid for a year or so?'

Sandra bristles, her brow furrowing into a tight little line. 'That was different. He told people he was going to do it. He made preparations. He didn't just up and leave and disappear into the great blue yonder.'

I shrug and bite at my lip. 'I'm really sorry, but when he left here after threatening me, he was no longer a part of my life. I'm not sure what it is you want from me?'

'Threatening you?' She is sitting up straighter now, her spine rigid.

'He called me a horrible bitch and threatened to hit me.' I feign sadness, lowering my gaze and sighing as I fiddle with my sleeves, tugging at a loose piece of thread. Tom didn't threaten to hit me at all. We did argue; that much is true. And he did call me a horrible bitch but I suppose he had every reason to after finding out about me. My capabilities, my past deeds. I like to think of them as strengths. A way of smoothing out the kinks of my disturbed life.

'Why? Tom was always so kind when he was younger. Why would he suddenly turn into this monster that you're describing?' She begins to cry again and I now want her to leave. Her blubbing is grating on me. I planned on having a peaceful evening with a glass of wine. Not sitting here opposite a grown woman who can't hold it together.

We sit for the next few minutes, Sandra oscillating between being positive that her brother has taken himself off into the wilderness for a break to thinking that I have murdered him and buried him under the patio.

'Keep me updated on what the police have to say.' I stand up and briskly rub my hands together.

She looks me up and down before getting up and heading out into the hallway. 'I'll definitely keep you informed.'

'Please do.'

She wants me to be afraid of her, of what she is capable of doing. I'm not. She doesn't know me, what I too am capable of. I am more than a match for her and her anger.

'They might even want to come round to speak to you about him.' Her voice echoes, bouncing off the bare walls and floor.

'That's fine. I have no problem with that at all. We all want to find him, don't we? Make sure he's safe and well.'

She doesn't reply, stepping outside instead into the setting sun. We stand together, buffeted by the warm breeze, our inner thoughts silenced by our dignity, our tongues too polite to say what we really think of one another.

'I'll be in touch,' she says before walking away and slipping through the narrow gate.

I close the door and head back out into the garden, stopping to pour myself a large glass of wine. Sandra can come back as often as she wishes and bring the whole of the North Yorkshire Police force with her. They won't get anything out of me that they don't already know.

The glass soon empties. I refill it, my mind raking over my day with Jack Downey and wondering how tomorrow will pan out. I think about Peter and decide to send him a message asking when we can meet again. I can't let him forget about me. Not when we've made such a strong connection. Tom is in the past. Peter is my future. A future I planned and not one I am prepared to let go of so easily.

By the time I have finished the bottle, the rough edges of my thoughts have smoothed themselves out. My mind is wrinkle free. No kinks or unwelcome curves or bends or undulations. The ground tilts ever so slightly as I stand up and step over the grass, pressing down any raised pieces with my feet, stamping on them and pushing them back in place with a smile. I kick off my shoes and use my bare feet, enjoying the sensation of the grass against my skin, then make my way back in the house, closing the patio doors behind me.

* * *

'Morning, Jack.' I smile at him as he unlocks the door and lets me inside, our bodies almost brushing as I pass through the doorway and kick off my shoes. 'I take it Mrs Downey enjoyed her time at the spa?'

His lips are thin, his hands tight at his sides as he replies to me. 'She isn't back yet.'

'Oh,' I say cheerily, even though I have a residual hangover after the wine last night. 'I saw her car outside and thought—'

'It's not your place to actually think anything, Alice. It's your place to look after the children and clean this house. If you must know, Elizabeth's car was in the garage getting some work done. I dropped her off at the spa and will be picking her up when she returns.'

'Which is?' I raise an eyebrow at him and even manage a coquettish grin.

'Which is none of your fucking business, okay?'

'Daddy?' Fionn is standing in the doorway of the playroom, his eyes wide. He sees me and comes running over, throwing himself at me with force. I laugh and step back, running my hand over his soft, featherlike hair. 'Daddy said a rude word,' Fionn says with an outraged squeak. 'I heard him.'

I don't look at Jack, staring instead at Fionn, who hugs me with an alarming amount of gusto, his little arms pressing into my midriff. I can imagine Jack's furious expression, his narrowed eyes and augmenting anger. I am willing to bet his blood pressure has spiked in the last few seconds, making him dizzy, knowing his son has a deep attachment to me instead of him. Maybe he should try being a father to him instead of batting away the poor boy's advances.

'Come on, young man,' I say, laughing loudly. 'Let's get you ready for school.'

The walk there follows the usual pattern – Fionn chatting animatedly about anything and everything, and Yasmin doing her best to be pleasant even though every muscle in her face is twitching to scowl at me and tell me how much she hates me. The feeling is mutual. I wonder if she knows that or simply thinks of me as a browbeaten, permanently angry adult.

It's once we get to the gates that she unleashes her tirade. Fionn runs off, waving goodbye and is more than halfway up the path when Yasmin turns to me and lowers her voice to a growl.

'I don't like you. You're a horrible woman. I don't care if you tell my dad about those messages. And when Mum gets back, I'm going to tell her to get rid of you and that you tried to hit me.' She looks at me, a triumphant expression in her perfect little features. I actually rather like this girl. She's gutsy. But she isn't me and never will be. I lean down and rest my hand on her arm, my forefinger and thumb gently stroking her skin.

'Shh. Don't be silly, Yasmin. You need me. And when you get home tonight, there will be a little gift for you under your pillow.'

Her eyes widen then narrow again, her faith and trust in me shaky and uncertain. As it should be. She is a wise one. I lean down and whisper in her ear. 'I know that your parents have lots of money but wouldn't you like some of your own to spend on computer games?' She stares at me, waiting for me to continue. 'I've bought you some gift cards for your Xbox and PlayStation. How does £150 worth of vouchers sound?'

Her mouth is slack as I pull away and look in her face. I push a stray lock of hair out of her eyes and smile at her. 'Our secret, okay?'

For all their wealth, I know that £150 still sounds like a lot of money to a nine-year-old, even one like Yasmin who attends private school and lives in a large, luxurious house. She is nodding at me now and even manages a small smile. I know I've hit the right spot when she skips up the path towards the school, turning to wave at me meekly before mingling in with the swaying throng, her form disappearing amongst the outline of young bodies.

30

PETER

The tense atmosphere in the house has softened with everything back to how it was before the incident with the books.

He leans towards Alice and refills her glass, her face coming into focus with breathtaking clarity. Lauren peeks her head around the doorway of the dining room and waves, her slender fingers gently massaging the air.

'Come and join us!' Alice pats the seat beside her and to his surprise, Lauren takes it.

'Now, as a responsible father, I shouldn't really be doing this,' he says, his tone mocking. Teasing. 'But would you like a glass of wine?'

She screws up her face and shakes her head. 'I'd rather have one of your beers. Wine gives me a headache.'

He sighs, cocks his head to one side. Relents. 'Go on then. Go and grab yourself one out of the fridge.'

She jumps up, thanking him profusely and dashes away, coming back seconds later with a beer in her hand. No glass because she's seventeen and it's way cooler to neck it straight from the bottle.

'So, Lauren,' Alice says as she sips at her Chardonnay. 'How's college?'

'It's fine,' Lauren replies. 'No, actually, it's better than fine. I really enjoy it. The teachers are great. Really approachable and they want us all to do well.'

'What are you studying?' Alice angles her chair closer to Lauren, her smile and happiness tangible, her charisma mesmerising.

'English and History. I want to do a degree in English Literature and go on to become a teacher.'

'That sounds amazing. It's good to have goals to work towards.' Alice is nodding, her face flushed with the wine.

Peter stands, raises his glass in a toast, acutely aware that his actions are both ridiculous and heart-warming. 'To the future,' he says loudly.

Lauren and Alice roll their eyes and giggle, Alice lifting her glass and chinking it against Lauren's bottle then reaching across and touching his goblet of wine, a marginally seductive act that sets his pulse racing.

'To us,' Lauren murmurs as she sips at her beer, a contented glaze in her eyes. He's relieved she has moved on from her thoughts about Alice. It could have formed a barrier between them. It hasn't and for that he is thankful.

'I've done enough food for three, Lauren if you would like to join us?' He winks at his daughter, hoping she accepts. They need to bond, the three of them. He needs her to see that Alice isn't capable of ruining anything. She is everything Sophia wasn't. They need her. *He* needs her. Deserves her, even. Maybe they deserve each other. Two grieving people, happy at last.

'Are you sure? I wouldn't want to intrude.'

'You're not intruding!' Alice half laughs, placing her hand over Lauren's. 'Please stay and eat with us.'

'I'd love to.' Lauren gives her father a sideways glance and smiles, running her finger around the neck of her beer bottle, the moisture against her skin making a dull squeaking sound. 'As long as Dad doesn't try to see me off, that is.'

Peter and Lauren smile, Peter letting out a dry, embarrassed cackle. He stops and grimaces, the memory of that evening coming back to him in a painful, embarrassing rush.

He observes Alice's bemusement, notes her perplexity. Decides to enlighten her. 'Lauren has a severe nut allergy. I once cooked us both a meal that, unbeknownst to me, had nut oil in it and we ended up having to call an ambulance.' He rolls his eyes, self-deprecation stamped into his expression, the way he shifts in his seat, and the perspiration settling in an arc around his hairline. 'It was all fine in the end,' he says a little too rapidly. 'I gave her a jab of her EpiPen and the medics gave her something to make her vomit but it was rather scary at the time.'

'So we now scrutinise every bit of food that comes into this house, don't we, Dad?' Lauren wags her finger and watches him, seemingly enjoying his discomfiture. 'Dad sometimes has takeaways but I steer clear of them just in case.'

'Yes, we do indeed scrutinise the food.' He gulps down the wine, his glass making a loud smacking sound as he places it on the table. 'And on that subject, I'll just go and get the first course.'

Peter strides out of the room, leaving Alice and Lauren together, their voices ringing in his ears as he checks the food and carves up slices of salmon.

He takes his time, arriving back and handing out plates a good ten minutes later. They eat and chat easily about everything and anything, the conversation and alcohol flowing freely. Peter keeps a close eye on how much Lauren is drinking. He counts four beers but thinks perhaps it may have been only three, his own consumption diminishing his capacity to keep an accurate count.

By the time they finish dessert, the world has been smudged into near obscurity by a cloud of food and alcohol. They retire to the living room, bellies full, limbs and hearts soft with wine. Lauren takes herself off into the kitchen, insisting she clear the kitchen and load the dishwasher, batting away all offers of help.

Snuggling up on the sofa next to a warm body is something he never thought he would ever do again, but here he is and here Alice is, next to him, her head resting against his chest as if it is the most natural thing in the world. They sit, comfortable in their companionable silence, their breathing the only sound to be heard in the room; the thud of their two hearts, the proximity of Alice turning him into a lustful teenager.

Later, they climb the stairs to bed. It feels natural, he thinks, as if Alice has lived here all her life. Their lovemaking is a quiet, sombre affair, both of them acutely aware that Lauren is in the room next door. It doesn't matter to him. It is good to have her warm skin next to his, to feel her breath on his neck, her fingers resting against his flesh as she drapes her arm over his chest.

'I have to go soon,' she says, her words cutting through his fantasy that she will stay the night and he will wake with her still there in the morning.

'Stay,' is all he is able to utter, alcohol and exhaustion and a post-coital mist clogging up his brain.

But within five minutes, she is up and dressed and calling for a cab.

'Always so eager to get away.' His voice is thick with sadness. Near despair. 'You're always too eager to leave.'

'Shh.' She leans down and kisses his head, his eyelashes, his mouth. 'We'll see each other again soon enough. Call me tomorrow when you can.'

And with that, she is gone, vanished like a thief in the night. Despite his uneasy state and despite missing her so much, it is like a physical body blow, sleep comes quickly, dragging him off into a world of darkness where nothing and nobody matters. Not even Sophia. Not even his possible arrest for her murder.

31

ALICE

Scrub, rinse, repeat.

Scrub, rinse, repeat.

The shower is so hot, my skin is almost vermillion when I step out. Red and sizzling and scrubbed raw. My bed is the most welcoming thing I have seen all day. I slide into it, the coolness of the sheets a sharp contrast against my burning flesh, and sleep soundly until the morning, the birds waking me from the deepest of slumbers. The sleep of the just.

Despite it being the weekend, I ignore Peter's text message. I am ready for a break from that man, ready for a break from the Downeys. I need some space from all of them. They take enough from me day after day, hollowing me out, each of them carving a deep void in my heart and brain. Soon there will be nothing left of me. I will have sacrificed my entire body, my values and integrity in the name of revenge. Will it be worth it? I hope so. Would I do it again if I had to? In a heartbeat.

I take a taxi into town, passing the local school along the way. My eyes are glued to it as we sail by. I'm tempted to rap on the glass of the cab, ask the driver to stop so I can get out and look at it, knowing I am finally free of its constraints and demands. But I don't. My memories of that place are tinged with darkness. I turn away, my face hot, fear and resentment building inside me. A bubbling cauldron of hatred and anger and bitterness.

We pull up outside the city walls with a slight screech. I lean over, pay the driver and step out into the hustle and bustle of York. It feels good to be away from everybody and everything, to be my own person and not be beholden to anyone at all. Today, I am free.

My phone continues to ring in my pocket. Peter has already called me once this morning. If only he knew, then he wouldn't be so keen to be associated with me. If he could climb inside my head and see the world through my eyes, he wouldn't be trying to get hold of me, wooing me, luring me into his bed, trying to keep me in his life. He would turn and leave, walking in the opposite direction as quickly as he could. I'd do the same, if I knew me, could foretell what I was about to do.

I weave my way through the crowds until I find myself wandering down The Shambles, one of York's tiny, iconic streets of timber-framed houses, some dating back to the fourteenth century. I have no idea why I am even here today. Something compelled me to come, to escape from the house and everything that has happened recently. I have money – Jack Downey's silence money – but don't particularly want to spend it. My time as a nanny in his employ is now limited. I need to start keeping a close eye on my finances and yet a small part of me is reckless. The money is as heavy as lead in my purse. It's mine. Every single penny of it. I've earned it. Instinctively, I place my hand over my handbag, smoothing down the fabric, checking the clasp is fastened properly, the sheer bulk of it making me euphoric whilst also filling me with a small amount of fear.

My heart starts up. The streets appear even narrower than they already are, the pavements uneven and slippery with heat and years of use. A bout of dizziness catches me unawares. I stop, stepping aside to let the snaking line of people past, and then lean against a wall until the moment passes. This is a moment of clarity, a time to start thinking about my actions. What I have done. What I'm about to do.

I take a few long gasps, weak and winded. This is silly. I have to pull myself together. This money is mine. I earned it. I've done nothing wrong; I have nothing to be ashamed of. I'm not the one stashing drugs in the house.

I'm not the one having extra-marital affairs. I'm the victim here, the wounded party.

I wait until my vision clears and the swaying dizziness leaves me, then move on. I stop every couple of minutes to stare into shop windows, but the compulsion to spend the money is diminishing. The goods now appear tacky and pointless, surplus to my life, my needs. I have no desire for any of it, yet something in my gut is forcing me to do it, to waste all my money just because I can.

My feet are hot and restless as I carry on walking, people behind me rushing past, people ahead of me moving too slowly. I keep on, turning onto Kings Square and then right onto Goodramgate where it is quieter. Cooler and less frenetic. I am fuelled by a need to hide from a sound that filters over to me, a noise carried along by the breeze, echoing somewhere behind me. It's somebody calling a name. Not my name. I keep on walking, eager to be alone. It was a bad idea coming here. The lure of the city that seemed so appealing only an hour ago now leaves me cold. I want to be back at home, away from the crowds, away from the noise. Away from this person behind me that is shouting and calling my name. Except it's not my name. Not any more.

The sound trails after me, louder and louder. Urgent, demanding. The distance between us closing. I hurry, driven by that need to be alone, to sit somewhere quiet and gather my thoughts. Driven by a deep desire to shake off that voice.

It continues, calling, asking me to turn around, to speak with them.

'Jade!'

I don't know anybody called Jade. I am Alice. Alice Godwin. Why is this person following me? Dread and anger shroud me as I slip down a narrow opening and into a churchyard where the only sounds to be heard are the rustle of the wind passing through the trees and the occasional chirrup of birdsong above me, the combination of gentle susurrations and trills doing little to still my pounding heart.

My breath comes out in ragged gasps as I swallow hard. Fear grips me. Sweat coats my back, my throat, running down my face and into my mouth. I grab at a tissue and dab at myself, craning my neck upwards to catch the cool breeze, settling myself on a bench behind a line of tangled shrubbery.

Hidden. I want to be hidden from everything and everybody. From this person.

And then it comes again, that name, the echo of a shrill voice coming from somewhere behind me. A voice from another time, another life. A voice from a past that I am desperate to leave behind. A past I am doing my best to escape.

'Jade! I've been following you for ages. Did you not hear me calling you?' She sits down next to me, this persistent person who refuses to leave me be, a smile spreading over her reddened face.

'Sorry,' I say, simply because I don't know how else to respond. I think about getting up and moving away, pretending she isn't here but my bones are weighted to the ground, my limbs too heavy to move, so I sit instead, wrapped in a tight smog of anxiety and confusion.

'It's me,' she says, cocking her head to one side to catch my attention. 'Jeanette, from the school. I was the secretary. Remember me?'

Of course I remember her. What does she think I am, some sort of idiot? I find myself nodding in agreement even though every nerve ending in my body is screaming at me to turn away from her and run until I am weak with exhaustion, my legs buckling beneath me.

'I just want to say that I'm really sorry for what happened. None of it was your fault. I wrote you a letter but I don't suppose you were up to reading it, were you? Everything must have been a bit of a blur.'

I stare at this woman's face, at her probing gaze and her portly midriff, and feel a tsunami of bitterness towards her. She needs to leave me alone, to get up and walk away. I barely know her and I don't want her here asking all these questions, making bland, uninformed statements about my life. Who the *hell* does she think she is? I don't know her. She doesn't know me.

'Phillip used to sometimes chat about you, Jade, when I saw him in the school. He said you were getting a lot better, that your therapy sessions seemed to be having a positive effect.'

I feel her touch my arm, the heat of her hand seeping through my skin, mingling and fusing with my blood. *Getting a lot better*. What does that even mean? Getting better from what? Have I sustained an injury of some sort that I know nothing about – a broken hand, perhaps? Maybe a broken arm? Or is she referring to my broken mind? I am suddenly cold, the breeze now an Arctic gust as it wraps itself around me, an icy shroud of hatred and resentment building and rising within me.

'I hope you don't mind me mentioning this? Phillip did say that you had had a tough time with all your issues and of course, the last time I saw you was after the court case...' Her voice tails off which is just as well. I want her to stop talking, to close her stupid mouth and leave me alone.

'I'm fine,' I murmur. 'We're fine. We are all just fine.' An ache sets into my jaw as I clamp my teeth together, wishing her far away from here, wishing her gone altogether. Why is she here? What was the point of following me and what does she even want from me? She needs to leave. Now.

'Oh, that's good to hear. Listen,' she says, oblivious to my cool, detached manner, to the fact that I am impervious to her words and am refusing to meet her gaze, 'maybe we could meet up for coffee one day? It would probably do you good to chat about it all. It must be a heavy burden to bear.' She stops and touches my arm. I recoil, my head buzzing with hatred, a wave of revulsion rippling over my flesh. 'Not that any of it was your fault, of course! Far from it. Or I could call around your house. Are you still at the same address?' She continues talking. Babbling. Not detecting my mood, my wish for her to walk away and leave me be. She just goes on and on and on. Words floating around me, over me. Piercing my thoughts. My heart. Skewering me. Making me bleed. 'How about next week? Coffee and a chinwag? I know some people took Sophia's side but I always think there's more than one victim in these cases. I mean, look at you, sitting here all alone. It's all so very sad, don't you think?'

Perhaps it's her intense stare or her empty chatter. Or maybe it's her inability to pick up on my deteriorating mood or maybe it's just because I cannot control myself, but before I know it, I have pushed her onto the ground and have my hands around her throat. She struggles as I lean over her and pin her down but for all of her extra weight, I have the advantage. I am younger, stronger, fitter. I am everything she isn't. And I am angry. The more she tries to push me away, the angrier I become.

We're hidden behind the bench as we struggle and squirm, her body pressed up against the metal frame, pinning her in place. I am abruptly made of iron; my mind, my body fortified and solid. I have the strength of a hundred men. She is losing and she knows it.

'I'm Alice,' I hiss, my voice low, almost a whisper, loaded with fury and bitterness and loathing. 'I don't know anybody called Jade. Stop saying it. Stop fucking calling me Jade! I am Alice and I don't know anybody called Phillip so just stop fucking talking, okay?'

My fingers are powerful around her neck. My knee is on her chest. Her eyes are distended, her fingers clawing at my hands. I can feel the thud of her body, the weight of it reverberating through the ground when she kicks out, her legs flailing as she struggles to breathe. I press down harder, tightening my grip, a strength I didn't realise I possessed surging through me. Her attempts are futile. She knows it, I know it. She may as well just accept her fate.

Seconds pass, maybe a minute. Perhaps even longer. We continue with our power struggle, heat billowing deep within my muscles. And then nothing. A sudden flop as she stops fighting, her body now limp beneath me. After the initial rush of power, I am overcome with exhaustion. I drop to one side, my eyes roving around the churchyard for anybody else. We're alone. I pull myself back up, kneel by her body, my lungs burning, and study her face: the way her eyes stare up at me, her tongue as it lolls out of the corner of her mouth. Her skin is mottled, a purple tinge spread over it. With fumbling fingers, I close her eyes and spin around looking for something, anything I can use to cover her body. There is nothing. Instead, I take hold of her arms and drag her farther around the back of the church, her body heavy and cumbersome, even more weighted in death than it was in life.

I lay her behind a row of gravestones, pushing her legs up to her chest, dipping her head away from the sky, then step back and glance over my shoulder. I'm still alone. Only the birds know what I have done. What she made me do with her constant intrusions and demands. She brought this upon herself. It was not my fault. These happenings rarely are. Events are foisted on me and I have to do things to limit the damage. It's just how it is. I've learnt that much in the past year. No number of therapy sessions can teach me what I have learned since the murder. It's a form of survival. A way to get by and keep my dignity and my current life intact. I refuse to be dragged down by things that have nothing to do with me. And Sophia Saunders' murder was not my fault, yet it has impinged on my life in so many quantifiable ways, too many to count. Nobody knows my pain, my suffering. Nobody.

Jeanette looks as if she is curled up sleeping as I move away and head out of the churchyard, keeping my head low. I stroll back down Goodramgate, dipping into as many alleyways as I can until I am back at the city walls, ready to flag down a taxi. Ready to get as far away from this place as I can.

I should be nervous, agitated or perhaps quite sick. I don't feel any of those things. It's surprising really. I don't feel anything at all. But then, I didn't expect to. It's not as if this is a first for me.

A passing taxi comes to a halt as I stick out my hand, open the door and jump inside.

We pull up outside my house just fifteen minutes later, the traffic flowing easily. I pay the driver and step out into the soft, midday sun, thinking I should perhaps call Peter after all.

32

LAUREN

I am a spare part but Alice insisted I come along. I don't mind accompanying them if they don't mind me being here. I just presumed they would want some time alone together, not have me hanging around spoiling their fun but it appears they actually enjoy my company. I suppose it's a chance for us all to bond. I almost laugh out loud at that thought. God, it sounds crass. Mad and old fashioned. Bonding. What does it even mean? That she will become my new mum? My face heats up. Images of Mum's dead body balloon in my mind. I close my eyes, will them away.

I need to know more about her, this Alice, dispel any nagging doubts I have about her background, her intentions. It is a weird time in our lives, lots of changes, a shifting of roles and expectations.

'More coffee?' Alice is holding out the flask to me, the cup in my hand now empty.

'Yes please.'

We're sitting in the middle of the North Yorkshire Moors, a blanket draped across the rough terrain, our picnic spread out before us. To the south of us is Rosedale Abbey, to the west, The Lion Inn at Blakey Ridge, another of Mum and Dad's favourite haunts before their marriage fell apart, and a place that I remember visiting as a kid. The sun beats down on us, a brisk wind cooling our faces as we eat and chat. I'm surprisingly happy and relaxed. I think about the faces of my friends when I tell them I spent the day up on the moors having a picnic with two oldies. They'll think I've flipped, gone soft in the head. Right now, Jessie and Allegra will be sitting on their beds, painting their nails, music blasting out in the background as they chat all kinds of shit about who's going out with who and who's sleeping with who.

'How do you manage your nut allergy, Lauren?' Alice drains her coffee and places the cup upside down on the grass. 'It must be a real worry when you eat out at restaurants.'

I shrug my shoulders. 'I guess we've just got used to checking everything. And most places are getting better at labelling and making sure food is properly separated. Apart from Dad's mistake, we seem to manage it really well, don't we, Dad?' I nudge him and he leans into me, a smile twitching at the corners of his mouth at the memory.

'I'm never going to live this down, am I?'

'Nope, you old poisoner, you. Never.' I reach up and give him a kiss on his cheek, his stubble scratching my mouth. I turn and look at Alice. 'Apparently, he's likened himself to some Dr Crippen dude from years and years ago who poisoned his wife.'

We all laugh, finish eating and pack everything up in our backpacks, the walk back to the car more like a trudge now my stomach is full and the length of the walk here has begun to bite at me, exhaustion flaring in my legs and up and down my back. I'm young. I should be fit and healthy but I'm definitely not: lazy and slovenly more like. Guess I'm allowed to be; I'm an idle teenager, after all.

There are so many things I want to ask Alice but the time never seems right, like how long was she with Stuart for? Where did the accident take place? We don't even know where she lives. Although almost now a part of our family, she is still a mystery to us.

I spoke to Dad about it and he said we need to give her time. I like her, I really do but am curious, or maybe I'm still a little bit suspicious. He thinks that perhaps she is embarrassed about where she lives. She shouldn't be. We have a nice home but it's not a palace. It's just a house, after all.

I know that people handle grief differently but I do wonder if she is still reluctant to get fully involved with us. I mean, could she really be the one who ruined those books, threw a rock through our window? It seems an insane thought and so unlikely but it's not impossible. Alice is a middle-aged woman, for God's sake. An image of her doing such stuff simply doesn't fit. Maybe if we knew more about her, it would dampen all my fears and doubts.

Hopefully, she can also meet Grandma, forge a relationship with her. It seems like the natural thing to do. I think that perhaps I do want her in our life, this Alice woman, but not as a stranger. I want to know who she really is, what she has in her past that makes her so secretive and evasive. It might be something, it might be nothing but I won't settle until I know. Unlike Dad, I'm not so eager to ignore her silences and coy glances when questioned. I have to get to the bottom of things. It's just how I am.

'Whereabouts do you live, Alice?' I can't help myself. What if this lady does become my stepmum? I have a right to at least know where she lives. She knows plenty about us, has been in our house, eaten there, slept there. I use the term 'slept' very loosely. I heard them creeping up the stairs last week, listened to her sighs, to the rhythmic squeak of the mattress. I'm seventeen, not seven.

I can't work out if it's an accident, ill-timed or deliberate but she goes down and hits the floor with a clatter within seconds of me asking the question. Dad rushes over to help, lifting her up by her arms and brushing down her clothes as she stands again, her hair mussed up, groaning that she has hurt her knee.

I do nothing. Is it me or is it Alice? My confusion is a solid lump in my chest. I swallow and try to reason with myself that this was no more than an accident, that she is hurt and that I need to stop being such a selfish cow, constantly doubting her, expecting things from her that she is not yet ready to give. She lost her husband in a car crash and is just treading carefully around us, that's all it is.

And yet there is something, a sensation deep in my guts that refuses to go away. I wish it would, I really do, but I can't seem to shift it. Before she drifted away from us, doing her own thing with somebody else, Mum used to say that I had a knack of seeing through people, was able to suss them out and could see beyond their tricks and deceptions. I hope this isn't what it is with Alice. I hope she isn't using Dad, getting what she wants before kicking him to the kerb when she's done toying with his affections, leaving him miserable and bereft once more.

A thought occurs to me – what if she's one of those strange types who is attracted to tragedy? I've read about them: women who actively seek out widowers and prey on their misery, using and abusing them then casting them aside once they have had their fun. And taken their money. I almost laugh. She will have to look hard for that. We're comfortable, not immensely wealthy. We don't have enough for Dad to be able to give up his job at that shitty little firm that employs him.

And then I think of the letter I wrote to Phillip Kennedy. Is that what I'm doing? Am I one of those strange types who attaches themselves to prisoners, sending letters and striking up a relationship? Fucking hell, that isn't it at all. I'm not some deranged individual desperate to hook up with a jailbird just for the fun of it. I have my reasons for writing to Phillip Kennedy, not that I'm prepared to share them with anybody. They are mine and mine alone, a form of insurance should things turn bad. Should any of my secrets come slithering out.

These are the thoughts that are whirling around my brain as we plod along the moors, Alice limping badly, Dad holding her hand and letting her lean in on him, using him as a human crutch.

'I'm going to go ahead and get the car then drive back and pick you both up. You can't make it with your knee, Alice.'

She protests but Dad is insistent. He shakes his head and pulls the backpack off Alice's shoulders, placing it on the ground at his feet.

'Here,' he says, laying out the picnic blanket and patting it gently. 'You sit down here with Lauren. It'll only take me twenty minutes or so to walk to the car and another couple of minutes to drive it back.'

She drops down on the blanket, her leg jutting out in front of her. I stay where I am. I want to offer to go with him but know that he'll refuse. Besides, despite my mixed feelings about Alice, it doesn't seem right leaving her here on her own in the middle of the moors. It would appear churlish, uncaring and I'm not the one who started this weird little charade. I have to act normally, go along with it. It's also a chance to ask again, to get the answers I need before I open myself up completely to this woman.

'Right. Won't be long.' And with that, he is gone, walking at a brisk pace, his figure already a speck in the distance as I sit on the ground opposite her and shield my face with my cupped hand against the glare of the sun. There is now a barrier between us, as if somebody has dropped a metal shutter, cordoning us both off into separate annexes. A strange kind of silence settles. An uneasy, palpable heaviness that is stained with something that I can't quite put my finger on. Something grey and murky that is pressing down on me.

'So,' she says brightly. 'I certainly didn't plan on damaging my knee. What a daft thing for me to do, eh?'

I pull my face into a grin, the feel of it making me sick, and lower my hand. 'So, where *do* you live then, Alice? Are you local? What's the name of your street?'

For some reason, my heart is battering about my chest. Maybe it's the thought of pushing the subject, maybe it's because I'm imagining this secretive life she has, how she has decided to target us. Or maybe it's because I can see the way her face changes, as if she is removing a mask to reveal something more sinister underneath, something dark and ominous that fills me with complete dread.

'You know, sometimes, Lauren it's better to not know these things. Why are you so concerned with where I live?'

I'm not immediately certain how to answer this. It's now obvious she isn't going to reveal her address, but why? What exactly is she hiding? I pick at a loose thread on my hem and try to turn away from her. She's watching me closely. I can feel it. My face burns, my throat thickens. My pulse, solid and rhythmic hammers away in my neck. Does she know about us? About Dad and me and Mum getting murdered? She has a plan. I'm now sure of it. I just don't know what it is yet. I need to get inside her head, read her thoughts. Find out who she really is, see if she's as fucked up as I first thought.

'Who *are* you, Alice? It just that it seems you know so much about us and yet we know nothing about you.' I don't inject any friendliness into my voice. Perhaps I should. If I play the innocent victim, she might be more likely to open up to me. Or not. I'm not prepared to be manipulated by her. All I want is the truth although I think the chances of that coming out are slim and shrinking rapidly with every passing second. I know now that there's way more to this relationship with Dad. She has an ulterior motive for being here and the possibilities of what that motive could be cause me to feel sick with dread.

'I'm Alice Godwin. There's not a lot else to know.' Her voice is even, no hint of distress or anger. No hint of anything at all. She sounds robotic as if this moment has been rehearsed many times, the lines played out in her head to perfection. An a-emotional woman playing at being caring.

'So, where do you live, Alice Godwin?' I'm going to keep at it. I too, can be polite and well-mannered when required but I'm also tenacious and I'm definitely nobody's fool.

She shuffles closer to me. I can smell her perfume, even the occasional waft of coffee as she leans in, her fingers now gripping my arm with force, her nails digging into my exposed flesh. 'Don't ask so many questions, eh, Lauren? Let's keep everything just the way it is and that way nobody will get hurt.'

I spin around, my heart now a galloping stampede beneath my ribcage, and stare at her. She's smiling. Not a smile. A grimace, her eyes narrowed into tiny slits as she stares at me and nods.

'What?' I shake my arm loose from her grip and shuffle away from her, putting some distance between us. The ground is soft under me. I try to stand up but my balance is out of kilter, the earth tilting and rocking, throwing me about as if it is trying to tip me out into deepest space.

'As I said earlier, except you refused to listen, you have no need to know anything about me. So why don't you stop asking questions and just shut your fucking mouth, eh? There's a good girl. Now sit the fuck back down and let's wait for your father to turn up and then he can take the two ladies in his life back home.' She looks away into the distance. No pulse in her neck. No sheen of perspiration coating her face. No signs at all that she is unnerved by any of this. Cool, calculated. Deliberate. Dear God, what are we dealing with here? Who *is* this woman, this Alice? Who the fuck is she?

I remain silent, a wall between us. She makes no attempt to say anything else and I make no attempt to speak to her. Two disparate souls sitting close together yet miles and miles apart.

I haven't the first idea what her agenda is, or who it is I'm dealing with here. But then, neither does she. We all have something to hide, things we would rather keep hidden, tucked away from the prying eyes of the world. Alice Godwin, or whoever the fuck she is, may just have met her match.

Dad arrives with a flourish. Red-faced and concerned as his car shrieks to a halt beside us, he takes Alice's arm, helping her up as if she were made of porcelain. I open the car door and slide into the back seat, unable or perhaps unwilling to take part in this sick little farce.

'Lauren, can you help out here, please? Get the blanket and fold it up. Put it back in the bag.' His voice is sharp, turning soft again as he helps Alice into the front seat, cooing and shushing her gently when she cries out in pain.

I throw the bag and blanket into the back seat and get in, unable to look at either of them. I can hear her as she settles down into the leather seat, sighing softly. She rests her head back and turns to look at Dad. 'Thank you so much, Peter. I hope the walk didn't tire you out too much. I feel like such a nuisance.'

'You are anything but that, my love. Now let's get you home and sort out that knee, shall we? And I insist that you stay over at ours tonight. You can't manage on your own.' Dad looks over at me and gives me a half smile. 'Lauren and I will spoil you, won't we, Lauren? You can sit back and we'll wait on you hand and foot, if you pardon the pun.'

He chuckles at his own joke then leans towards her and they kiss and all the while I want to vomit, to leap in and drag them apart, screaming at him that she isn't who she claims she is, that there is something else going on here. Something deeply menacing and underhand but I know he won't believe me. He will take her side because he is well and truly smitten. And I also don't know what that something else is and until I find out, I am onto a loser. I need more evidence that she isn't the sickly-sweet individual she claims to be.

I just don't know where to look to find it.

33

PETER

Lauren has turned sullen, shrinking away from him and Alice and holing herself away up in her room as soon as they arrive back at the house.

He noticed it first in the car on the drive back home – the pout, the dark looks, the truncated sentences. Disappointment had rippled through him. He thought her better than this. Better than other teenagers who flounce around the house, grunting and answering in monosyllabic tones and yet it appears she has suddenly morphed into just that.

It disappoints him. He wants them to gel as a family because they fit together, him and Alice, and deep down, he thinks Alice knows that too but also knows that she is holding back, still too scared to commit herself fully. He isn't about to pressure her. That would only fuel her fears and frighten her off. She just needs a little time and careful handling, that's all it is. They've both been through a lot. More than most. He thinks about the sessions at the church, how quiet she was, almost disappearing off his radar. Demure and sensitive. He needs to tread carefully around her. She's a quiet one. Deep and thoughtful.

Months from now, they may look back on this delicate period in their lives and smile, recalling how they tried so hard to treat one another with the utmost care, how he handled Alice with kid gloves. Like fine bone china. But that's okay with him. That's all he can do: show her some decency and let her know how much he cares about her and then everything else will fall into place.

Except for Lauren's rapid and unexpected change of mood, that is. That has put a big dampener on things. Maybe it's something different – a boyfriend issue, a girlfriend thing, some kind of fall-out. Or maybe it's Alice. He doesn't want to think about that. She is here to stay and his daughter had better get used to it.

It starts as soon as he gets back in after dropping Alice off home. She declined his offer to stay over at his house, telling him she had work in the morning, insisting she would manage just fine. All the way home, she had regaled him with tales of her employers, telling him how lucky she is that they treat her so well although she fears that a redundancy may be on the cards as his business is in trouble, this Jack Downey. Thoughts and visions had flitted through Peter's head as she spoke – visions of Alice moving her things into his house and settling there with him and Lauren; waking up next to her every morning, staring into her eyes, the lingering scent of her perfume on the pillow.

He had had to force himself to stop. Jumping ahead would do nobody any good. One day at a time, that's what he told himself. One day at a time.

'What did Alice say when you dropped her off?' Lauren is standing in the hallway, hands on hips to greet him as he shrugs off his jacket and hangs it over the newel post.

'Nothing of any real importance. Why?' He keeps his voice even. Measured and controlled. He refuses to get into an argument with her. She has the same attitude she had that day she discovered the damage to the books. A dark, simmering fury located somewhere deep inside her. He has no idea where it has sprung from, why she is being like this. She needs to try harder, be more accepting, throw off the shackles of distrust, have fewer misgivings.

'She didn't say anything about me and our conversation when you went to collect your car and we waited behind?'

'No?' Peter furrows his brow in confusion, exasperation creeping into his tone. 'Why would she?'

He refuses to second guess what Lauren is about to say and will not get involved in a spat with her. Things were looking up, almost damn near perfect. She will not spoil it. He won't allow it. He will shut her down before she has the chance to even begin.

She shrugs and bites at her nails feverishly. 'No reason. No reason at all.' Her head is shaking, despondency evident in her stance as she turns and heads upstairs.

'What, Lauren? What is it you're trying to say?' His voice echoes up the stairs, straggling behind her as she reaches the top and spins around, her face half hidden in the shadows. A cold feeling clings to his skin. It's like looking at Sophia – a younger Sophia, but Sophia all the same. Peter shivers, bats away those thoughts: Sophia crying out as she slid down the riverbank, that strangulated cry, the echo of it as he turned and fled.

Lauren's eyes are dark, her voice low, peppered with anger and, he thinks, possibly an element of desperation. Her words hit him with force, a punch to the gut that blindsides him. 'Dad, you need to watch out. I don't want to say anything else because I know you won't believe me anyway, but something happened between Alice and me when you went to collect the car. Something really unpleasant. She'll deny it if quizzed, but you have to believe me when I say that she is a very, very nasty piece of work.' Lauren waits, her breathing irregular. Ragged. 'She is hiding something, Dad and she's mean – really, really mean. Just be careful.'

The door doesn't slam as she goes into her room. It's more of a dull thud that accentuates the instant silence around him. He stands, her words still ringing in his ears, thinking that he should go in there, demand she elaborate, speak to him, tell him what the hell that was all about, but then he thinks better of it. It won't solve anything. In fact, it will probably escalate the situation, make things a hundred times worse.

Instead, he sits himself down in the living room, tries to work out what is going on in Lauren's head. Did she misconstrue something innocuous that Alice said to her? Did Alice commit the terrible sin of speaking about Sophia and Lauren has taken it to heart, convinced Alice is the Devil incarnate for daring to do such a thing? He thinks not. Lauren loved her mum but he knows now that she knew about the affair, knew that the marriage was coming apart. She is all too aware that Sophia was not a saintly figure but simply a woman with flaws. So what did happen back there on the moors in his absence? What exactly was said?

Alice's face implants itself in his mind – her gentle smile, the way she waved and blew a kiss as she stood at her gate, her hand resting on the latch. And he was right about that too. The house, whilst not completely rundown, needs repair. A small, terraced property, it had a postage stamp sized front garden and looked as if a lick of paint wouldn't go amiss. Even the gate was looking the worse for wear with rusty hinges and paint flaking off in huge chunks.

Peter sighs. Poor Alice, having to endure the wildly oscillating moods of a resentful teenager. He needs to do something to bridge this gap because Alice is going nowhere and Lauren had better get used to having her around.

He glances at the clock, wondering if it's too early to crack open a beer. It's earlier than he imagined but as the lyrics of the song says, it's five o'clock somewhere. He opens the fridge door, grabs at a bottle, snaps off the lid and takes a long and welcome slug of the freezing, amber liquid.

34

ALICE

I wait until his car drives off, disappearing around a corner, and then I step away from the gate, hoping nobody inside saw me loitering outside their house. I'm pretty sure this is the same place where the taxi dropped me off when we were out together but I can't be certain. Both Peter and I had had a drink, it was dark and if he questions me, I am a bloody good liar. One of the best. I could easily bamboozle him. He is naïve to the point of being childlike. It's as if he was desperate to fall in love with somebody and I happened to be that somebody. I had to get to him before anybody else did. It took time but I managed it in the end. I guess I would have found another way had he not succumbed to my charms, but he did and now we're a couple. A couple with a shared past. A dark, troubled one.

I continue walking, knowing I have a fairly long journey ahead of me but the weather is mild and I have plenty of time. Nobody waiting at home for me. Nothing pressing. Nothing at all.

I wonder if Lauren will mention our little chat to her father. I suspect not. We have quite the connection, Peter and I, our chemistry flowing nicely. If she does, he will undoubtedly take my side, thinking she is jealous of his new-found love, knowing she is still grieving for her mother. He will forgive her but he will not tolerate her berating me or blackening my name. As I said, Peter and I have forged a good, solid connection. He hangs onto my every word. It's rather flattering really, if not a little disconcerting. Like a child clinging to its caregiver. Quaint and yet at the same, utterly grotesque.

The streets are quiet as I head home. Only the occasional teenager hanging around or the odd smoker loitering outside their doorway blowing grey trails into the air as they stand, banished from their own property because of their stigmatised habit.

My feet are aching by the time I get in. Faking a limp has put a strain on my leg and now I am paying the price. It seemed like my only option at the time. Fucking stupid Lauren and her relentless probing into my affairs. She wasn't prepared to let it go. I had to do something to curtail the conversation. I just hope she's now got the message that my private life and where I live is none of her fucking business and definitely not up for discussion.

I rest my feet up on the sofa and glance at my phone, looking specifically for the local news. I've been checking sporadically throughout the day and so far, there has been no mention of anybody finding a body in the churchyard. No missing persons either. I suppose I should feel relieved but actually, I feel nothing at all. Perhaps a little intrigued at how it will all pan out, but as for guilt and remorse and shame and all those sentiments that should be currently burrowing their way deep under my skin and into the very heart of me – they are absent.

Maybe my family were right all along and I am damaged and in need of help. I had to do something to stop that woman's probing. Just like Lauren, she thought she had every right to investigate the goings on in my life, assessing and judging, paying visits to check that everything is as it should be, and I had to stop her. If people made the decision to get on with their own sad little lives and to leave mine alone, then none of these things would have happened. It's been a damaging turn of events and it began with Phillip, telling me that I should see somebody about my declining mental health, his sister wading in on the argument, agreeing with him, backing him up. How dare they? How fucking dare they? I went along with his suggestions to keep him happy and he went behind my back and slept with another woman – a colleague. The indignity of it still makes my scalp prickle with horror. Initially his friend and purported confidante, she soon became his lover.

I stop scrolling as I stumble upon a headline about a death in York and read the story beneath, marginally disappointed that it's not about Jeanette, but a homeless man instead, who was found slumped and freezing cold in a shop doorway by an unsuspecting young woman who had turned up early to open up for work. Surely somebody has been in that churchyard since I was there? It's a tiny, overgrown area accessed down a small alleyway but still, local people know it's there and what about the priest? Hasn't he been and seen something? Small animals will be foraging by now, nibbling at her skin, tearing off strips of her flesh. That will surely draw attention to her, won't it?

The walk home and the constant pretence I have to maintain in the presence of Peter and Lauren has exhausted me. I lie back on the sofa and drift in and out of sleep, dreaming of Tom and Jeanette, their faces leering at me, furious and ghost-like. I dream that Jack Downey asks me to marry him and that Elizabeth never returns home and I take her place as the woman of the household.

When I wake, the darkness has begun to set in, a veil of grey obscuring the sunlight and stealing the remnants of the day. I sit up and yawn then feel around for my phone, finding it lodged down the side of the cushion.

My eyes are misted over as I look again, scouring local pages for news of a body. And then I see it.

Body Found Near Local Church

I read the article but it gives little away, stating that it was found by one of the gardeners and that police are conducting enquiries into the identity of the deceased.

So little to go on. Still, it's none of my business, is it? I barely knew the woman except for her connections to Phillip, to that damn school.

The knocking causes my skin to prickle. Not Sandra at the door. Not again. I've had about as much as I can take of that woman. I stumble through to answer it and am knocked sideways to see Tom standing there, his face set like stone as he watches me carefully.

'Your sister thinks I've murdered you and buried you under the patio.' I laugh and take a step forward to block his entry into the house.

'As far as you're concerned, anything is possible. I've come for my jacket.

I left it here the last time I visited.' His voice is like gravel, rumbling and bouncing through the hallway.

'You'll have to wait here while I get it.' I try to close the door but he jams his boot in it, stopping it from shutting properly.

'Look, let's not start on the wrong foot, eh? Please, Jade. Let's give it one more go. I'm sorry, okay? I'm sorry for accusing you like that. I was drunk. I was upset. It's just that I worry about you.' He tips his head and smiles at me. 'How are things with you at the minute? You managing okay?'

'Wait here,' I say, ice in my tone. 'I'll go and get your stuff.'

He stands there, his limbs locked solid as I reach into the cupboard and grab at his beige, cotton jacket.

'Where have you been? Sandra said you weren't answering your phone.'

He shrugs and stares down at the floor as I hand it over to him. 'I just needed to get away, give myself some time to think.'

I consider Tom's circumstances, so different from mine. He has money to keep him going, cash inherited from his parents. He is a drifter, going where the breeze takes him because life has given him the opportunity to be one. The rest of us need to work, to generate a regular income with which to pay our bills.

'Well, you've had time to think and so have I. Nice seeing you again, Tom.' I slam the door, remembering our last argument, his words lodging themselves in my head, telling me that I was unhinged, that I needed to see a shrink. That I used Phillip's imprisonment and my subsequent shock and despair as an excuse for my deteriorating behaviour.

He was wrong. So very, very wrong. I had had a bad day, was really low, my sensitivities heightened and raw. Tom said the wrong thing at the wrong time and I flew at him, threatening to hurt him, to maim him. I recall him having to peel me off. I remember blood under my fingernails, smeared on his face, down his shirt. Everything else afterwards is a blur. He left. I didn't see him again. And now he's back, a face I thought I'd never see again, staring in at me as if nothing happened between us. As if we can pick up exactly where we left off. Why on earth would he ever want to be connected to me? Maybe I misjudged him. Maybe he's as devious and damaged as me, although I very much doubt it.

I put the chain on the door and shuffle back into the living room, pushing people and recent events to the back of my mind – Phillip, Peter and Lauren and the Downeys. Jeanette. And Tom. He's history now, another part of my life I would sooner forget.

The television is the usual stream of nonsense – game shows, reality TV repeats, re-runs of sitcoms that weren't remotely funny the first time around. And then I spot it. An update on the local news. The police are asking for anybody who saw the deceased entering the graveyard of Holy Trinity Church on Goodramgate to help with their enquiries. The police officer stares at the camera, his look sombre and professional. 'We are keeping an open mind but would ask that anybody who has been in the vicinity of Goodramgate in the past few days to get in touch.'

I wonder if they have CCTV cameras on that particular stretch? It doesn't matter. Their images will be grainy. I kept my head low, desperate to escape Jeanette and her incessant hollering. Nobody is going to suspect a nanny in her late thirties of a violent crime. They will be out looking for druggies and dealers and other known offenders, scouring their records for the names that come up on their systems time and time again.

I'm not scared and I am not about to lose sleep over a woman who didn't know when to keep her sticky beak out of my business. Besides, I don't remember much about it. Perhaps she fell, hit her head and passed out.

I'm putting all the pieces together in my mind as I'm sitting here and it's all so fragmented. I'm not entirely certain what happened, if I'm being honest. I thought that maybe I'd hurt Jeanette but now I'm not so sure. Maybe I imagined it. Maybe she isn't even dead and this is somebody else they are talking about.

Or maybe Phillip and Tom were both right and I'm losing my mind, slowly slipping away into a pit of total madness.

I stare down at my hands, a fleeting memory nudging at the edges of my brain – shouting and screaming. A gurgling sound, unseeing eyes staring up at me. Water. Lots of water. Then silence. No movement and no sound. Just the wild thrashing of my own heart. That wasn't Jeanette, was it? I know it wasn't. I'm certain of it. So who was it?

My legs are still weak as I head into the kitchen and pour myself a glass of chilled wine, sipping it at first, then tipping my head back and drinking it all in one go. It travels down my throat, icy and refreshing with a slight acidic kick. I refill it and sit at the table, drinking and reassessing the past few days, thinking about tomorrow and what it will bring. Thinking about the awful images that fill my mind. Everything seems unclear, murky and misty as if I really am losing my grip. I can't allow that to happen. I have to stay sharp, alert. In control. No room for error. My life is a fine balancing act. I need to keep it that way.

I glance down, see that the bottle is empty and resist the temptation to open another one. A clear head for work tomorrow is a must. Facing Jack is no longer the easy, forgettable task it used to be. I have to keep my wits about me, be one step ahead. I need him to need me. And once I have his money, that need can be severed and I will be on my way. But not just yet. There is more to do. I got lucky with my chance finds in that house. Those items are a way out of that place, a way out of the daily grind. A way out of cleaning up after people who couldn't give a shit about me. Like everybody else in my life, they trample over me and expect me to smile while they do it. But not for much longer.

* * *

The morning arrives with more of a squeak than a bang, with faint strips of amber light filtering in through the curtains. The wine had the desired affect and I slept soundly, dreaming of nothing, my mind flattened into submission by the alcohol.

I shower, dress and eat a slice of toast, swigging back a cup of tea before leaving the house, ready to make the mile and a half walk to the Downeys' property. Our lives couldn't be more different with their large, sprawling house compared to my average, three-bed semi. Do they know how I live now that I no longer have my husband's income to help me get by? Do they have the faintest idea where I come from and who I really am? I think of Elizabeth at her spa, being pampered and massaged to alleviate the stress she doesn't have to endure, and curl my fingers at my sides, my nails digging into my palms.

By the time I reach their house, fury has swollen and multiplied in my chest, a growing, spreading furnace, ready to burn everyone within its reach, to scorch and maim them. I imagine driving my fist into Jack's face as he opens the door, kicking at his shins, telling him how much I loathe the sight of him, but that doesn't happen. I keep it together. I maintain the illusion of being the perfect nanny and cleaner and am the person they expect me to be. With a slight edge of course. Always the edge. It's what keeps me sane.

'Morning, Jack,' I say lightly, making sure my eyes reflect my measured yet pleasant tone. 'Another day, another dollar, eh?'

I take off my shoes, smile and hold out my hand for his payment.

35

LAUREN

I didn't expect a reply. Jesus Christ, I didn't *want* a reply. I should throw it away, pretend I haven't seen it. Burn it. Do anything but open it. I did my bit, wrote the letter, kept a copy to show to anyone should they ever ask to see it.

Dad has left for work and I've got a later than usual start at college. I got lucky, getting to the post first. After my run-in with Alice on Sunday and the subsequent fall-out once Dad got back home after dropping her off, I don't think him seeing this envelope would have helped matters any.

I stare at the letter, my fingers itching to open it, to grasp it tightly and tear it up into a thousand little pieces before I have chance to read his reply. I take a long breath, air concertinaed in my chest, then pick it up.

My hands are trembling as I tear open the envelope before stopping and placing it on the bed without removing its contents. My stomach is in knots, my skin prickling. I don't know if I've got the nerve to do this. Writing a letter is one thing; receiving one back is another thing entirely. A whole new level of tension and terror. A reply from a convicted murderer. I'm pushing my luck here, running the risk of making a stupid mistake, ruining both mine and Dad's lives.

I'm not ready for this. It was an impulsive, reckless idea writing it in the first place. My head is thumping. A pain travels up the back of my neck.

I swallow and tug at strands of my hair, waiting for my body to calm itself down, for my brain to start functioning properly. I focus on my breathing, telling myself that nothing bad is going to happen. The worst that could happen has already taken place. Everything else is just dust and detritus. It's only a letter, for fuck's sake, a message from a man I wrote to. A message from a prisoner. Somebody who is inside for killing my mother. Nothing he says is going to drastically alter the trajectory of my life. Whatever is written inside this envelope makes no difference; he'll still be in prison, Mum will still be dead and Dad and I will still be here, me wondering how to best convince him that Alice is a toxic presence in our lives. Unwanted and a possible danger. I admit that I initially thought she was great – warm, generous and easy going but since last week, my opinion of her has altered. She has a dark side, a secretive other self that she is adept at keeping hidden. Maybe we're just too alike, Alice and me.

I decided yesterday to do some digging around on her background – find out who she is, discover more about her dead partner. Car crashes are generally reported in newspapers, aren't they? Especially when there's a fatality, and the scary thing is, I found nothing. No car crashes involving somebody called Stuart. Not a bloody thing.

No news stories, no mention of any accidents around the same time Mum died. In fact, I couldn't find anything on her at all – no Alice Godwins that match her on any of the social media sites, which isn't so strange as many people of Alice's age shun having an online presence, but what is odd is the fact I couldn't find anything at all. It's as if she doesn't actually exist. Everyone has some sort of online footprint, yet Alice seems to be invisible. I paid to view some names and addresses on 192.com and the electoral register but again, came up with zilch. She's a ghost, an intruder in our lives. I've come to the conclusion that Alice Godwin is a bloody big fat liar.

Maybe she really is some sort of gold digger? She's onto the wrong family if that's case. Dad doesn't have a lot of money but we're not exactly poor either. I know he got some insurance money after Mum died which paid off the remainder of the mortgage; the rest he split, putting some away into his pension and some in a trust account for me which will help fund me through university, so although we're not poor, we certainly don't have lots of cash which we can splash about. If we did, Dad would have retired from his shitty job by now and would be pottering around the garden rather than dashing up and down the motorway in his car day after day to see customers and his managers at the other end of the country.

Maybe she saw him at the grief sessions at church and thought he seemed like a catch? Handsome widower with a nice car and a hefty insurance pay-out? It's possible, even though it sounds like some flimsy plot from some stupid, shitty, second-rate movie. And if she isn't after his money, what exactly does she want?

I've tried to think of loads of ways in which I can raise it with him again but there seems like no easy option without him blowing a head gasket. After the conversation last week, everything is still too raw. He would react badly if I were to start throwing accusations around without any solid evidence to back them up. And anyway, he's been really busy at work all week so we haven't had chance to discuss much at all. He stayed overnight at a conference in Birmingham and has been driving to see customers in Northumberland and Sheffield so he's been too tired to engage in any sort of conversation about anything really. It's no big deal. I'm more than prepared to do this thing on my own. I will dig and dig and dig until I strike gold. And once I find Alice's hidden treasure, I'll present it to him, see what he says. Because there is definitely something disturbing going on with that woman. We all have hidden secrets and I am going to dig up hers, see what her motive is, what it is she really wants.

The envelope seems to glow hot. I pick it up again and slip the letter out, opening it and scanning the words written there. As expected, it's a bland, non-committal reply, acknowledging my original letter but not actually saying anything at all. Except that he is innocent. A wrongly accused man. A huge miscarriage of justice. Blah, blah, blah. I set it down next to me, then read it again.

> Hello Lauren,
>
> Thank you for your letter. I don't really have anything to add to my initial statement. I am terribly sorry about what happened to your mum but you have to believe me when I say that I did not kill her.
>
> I admit that I was having an affair and she broke it off. I admit that I was angry but I do not admit to killing her because I didn't. I have been

wrongly imprisoned and will fight to clear my name. My being here is a huge miscarriage of justice.

You lost your mother; I have lost my freedom. We are both prisoners of fate.

Yours sincerely,

Phillip Kennedy.

I roll my eyes, tear up his reply, and then thinking better of it, pick up the pieces and place them in a drawer for safekeeping. For the future. My future.

I get ready and tidy my room, ready to go to college where I'll listen to teachers and hang out with my friends and act all normal and stuff, as if everything is right with the world when in reality, it's far from that. Not with having Alice around. Not until I find out who she is. And what it is she wants from us.

Even going out and seeing Josh didn't make me feel any better. We might see one another again or we might not. My heart isn't in it right now. The timing is all wrong. I'm losing the relationship I had built up with Dad. I'm losing him to Alice and I'm not prepared to sit back and let that happen. Not now. Not ever. And not to her. We need to stick together, Dad and me. We have a bond. Something that ties us together. It's just that he doesn't know it.

I pack up my bag and stop for a second, looking around at my room, before closing the door and heading off to college.

36

ALICE

In the last few days, Jack has handed me just short of £1,500. I have told him that it's not enough for me to keep silent about his little habit and yesterday, I threatened to pay the headteacher a visit, telling him that if they didn't take me seriously then I would alert social services to what goes on behind the closed doors of this purportedly decent house.

Today, I am expecting a larger payment, something substantial that will keep me from passing on the photograph to the relevant authorities.

'Still no Mrs Downey, eh?' I smile as he opens the door and I bustle my way inside. 'Or is she back from her little break and is resting up after all the stress of packing and unpacking? She must be exhausted, poor thing.'

He glares at me, hatred oozing out of every pore. I'm pushing my luck now. I know it but can't seem to help myself. Naughty me. We are past the social niceties phase now, beyond being pleasant and enduring forced conversations that go nowhere. There is little point in pretending we are anything other than arch enemies.

'Elizabeth is still away. She has extended her stay which is probably for the best given your presence in the house and your unreasonable demands. I want you gone when she arrives back. We'll manage just fine without you.'

Fionn comes running through, throwing his arms around me and pushing his face into my midriff as I bend down to greet him.

'Yes,' I say, looking up at Jack, enjoying the anger in his expression. 'I can see that you'll manage perfectly in my absence. Fionn will be delighted to see the back of me, won't he?'

The young lad looks up at me, doe-eyed and perplexed. 'Where are you going, Alice? You have to take me if you're going somewhere! Can I go with you?'

'Fionn, go and finish getting ready for school. Tell Yasmin to get ready as well.' Jack's voice is gruff, weighted with hatred and resentment.

The little boy pulls away from me reluctantly and traipses upstairs out of view, Jack's eyes fixed on his son before moving nearer to me. He steps closer, shoving an envelope in my hand, his voice a rumbling whisper. 'Here. This is the fucking last. I am done with you. Take your money and fuck off out of our lives. This is your last day in this house. I don't want to see you here tomorrow or any day after that. If you try to come in, I'll call the police.'

I step back and widen my eyes dramatically. 'Really? Are you sure about that? Maybe while the police are here, I can show them the photo, tell them about my little find and your filthy little habit. I'm sure they'll be very interested in what you get up to in your spare time. Let's see how your business copes once word gets about, eh?'

Jack shakes his head and laughs, his eyes crinkling up at the corners as he watches me closely. 'Oh, Alice, you think you know everything when in actual fact, you know nothing at all. You don't have a clue, do you? Not a bloody clue. You are utterly blind to it all.' His cut glass accent rings off every wall, every bare, polished surface.

I scrutinise his every move, wondering what the hell he is talking about. He continues to laugh, looking at me as if I am a piece of dirt stuck on the underside of his shoe.

'Where do you think Elizabeth really is? Come on, Little Miss Know-It-All. You think you've got it all figured out, don't you? I mean, do I really have to spell it out for you? Why do you think that packet was hidden behind those books? If it was mine, do you not think I would have locked it away in my study? How often did Elizabeth go in the library? Go on, think about it. Have a guess. Where is the one place I could hide something from her? Not my workplace. She has keys for that room. She would have found it in a heartbeat.'

A pattering sensation thrums in my chest, crawling up my neck, growing and accelerating until it is pounding in my ears. I think about Jack's words, the look on his face, and Elizabeth's prolonged absence and everything suddenly slots into place.

'Yes,' he says, watching me closely for my reaction, nodding and smiling as realisation dawns somewhere deep in the recesses of my brain. 'Now you've got it. Took a while but you got there in the end, didn't you? Poor, dim Alice. You know everything and at the same time, so little.'

'Elizabeth isn't at a spa at all,' I say more to myself than anything. 'She's in rehab.' My voice sounds disembodied, rattling around in my head. I didn't see that one coming. I've been remiss to not pick up on that fact. Anger at my own stupidity scores at my skin, little blisters of shame at my own stupidity burning at my flesh.

'Bingo.' Jack's eyes are glistening. He's enjoying this. My threats about exposing this family, however, still stand.

'That won't stop me going to the police and the school and telling them what a bad mother Elizabeth is, how she takes drugs while the children are in the house.'

'She's in fucking rehab, Alice. She is no longer here so is no longer a threat. I'm as clean as a whistle. Test me and you'll find nothing. What reason has anybody got to take the children from us? You really think the school is going to start smearing our name when we pay them tens of thousands to educate our children? Get real.' He crosses his arms and steps away from me, looking me up and down as if I am a lab specimen about to be dissected solely for his pleasure. 'I have to admit, at first you got me. I panicked and handed over that money but after giving it some serious thought, I've decided that enough is enough. A shitty little gold digger like you doesn't scare me. Who are people going to believe anyway – a sour-faced little nobody like you or a professional, successful businessman like me?'

I open the envelope and stare down at its contents – a letter telling me that my services are no longer required. The letterhead is that of a firm of lawyers with Jack's signature at the bottom. No money. Not a fucking penny.

'Yes, it's empty. As you can see, you'll not get anything else out of me. Your little game is up. I've packed up your measly belongings and stacked them in the utility room. Now if you wouldn't mind collecting them, you can be on your way.' He sounds triumphant. His skin has taken on a golden hue, flushed with a tinge of pink. The complexion of somebody who has hit the jackpot. The complexion of a winner.

A noise comes from upstairs: a creak followed by the sound of somebody running. Fionn comes barging into the hallway, his face lined with anxiety. 'Daddy, it's Yasmin! She's been sick all over the bedroom floor.'

I stand rooted to the spot, enjoying the concern and disgust on Jack's face. I make no attempt to move, to race up there and clean it up. Instead, I wait, savouring the power that is rising within me. I doubt that Jack Downey has ever had to clean up anything in his life, especially piles of vomit.

'I presume you'll be gone by the time I get back down here?' He raises an eyebrow, and without giving me a chance to reply, he disappears upstairs, his footfall heavy and clumsy, borne out of anger at having to actually care for his own children.

Fionn is staring up at me, his eyes wide and innocent. 'Are you taking me to school? Yasmin can't go. She's sick.'

My chest expands, my heart throbbing wildly beneath my ribcage. 'Yes, I am. Come on. Grab your coat and bag. We don't want to bother Daddy, do we? He's busy looking after your sister.' I'm whispering now, my words fast and urgent.

Fionn smiles and scoops up his bag and coat that sit at the bottom of the stairs. We are out of the door and down the road in seconds, his little legs running to keep up with my hasty pace.

'You're going really fast, Alice!' He giggles and I squeeze his hand tight and wink.

'Well, I have a secret to tell you, but you mustn't tell anybody because it's just between the two of us.' We turn right down Pendlestone Avenue and take a left onto Marsden Road where the streets are quieter and we can slow down.

'A secret? I love secrets!' He is almost squealing, his face full of joyful innocence. This boy. This wonderful, wonderful child. I wish he were mine.

I lean in to his ear, my voice a thin low whisper. 'We're not going to school today. Daddy said you can have a day off.'

'Really?' His brow is knitted, a small line of discontent settled deep in his skin. 'Is that because Yasmin has been sick?'

'Yes!' I say excitedly. 'He said that you can have a day off for being such a good boy all the time. That's what we were talking about when you came down the stairs. Yasmin was going to have a day off as well but now she's ill, she has to stay in bed and Daddy has to look after her.'

He thinks about this for a second or two, then seemingly satisfied with my explanation, smiles and skips along the road beside me, his little, hot hand firmly locked with mine.

I think about how it would feel to have my own child, to have somebody look up to me, to rely on me and for me to be their only carer. A warm sensation shifts and curls somewhere deep inside my gut, coiling around my muscles, settling in my bones. I would be everything they would ever need, always there for them, ready to attend to their every want and desire. They would love me unconditionally. I would have a family again, a proper family, somebody amenable and loving, not somebody who continually questions my movements, my decisions, my state of mind, reminding me how fragile I am, how close I am to tipping over into a void of madness.

An image of my young sister jumps into my mind, the way she splashed about in the bath while I crouched by her side watching her, her stricken expression as she slipped under the water, then the apportioned blame afterwards. The horror on the faces of my parents and the subsequent decision by the coroner that it was an accident, that there wasn't enough evidence to say anything untoward took place, that I had possibly tried to save her and wasn't necessarily responsible for her death. Her passing was the beginning of the end. The end of me. Everything took a downwards spiral from that point on. I was ten years old.

My life as an adult improved little. In the beginning, Phillip helped me, guided me through the perils of university, assisted me when I tried and failed to conceive a much-wanted child. I figured if I had a baby of my own, I could replace my sister, bring another child into the world to make up for the one who died. It didn't happen. I sunk into depression. Phillip became tired of me and my demands. Tired of having to prop me up: be my carer as opposed to my husband. He turned to friends and colleagues for friendship and support. He turned to Sophia.

It wasn't all bad. At one point before everything fell apart, my job as an assistant at the kindergarten was a really positive thing. It was a chance to better myself; there were opportunities for promotion, people I imagined were my friends. I thought it would help. And for a while, it did. But then one day, it didn't. I lost that position after being there for just one year. They made erroneous claims that I had hurt a child, grabbed them, shook them about. Badly injured them. It was nonsense. I would never do such a thing but another staff member said they had seen me hit the youngster and so their decision was made, regardless of my protestations. No legal action was taken as they didn't want the bad publicity, but what they did want was for me to leave with immediate effect. Which I did. I recall Phillip's reaction, his despair. His elongated disappearances as he lost faith in me and slowly drifted into the arms of another woman…

I squeeze Fionn's little hand. The way he looks at me, the trust he has in me and me alone, tells me everything I need to know. I realise at that point that I don't need to take him back. He deserves better than being forced to live in that house with those cold, uncaring people. His mother is a drug user and his father an aloof, heartless individual who cares more about money and status than he does his own children. Fionn is better off with me. We're friends, he and I. He will understand once I explain what is going on. I'll tell him he's having a sleepover at my house. We'll get pizza and watch TV together. We will do fun things: thrilling, exhilarating things. He will love me and I will love him right back. Excitement fizzes inside me, warming my blood, settling and soothing my permanently frayed nerves.

'Where are we going?' His voice cuts into my thoughts, dragging me back to the present.

I look around. I have no idea where we are going. We have wandered aimlessly, dashing and running to be far away from the Downey house. In the distance, I spot the spire of St Martin's church and feel drawn to it. The church where I attended the counselling session, the church where I met Peter. The church where the idea of Alice was initially born.

'I'm going to show you something exciting.'

'Are we going to get an ice cream? Is that where you're taking me?' The joy in his voice is like being immersed in a warm bath on a cold winter's day. I shiver, my flesh tingling with delight.

'In a while. First, I want you to see something. I think you'll like it.'

We stroll along as if we haven't got a care in the world. People pass us by and I wonder how many of them think that Fionn is my child. It makes me feel like a whole person, the thought that anybody would think such a thing. We fit well together, this boy and me. His parents don't deserve him. I do. He makes me feel complete again. I can give him a much better life, provide him with the love and attention he lacks at home. One day, he will thank me. I have a sense for these things. Soon, he'll forget all about his parents and his spoilt sister and will look to me and me only for comfort and happiness and I will be here for him – my little boy. My lovely Fionn.

37

LAUREN

It's good to hear Grandma's voice, her gentle and reassuring lilt bringing a lump to my throat.

'Hello, love. Everything okay?'

I nod, blinking back tears as I stop and sit on a bench at the side of the road, my phone practically glued to my ear. 'It's fine, Grandma. I'm fine. Just thought I'd give you a ring to see how you're doing.'

'Oh, you know,' she says lightly, her voice reminding me of gentle rain on a soft, spring day. 'All's good here. I've been going through some old photographs and there's one of you as a toddler in the garden running across the lawn with your chubby little legs and that wild tuft of hair that you had at the back of your head.' She laughs and sighs, her voice full of contentment and hazy memories. 'It looked like a piece of candyfloss attached to your head. You were such a cute little thing. Always happy. Always smiling.' She stops and I can tell that she's thinking of Mum, thinking of how our happiness ended a year ago after Mum's death. Little does she know it ended long before that with Mum's affair and her secretive, furtive ways. 'Anyway, enough of me rambling. I'm going soft in my old age.'

'Still got the candyfloss hair and I'm still happy, Grandma. Life goes on.'

Above me, a bird flaps its wings furiously, fighting for its share of a branch as another bird settles beside it and nudges its way in.

'It does indeed, love. How's your dad? I've not heard from him for quite a while.'

I think about how Dad is so wrapped up in thoughts of Alice that he has forgotten to keep in touch with his own mother, and shiver. 'He's okay, Grandma, busy working and even busier falling in love, I think.' There is a brief silence as I realise that I've let the cat out of the bag. 'He didn't tell you he's seeing somebody?' I've done this deliberately. I knew she didn't know and right now, I need an ally, somebody who can see things from my point of view.

She brightens, a cautious attempt to cover the awkwardness in our conversation. 'No, but he's a grown man and it's time now to move on, isn't it?'

I want to say yes, to agree with her and tell her that things are great, never better. But I don't. My mouth runs away with me and before I know it, I'm being ruthless, spilling everything out to her, heaping my problems onto my poor, ageing grandmother and burdening her with my issues, telling her about my suspicions, how Alice is untraceable. How she spoke to me that day on the moors.

'I don't like her.' I'm breathless and now I'm late for college but I don't really care. 'I used to like her but then things have happened, weird, unexplainable things and I just know she's behind them, although Dad thinks not.' My vision blurs and my head swims as I tell Grandma all about the books and the even the stone getting thrown through the door. I know that I should stop, that I'm causing Grandma unnecessary worry but I can't seem to help myself. It's cathartic, opening up, speaking to somebody about my concerns. I can't talk to my friends; they wouldn't understand and besides, I don't want our family business known to others, not even Jessie, my friend of many, many years. This is a private affair, something that should be kept between us. All it would take is for a drunken Jessie to unintentionally say something, blabbing her mouth off without realising it, and then word would be all around town about how we've got a psycho in the family.

'I'm not sure what to say, love, except that she sounds like a nasty piece of work. What sort of person would swear at you like that?' I visualise Grandma's distress, her eyes wide with shock, her mouth puckered into a tight, thin line at the thought of somebody being mean to me. Poor Grandma. Poor, lovely Grandma. She deserves better.

'Please don't mention it to Dad. He thinks she's wonderful and I don't want to spoil that but I'm trying to tell him to be aware. He just isn't listening.'

We talk some more and I tell Grandma that we're fine and not to worry, even though I've just told her something that will cause her to lose sleep at night. She promises to say nothing to Dad and I promise to keep in touch on a regular basis to let her know how we're doing.

'I'll pop round this week, love. Leave your washing for me. I enjoy it. It gives me something to do. Going out shopping with Ruth and Bella gets boring and there's only so many places a person can go for coffee and cake before it starts to get a bit mundane.'

I laugh and she blows me a kiss down the phone before we finish the call. I hope I've done the right thing, telling her. It was a spur-of-the-moment decision and I'm slightly concerned that I've now made her worry about us. I just need her to know, that's all. I need somebody who's on my side.

Deciding that college can wait, I head back home, determined to do some more rooting around into Alice's background. My gut instinct about people is rarely wrong. I'm going to go with that instinct and use my time wisely and try to find out more about this Alice lady, work out who she really is and what her motives are.

It's me against Alice now. Just the two of us. A pair of devious souls pitted against one another.

* * *

I sigh, run my fingers through my hair, tugging at loose strands, remembering when I would yank at it with furious fingers, gleaning some sort of pleasure from feeling it come loose from my scalp. No more of that. I've moved on. Still nothing on Alice though, which pisses me off. Not even a local address. I wish I'd asked Dad where she lived. He's dropped her off and picked her up a few times but now that he knows I'm against her, it would look suspicious if I contacted him asking for a street name. There's no way he would tell me anyway. He would clam up, pull a face and that would be that. And the weird thing is, she's started to remind me of somebody but I can't think who. The shape of her face, her eyes, I felt sure I'd seen them somewhere but know that I can't have. I think maybe I'm just getting too agitated about her, seeing things that aren't necessarily there.

Once again, I scroll through social media looking for anybody that matches Alice's description and profile but find nothing. Not a damn thing. It just doesn't make any sense.

On impulse, and mainly because I've run out of ideas on where to search for more information on Alice and also because I have wasted enough time on her, I decide to look into Phillip Kennedy's background. He's there, on the electoral register as living not too far from here. I make a note of the address and without thinking, I grab my coat and am out of the house and on my way to his property. I just want to see what sort of house he lived in, try to get a feel for the man. If I can't discover anything out about Alice, the least I can do is find out how Phillip Kennedy lived his life before he went to prison. I've no idea why I'm doing it; it's like scratching an itch, and I know that it's just something that I need to do to clear my head of him.

According to the map app on my phone, it'll take me twenty minutes to walk there. I keep my pace brisk, keen to see where he lived. Perhaps I should have done it before now but that letter has opened up a cavernous place inside me that needs to be filled with as much information as I can cram in. If I can do that, it stops that particular hollow from screaming out at me that I'm a bad person. It stops my own demons from creeping in and settling there.

It's warm out, a lot warmer than I expected, and by the time I take the final turn before reaching the street where Phillip Kennedy lived, I'm sweating. My jacket is tied around my waist and I'm panting. I stop and pull at my hair, tying it up into a ponytail. The breeze hits my neck and I stop and shiver, enjoying its coolness. I twist my face to the wind to catch it again, and then set off, determined to see this house. To get a picture of the man before he was sent away and maybe see who he could become once again when he's released. Which he will be at some point. He's not in there for life. Someday, Dad or I could easily turn a corner and bump into him. The thought of it makes me shiver.

I look down at my phone, at the map grid on the screen and stop in front of an ordinary-looking, semi-detached property. This is it. This is his house. This is where Phillip Kennedy used to live. My heart pounds and despite initially cooling down, I am now sweating again. A tremble in my legs forces me to hold onto a wall for support.

It's an average house in an average street. Nothing more, nothing less. It doesn't make a statement; it simply blends in effortlessly with all the other surrounding houses. Disappointment doesn't cover it. I'm not sure what I expected but whatever it was, this isn't it. I wanted him to be a grubby little man who lived in a grubby little house.

I move away and walk over to the other side of the road, just to observe it from a distance for a short while. I spot a large shrub next to the street sign that's perfect for hiding behind. I salt myself away and stand for a couple of seconds, watching the house, waiting to see if anybody else is living there. He had a wife, that much I do know. I've no idea what happened to her, whether or not she moved away or whether she's hung around, has forgiven him and is doing the dutiful wife thing and patiently waiting for his release.

I scroll through my phone, studying the people who lived with him at this address and see that there is another female listed as residing here. Jade Kennedy, his wife. Her name rings a bell. She kept a low profile throughout the proceedings but then, so did we. The grisly, sordid details, it was too much for us so we kept our distance, attending only when necessary. We stepped back, kept a dignified silence and kept our heads low.

And now, I find myself wishing I had attended more, found out about Phillip Kennedy's life. Put a full profile to the person. Dad hid as much as he could from me, sheltering me from the media frenzy, keeping our identities under wraps.

There's no movement over at the house. His wife might not even live there any more. She might have sold up, moved on to somewhere new. My fingers itch to knock at the door, to stride over there and bang as hard as I can until somebody answers, if only to be able to see inside. It's silly really, this venture. Silly and pointless, and yet here I am, fuelled by a need to know.

I wait some more, hopping from foot to foot, sighing, chewing at a loose nail, biting at the inside of my mouth. I look at my watch, thinking how mad this is. I really shouldn't be here. It's all a waste of time. There's nothing happening in that house, nothing happening behind that door. His wife will be at work. She may not even live here any more. The place is empty. I really should turn around, head back home.

And then it happens. A flicker of a movement catches my eye, something in my peripheral vision as I stare down at my phone for inspiration. I glance up, suck in my breath, my skin burning with anticipation.

Standing at the living room window of the Kennedy house is a little boy. I can see his tuft of hair bobbing about above the windowsill and a pair of keen, roving eyes as he scans the street. I'm too far away to scrutinise any of his features properly but am transfixed, unable to look away, desperate to see more. Maybe he's their grandson? I'm not even sure whether or not the Kennedys actually had any children. I know so little about them. I've managed to compartmentalise my life since it happened, focusing on my studies at college, keeping an eye on Dad, making sure he isn't heading for some kind of breakdown. Making sure he doesn't know about me...

I watch as a shadowy figure suddenly scoops him up, snatching him out of view. The curtains are quickly drawn even though it's the middle of the day and I am left with nothing to go on, my mind buzzing with confusion.

I'm tempted now to knock at the door. Somebody is in there. If the Kennedy family did sell up, the stigma too much for them to take, then maybe this is another family who have since moved in. I could ask, couldn't I? Pretend to be a long-lost relative asking after them. Maybe these people have a forwarding address.

Or maybe it's Jade Kennedy in there with her grandson. What would I say to her if she opens the door and asks me what I want? If I tell her who I am, she could react badly, thinking I'm after revenge. I bite at my lip, tugging at a loose piece of skin. It's definitely not revenge I'm after. That's the thing – I don't know what it is I need or why I'm here. Just idle curiosity, I guess. After sending the letter to Kennedy,

He's locked up in a tiny cell with little access to daylight and all the other things we all take for granted day after day. So why am I here? Why would I take a chance and knock at that door? I've no need to pursue this, no need at all. I'm actually in danger of ruining everything. It's all worked out perfectly so far. Maybe this is guilt biting at me. So far, I haven't felt anything resembling remorse. Maybe this is it – a delayed reaction to everything that's taken place. I've got to stop it before our lives unravel and fall apart. Because if that happens, that is when the real storm will begin.

38

ALICE

'Who is it we're coming to see?' Fionn skips along, his attention fixated on the many rows of headstones that surround us. 'Is it a friend of yours? Is she buried here?'

I want to laugh but hold back, maternal love and happiness swelling within my chest. He is so perfectly innocent, so delightfully trusting that the rush of adrenaline that is coursing through me at the idea of keeping him with me forever makes me giddy. I am his now and he is mine. We're together for the foreseeable future. I think of Peter and reality kicks in. Maybe it's time to forget about him. But then, I've come so far, it would be churlish to ignore all the ground I've gained. I could do both – the Downey family and the Saunders family in one go. I could let them all know exactly who it is they're dealing with, make sure they know my name and make certain they never forget it.

'Not a friend no, but it will make you smile.' I squeeze Fionn's hand and ruffle his hair. He responds by stopping and throwing his arms around me. Such a tactile boy. So affectionate and well mannered. I think about his father and wonder how he is coping with the demands and messiness of caring for a sick child. He won't be finding it easy. Paternal instincts don't come naturally to him. Everything is forced and contrived. Then I think of Yasmin and wonder if in her muddled and bewildered state, she mentions our little conversations. Not that it matters. I'm done with that family, all ties well and truly severed.

'I like smiling. You make me smile, Alice. When are we going to get an ice cream?'

'Ah, here we are,' I say, ignoring his question. 'Take a look at the name on there and tell me what it says.' My finger is outstretched towards one of the headstones, next to the ones I was tending the day Peter finally noticed me.

Fionn gets down on his haunches and peers at the inscription, his eyes narrowed in concentration as he mouths the words slowly and precisely, stumbling over them, murmuring the epitaph until he's sure he has got it right. Then he turns to me, eyes bursting out of his sockets, his mouth gaping open, and lets out a long gasp. 'Is that you? Are you a ghost?'

'No, sweetheart. I'm not a ghost. Look, feel my hand. See how warm it is. It's just that I don't like my own name so I thought I would use this one instead. What do you think?'

He reads it out loud, his little voice a squeak in the emptiness of the graveyard. 'Here lies Alice Godwin. Born 1871 Died 1910. What does it mean, Alice? Is she one of your relatives? Is Alice your mummy?'

I melt as he stares up at me, incomprehension at this aberration evident in his little face. 'No, sweetheart. She isn't one of my relatives and she definitely isn't my mummy. I don't know her or her family at all. I just liked her name, that's all. I used to visit this church a lot so I could meet somebody and I didn't want that certain somebody to know my real name so I used this one instead.'

'Is that allowed? I mean, you're not breaking the law or anything, are you?' His chin wobbles as he speaks and my insides turn into to melted butter. Such a sweet boy. My sweet boy.

'No, honey, I'm not breaking the law. People can be called any name they want.'

'Like a nickname?'

'Exactly. Just like a nickname.' I take his hand again and trace my fingers over his soft, silky skin. Like rose petals on a warm summer's day. 'What would your new name be? If you could choose any name at all in the whole wide world, what would it be?'

He places his finger on his chin and makes a slight humming sound as he thinks for a short while. 'Maybe I could be called Jack, like my dad.' He flashes me a big smile, his small, pearly-white teeth glistening in the sun.

Ice pierces my happy little bubble, bursting it wide open as he says those words, that name. Misery rains down on me at the thought of Jack Downey.

'Let's be a bit more adventurous, shall we?' I'm trying to sound jovial but my voice is a little too loud, a little sharper than I intended it to be. It's knowing that Fionn's father is still on his mind, that's what is causing me grief. Fionn belongs to me now. He's going to have to learn to adapt to my ways and get used to not having his other family around. It might take a little while but he'll get there in the end. We both will.

'Hmmm.' More chin tapping as he squeezes closed his eyes and cocks his head to one side. 'I know! How about Luke Skywalker?'

'Yes!' I reply, my spirits lifting slightly as he learns how to play my game. 'Maybe that's what we should do. We should start calling you Luke.'

He is nodding now, his smile bright and enthusiastic.

'Right,' I say, my voice chirpy and light. 'Come on then, Luke. Let's go and get an ice cream. What would you prefer – chocolate sprinkles or raspberry syrup?'

'Both!' He is jumping up and down now, his hair bouncing around, his face flushed with excitement. 'I would like both!'

* * *

We get back home in the nick of time. Luke dashes off to the toilet, desperate for a pee after eating an ice cream and drinking two full cans of lemonade.

'Make sure you wash your hands!' I shout upstairs after him, remembering how sticky his fingers were after his many glutinous snacks. 'And give your face a rinse too.'

I lock the front door and turn on the television, searching for kids' channels that will entertain him. I find one that seems to have an endless stream of cartoons playing, the loud noises and bright, flashing colours irritating me after only a few seconds, and decide it will have to do. Things aren't going to be perfect for either of us and there will be plenty of hitches along the way but we will have to learn to solve them and be a team together. Alice and Luke. Luke and Alice. A perfect match.

He comes running into the living room, his face clear of the crimson syrup that was coated around his mouth. He holds out his hands and I inspect them, smiling and turning them over to look at the other side. 'Well done, young man. I have to say, Luke, you've done a fine job of cleaning yourself up.'

'Luke?' And then he giggles, his small fingers covering his mouth. 'I'd forgotten about my new nickname!'

'Ah, but you must never forget.' I reach over and tickle him, softly pressing at his tummy. 'You're mine now, young Luke. All mine!'

He lets out a squeal of delight and falls back onto the sofa with an exhausted sigh, his limbs spread out, gaze turned upwards to the ceiling. He's relaxed. That's good. He feels easy in this house – our house. Things are going to be just fine. I'll make sure of it.

I'm in the kitchen preparing us both a sandwich when I hear him calling out to me. 'Who's that over there, watching us?'

My heart jumps into my mouth as I hurry through to where he's standing. His head is bobbing up and down in an attempt to peek over the top of the living-room windowsill. I half turn away, refusing to look at who it is out there. I don't want to see them and I don't want them to see me. It's a female, that much I do know. She's standing over the road, half hidden behind a clump of shrubbery. I whip the curtains closed and carry Luke away from where he is standing staring out, fascinated. I find it hard to believe that Jack has already reported Fionn missing. It's only been a matter of hours. He thinks he's at school. So who is she? And why is she here?

I take a deep breath, tell myself to stop it, to calm down and start thinking rationally. She may not even be watching my house. She could be lost, waiting for somebody. A jogger catching their breath.

'Come on young man. Let's get you a snack, shall we?' Before I whisk him away, I pinch hold of the fabric of the curtains and as surreptitiously as I can, I peek out, my body rooting itself to the spot when I see her there. A wave of dizziness takes hold before I right myself and half carry, half drag Luke through to the kitchen, fear and anger blinding me.

I sit him at the table, my mind a vortex of dark thoughts. 'Come on. Eat up. Once you've had this, you can watch some TV.'

He eats and I wander back through to the living room, my legs liquid, my head a tangle of wild and insane ideas. What the fuck is Lauren doing here? She was desperate to discover my address and now here she is, waiting outside, watching me. What the hell does she want? There is no way she can know who I am. It's not possible. I've changed everything – my hair, my appearance, my name. So how in God's name did she find me?

My stomach contracts, tight with anger and disquietude. I peer out again and see her shadow shift as she leaves the street, wandering off out of view.

My phone rings and a million possibilities race around my head about who it could be – Jack Downey, Peter, even the police who know that young Fionn is in my charge. I snatch it up and stare at the screen, my anxiety loosening.

It's Peter, the lesser of all the evils, and my God, there are many. My thoughts slow down as I listen to his voice, his gently pleading tone. I know what he wants, his need to see me an all-encompassing, cloying emotion. I now have a child to think about, however. He asks if we can get together tonight. I spin around and gaze into the kitchen at little Luke, who is sitting eating his snack, humming away to himself like he doesn't have a care in the world.

I want to refuse, to tell Peter that I have other things planned but the words won't come. So I go along with whatever he says, a solution already implanting itself deep in my brain. I have no choice. This is just something that I need to do. I have set this whole thing in motion and now I need to see it through to its bitter end.

39

PETER

All the driving is starting to get to him. It's been a busy few weeks and he's ready for a break. A proper break, not just a couple of days off at the weekend. A holiday somewhere warm. With Alice. The thought of seeing her has kept him going, helping him to deal with awkward, irate customers and giving him the patience to smile and nod while being berated by his management team for countless imagined misdemeanours by the sales team who work under his direction. The guys in his team are a hard-working bunch who do a thankless task trying to bring in orders from an area that they as a company have yet to break into. It's a big ask but they are slowly getting there, although according to management, too slowly. They want results yesterday and aren't prepared to wait, talking already about possible redundancies if the team don't hit their ridiculously impossible targets.

Peter sighs, shuffles about in his seat, checking the time as he finds a more comfortable position to try and alleviate the ache at the base of his spine. Too much driving. Too much work-related stress. He thinks about ringing Alice, if only to hear her voice, the gentle lilt of it, the way it soothes him and helps keep him grounded. Sometimes, when she isn't able to speak on the phone, it makes him conscious that he comes across as too demanding: constantly leaving voice messages asking her to return his calls. She too, has a job and a life. He often reminds himself of this fact, aware that she is a grown woman who needs her own space. It's been a few days since they've spoken. It feels longer, time taunting him with her absence.

She answers after only two rings. 'Hi, Alice? It's me.'

'Hi, Peter.' She's breathless and sounds different somehow: cagey and out of sorts. Not the usual, calm, gentle Alice. Somebody caught on the backfoot. Somebody different.

'I'm on my way back from Sheffield after an early journey this morning and was wondering if you fancied a get-together later? Nothing too spectacular, just an easy meal and a couple of beers at mine?'

She says nothing. Her breathing is the only thing he can hear.

He knows she is reluctant and rather than give her space, he does the one thing he promised himself he would not do and tries to corner her into agreeing. 'Look, I tell you what, I'll pull up outside yours at seven o'clock and if you're not in the mood, feel free to come out and tell me to piss off. I won't be offended; it's just that I've had a sod of a day and, well, I've missed you.'

'Outside mine?' Her voice has a slight tremble to it. He ignores it, carries on regardless.

'Yes,' he replies, trying to sound laidback, affable, hoping this isn't the end of them, his desperation becoming too much for her, overwhelming her. Scaring her off. It's too soon. She needs to give them more time. It's still early days. This thing can work, he knows it. Panic grips him. He visualises her face, creased with doubt and concern. Already, he can hear her voice as she says those words: *sorry, Peter, this isn't working out for me.*

'Outside yours it is then. I'll see you at 7 p.m.' And before she can refuse or tell him to go to hell, he hangs up, heart thumping, blood running hot through his veins.

It was wrong, what he did, cutting her off like that, forcing her to go along with his plans but tells himself that tiredness forced him to do it. If she really didn't want to meet, she would ring back and tell him to go to hell, shouting at him that he is an arrogant bastard and that she won't be there for him later, that she has a life of her own that doesn't involve him. He has a feeling she won't do any of those things but spends the next twenty minutes gripping the steering wheel, bracing himself for her return call.

It doesn't come. He arrives home in a more buoyant frame of mind, time conspiring against him, pushing him into a tight deadline. He needs to shower, to change into clean clothes before heading off to Alice's house.

He calls to Lauren that he's home. She replies with, 'Hi, Dad!' and he goes about getting himself ready. On impulse, he pokes his head around her bedroom door to find her sitting on her bed, scrolling through her laptop.

'I'm going to pick Alice up soon. I've invited her here for some food and a couple of drinks.'

Without waiting for a reply or giving her a chance to protest, he backs out again, closing the door softly. What Lauren thinks about Alice is none of his business. This is what he told himself on the drive back. He is a grown man and deserves some happiness and regardless of what his daughter's opinion is of his new partner, he is going to take that happiness; he will snatch at it greedily and hang onto it for dear life.

He prepares the food and covers it, ready to heat up when they get back. His mood is still upbeat as he showers and gets ready. Once she gets over herself and her current mood, Lauren will soften. She will once again warm to Alice's gentle charm. He will invite her to join them downstairs for food, lure her into the conversation and get the two of them talking again.

* * *

Alice is standing outside the gate as he pulls up, looking as radiant, as alluring as ever. He senses an air of reserve as she climbs in the car but his fears quickly dissolve when she reaches over and places her hand over his, her voice soft and gentle. 'Lovely to see you, Peter. Thank you for picking me up.'

The remainder of the journey is quiet, the atmosphere sombre. The music is enough to quell his fears, to keep them at bay, and by the time they reach his house, she has softened and the old Alice is alive and well once more.

'Listen,' he says softly as he pulls up on the drive and turns to face her,

'Lauren has been rather down lately so don't worry if she appears a bit off. It's definitely not you. It's a family thing, a teenage girl thing. It'll pass, I'm sure.' He wants to add that she is possibly missing her mother but stops himself. Alice doesn't need to hear about Sophia. None of them do.

'I totally understand. Don't worry, I remember those years all too well. And of course, she'll be missing her mum.'

His breath becomes heavy. Erratic. He wants to wrap his arms around this woman, to hold her close for the rest of his life. So many women would shun a surly teenager, so many would lack compassion, be too fearful to mention her mother, but not Alice. Always warm and thoughtful. Always knowing what the right thing is to say and do. She is a gift and despite being a non-believer, he thanks whichever god is listening that he has her in his life.

'Right, come on then.' His voice is light, carefree. 'I don't know about you but I'm bloody starving. Let's get inside and eat and drink ourselves senseless.'

40

ALICE

Poor Peter. Poor, stupid, bovine Peter. So blind, so misguided and so desperately naïve. Child-like in his ways. Here he is thinking I am the best thing that has ever happened to him and here I am thinking of a thousand ways in which I can hurt him.

He trapped me, giving me no way of backing out of tonight but that isn't a problem. If anything, it works well in my favour. We have unfinished business, me and the Saunders family. It's just that they don't know it yet. But they will soon enough.

And then of course, there is little Luke to think about. Lovely, gentle Luke who is currently asleep in the spare bedroom of my home, dosed up with sleeping tablets. I had no choice. Not coming here to Peter's house wasn't an option. I have an opportunity to confront Lauren, to find out what she wants from me, find out why she was hanging around outside my house earlier today. I don't care for people spying on me and I don't care for her. My life is my business and nothing to do with an interfering teenager who has a high opinion of herself and ideas well above her station.

It's becoming tiresome, keeping up this pretence, being the sweet, docile, little woman, the mousy creature that Peter wants me to be. Perhaps that's how it was with Sophia. Maybe they lived their lives as a lovestruck couple, continually whispering words of affection into each other's ear.

Although I doubt it. Lovestruck wives don't fall into the arms of other women's husbands, do they? They stick with the one they have. So why didn't Sophia stick with Peter? If he had taken better care of her, made her happier, loved her a bit more then she wouldn't have sought it elsewhere. If Peter had been a decent husband to his wife, my husband would still be here with me.

I think of how he treats Lauren, like she is some sort of precious bird in a gilded cage and then think of how my parents treated me, and swallow. We are worlds apart. Memories of the many arguments we had and the acrimony that followed me into adulthood after the death of my sister filter into my brain. I try to stuff them down out of reach but they keep clambering back up, clawing their way out of the darkness. Memories of me as a child, being scolded at every opportunity, memories of me as an adult being told that I needed help, that the things I did weren't normal, that I was dangerous. Possibly unhinged. A coroner's report stating accidental death wasn't proof enough for my parents. That incident has followed me every single day, tainting me, taunting me, poisoning my life.

And then came the professional help I received as an adult, the forced assistance that achieved nothing. The very idea, the memory of it makes me want to retch. All that talking, raking over the worst times of my life, looking for clues, reasons why my brain doesn't work as it should. Sometimes, there are no reasons. Sometimes, we just are what we are.

I don't suppose Lauren will ever have to undergo any type of psychiatric assessments. She is too smart for that, too savvy and too damn perfect. Her life – up until losing her mother – has been a textbook existence. Completely and utterly faultless.

And then Sophia died. At that point, our lives took on a common theme – we have both lost somebody close to us either to death or to a life sentence in prison. I suppose that should make us alike, bring us closer together. Allies and partners. Except it doesn't. We are different. Very, very different.

She loves her father. I don't. I am here for a reason. I have a job to do here, in this house. All I'm doing is righting some wrongs, tipping the scales back and readjusting them accordingly.

I've got Luke now, and Peter and Lauren. I have plans for them all. It's just a case of rebalancing those scales. If Sophia hadn't got involved, then none of this would have happened. My world wouldn't have fallen apart. She came on the scene and that was the end of my little family. I was left with a gaping hole in my life. Why should the Saunders still have their own happy little family when I have nothing?

As we enter the house, I'm struck by how different it is to my own little place – warm and full of ambience. How have I not noticed this before now? The contrast is so stark, it stops me in my tracks, making me realise that I deserve some of this warmth in my life. Luke and I deserve it. He is my way out of this dispassionate, lifeless existence.

After I leave this house in a few hours, we can escape, Luke and I. We can leave this town, move south and live in anonymity in some decent village where nobody will recognise us. I'm not stupid. I know that the police will be out by now, searching for him, my boy. They can't have him. The Downeys don't deserve to have him back. He's better off with me. The crying and whining when I told him he was stopping over and spending the night at my house is just a phase. He'll soon become accustomed to his new life. Besides, the sleeping tablets soon stopped his protestations. I have my little ways of making everything perfect.

He's better off with me. I mean, his parents didn't even bother checking my true identity and references, for heaven's sake. What kind of people would do that? They were so desperate for a nanny, so desperate for somebody to look after their children that they agreed to pay me cash if I could start straightaway. Finding these people is easy. They're all out there, advertising in local newspapers, unwilling to go through the proper channels to avoid paying more than they need to for someone to take care of their children and do their cleaning and laundry: chores they deem to be beneath them. I got lucky. I found things they would rather had stayed hidden and managed to get enough money out of them to keep me going for a short while.

'I asked Lauren to join us but as I said, she's a bit out of sorts at the minute.' Peter is watching me, his words cutting into my thoughts, jolting me back to the present.

We are standing in the dining room. I have no memory of getting here. The table is set for just two people. It is surreal. Everything is odd and dreamlike, as if I've stepped through a portal into another universe, one where everything lends itself to my needs. I nod, smile, go through the array of expected social niceties, my movements soft and effortless.

'I've done enough food for all of us but she's adamant that she's staying put.' He eyes me cautiously. I suspect he thinks I'm upset by her absence. I smile and touch his hand softly, a reassuring stroke to counterbalance his anxious tone.

'Tell you what,' I say breathlessly. 'Why don't you put some on a plate and I'll take it upstairs to her room?' Eagerness grips me, an explosion of exhilaration pumping through my veins at what lay ahead.

His eyes are wide, dewy with gratitude. 'Would you? That would be great. I think perhaps a friendly face delivering it might be just the ticket.'

I know what he's thinking – that Lauren and I can make amends, be the solid friends he wants us to be. I am thinking very differently. And my God, these two are making it so easy for me. Far easier than I expected. I had all kinds of subterfuge planned and here they are, offering me opportunities on a gold platter. At times like this, life really can be so rewarding.

'Let's have a glass of wine first,' I say as he takes my jacket and places it on the back of the chair.

He nods and pours us both a glass of Chablis. We raise a toast. 'To us,' he says as he leans forward and kisses me on the lips.

'To us,' I reply and take a long, welcome swig, hoping to wash away the taste of him.

I place my goblet on the table, my hands steady and willing. 'Tell you what, if you give me Lauren's food now, I'll take it up and we can have a little chat before you and I eat together down here.'

* * *

Peter has gone to a lot of effort. He always does. Already, I know that much about him, that he doesn't hold back when it comes to cooking and trying to impress me. I scoop up Lauren's plate and leave him in the kitchen as he prepares the dessert. He's immersed in his cooking, too busy to notice what I am doing.

I stop in the dining room and adjust my hair, my clothing. Not too glossy, hopefully demure enough for her to trust me. I open my bag, take out the bottle of peanut oil, open it up and add a few drops to the food before heading upstairs and knocking on Lauren's door.

'Hi, Lauren. Just thought I'd pass this to you, see if I can make amends for our little misunderstanding last week.' I push at the door with hip and let myself in before she can answer. Before she can stop me.

Her hatred towards me is evident. Anger seeps out of her in bucket loads as I place the plate of food down on the end of the bed.

'Cooked for you by your dad. Don't worry,' I say holding up my hand as a peace offering, 'I'm not stopping. I just wanted to tell you how sorry I am for snapping at you and that what I said when we were alone together on the moors was unforgiveable.' I manage a meek and tender smile and back out of the room, closing the door with a muffled hush before creeping back downstairs.

Time is a hefty, tangible thing as I wait, my senses heightened, my ears attuned to every little sound. Peter and I have another drink together before sitting down to eat. The music is playing softly in the background. The lighting has been dimmed. Everything is perfect. And then I hear it – banging coming from upstairs, the rumpus of somebody staggering across the room, closely followed by the thud of footsteps as Lauren races downstairs and opens the door to where we are sitting. I see the look in her eyes. I see the incredulity and terror in her face. I smile because I know.

And that's when everything changes.

41

LAUREN

She knocks at my door and is inside within seconds. I want to push her away, to tell her go to hell and leave Dad and me alone, but she is so quick, so fucking adept at manipulating the situation that I simply don't have time to protest. She makes her false apology and is out of the room before I can say anything in return and I am left sitting here on my bed like a mute delinquent, unable to respond or do anything at all.

The plate of food beside me smells divine even though my stomach is tied up in knots and I feel mildly sick. I wish to God I could work out what is going on here, what her little game is, but my mind seems to be stuck in a rut. I'm going round in circles, covering old ground and getting nowhere fast.

A pain travels up the back of my head, lodging itself behind my eyes. I take a drink of water from the bottle I brought up here earlier and stare down at the chicken casserole beside me. It is betrayal of my own principles and instincts to eat any, however my body is telling me otherwise. I reach down and take a forkful of food and then another before opening my laptop and scanning the internet for inspiration.

My stomach ache increases and leaves me worn out. I eat some more and drink plenty of water until both the plate and the bottle are empty then continue scanning, unsure of what it is I am actually looking for.

I don't have to look far. The article finds me, knocking all the oxygen out of me, the story bold and unmissable at the top of the webpage.

The floor tilts and sways, my bedroom taking on different dimensions as I push everything away off the bed and try to stand. It's her face, there on the screen, staring out at me. This is it. This is what I've been looking for. I knew it. I just knew there was something terribly wrong and now I've found it. Alice's face on the news. It's her.

A searing pain claws its way up my throat from my stomach, a thick wave of discomfort, hot and prickly, forcing me to double over. My hands reach up to my neck. My eyes blur, a mist clouding my vision as I stagger across the room.

Dad. I need to speak to Dad. I have to let him know. We need to call somebody. Anybody.

The air in the room thins. My guts clench and become constricted. I can't seem to breathe properly. Why can't I breathe?

I stare down at the empty plate, at the remnants of the chicken and go faint.

No, please not that. Not again. Anything but that.

My legs are leaden as I stagger downstairs, too short of breath, too deprived of oxygen to cry out for help. A familiar tingle takes hold in my mouth, my lips suddenly hot and fat, my eyes itchy as they swell and close.

They're both sitting there at the table as I lunge forwards, my mouth agape, my throat becoming smaller and smaller, almost a pinprick. I look to Dad for help. His mouth drops open. I lurch over to him, my legs buckling, my breath coming out in short, screeching gasps.

'Dad!' I watch him rise from his seat, the world rotating in slow motion around me, his movements clumsy and laboured. '999. Call 999.'

'Lauren! Where's your EpiPen? Your adrenaline. Where is it?'

I shake my head and point to the sideboard, to the cupboard where it sits week after week, month after month doing nothing, and try again to alert him. 'In there. 999. Now.'

My hands are clasped at my windpipe, my nails digging into the soft flesh there as if it will help to get more oxygen into my bloodstream, as if it will stop my throat from closing up completely. An attempt to stop myself from dying.

He opens the door to the shelf where I store it and turns to look at me, shaking his head, his skin loose with shock. 'Where, Lauren? It's not there! Where is it?' His eyes bore into me. I can't speak, can't help him. I can't breathe. Everything drifting away from me. My vision attenuating. My world gradually coming to a stop.

'Is this what you're after?' Her voice is nauseatingly soft and sweet, her timbre slow and mocking.

Alice sits rigidly, the EpiPen clasped between her hands, her bony fingers gripping it tightly. She is smiling. *Fucking smiling*! And I am here struggling to breathe, my body slowly shutting down as it becomes deprived of oxygen, my throat swelling and closing until it snaps shut and I am unable to get any air in there at all.

'Alice?' I can hear Dad's voice. An echo in my head. A disembodied sound coming from somewhere in the room. 'The EpiPen. Can I have it, please?'

My knees hit the floor with a crack, my legs giving way under me.

My stomach roils, my guts churn and swirl. I feel it coming, travelling up my throat, thick, viscous fluid trying to escape, my body trying to purge itself of the toxins in there.

I listen to the silence, am still aware enough to detect Dad's shock, to sense his deteriorating mood and growing horror as it dawns on him what is happening here, what is happening to me. Does he know what Alice is doing? What she has already done?

'The food? Oh my God, the food!' His voice swirls around me, the air in the room shifting as he panics and thrashes about. 'What the fuck have I done? What the hell was in that food?'

I try to listen, to hear his words. I want to tell him who she is, that we need to call the police but nothing comes out. I can say the words in my head but my tongue is a thick carpet in my mouth, glued and set in place. I want to feel Dad's arms around me, to hear him say that everything is going to be all right but feel only my fear, my growing terror that tells me that this is it, the final moment of my life, that I am going to die. I'm frightened. Terrified, actually. But then something happens. A coldness sets in. I am in a tunnel, distanced from everything and everybody. Suddenly, I feel nothing, hear nothing, a silence settling far inside my head as my vision mists and fades and the darkness begins its cold descent.

42

PETER

He doesn't understand. Or maybe he does. Lauren tried to tell him. She tried on so many occasions and he just couldn't see it. He was blind to her words, her nuanced ways. His heart is pounding, his head buzzing as he stares at Alice. His Alice. The woman he thought he knew. The stranger before him. He doesn't know her. He doesn't know her at all. She continues holding the EpiPen. And she is smiling. *Smiling!* Lauren is lying on the floor, clutching at her throat, gasping for breath. She's dying. Sweet Jesus, his daughter is actually dying.

'Alice? The EpiPen! I need the fucking EpiPen!'

Without moving a muscle, she drops it at his feet, her body rigid, her face frozen into a grimace. Or is it a smile? It's too difficult to tell. He can't seem to think straight, his brain a fraught mess of terror and dread, confusion muddying his thinking.

With hands that are slippery with sweat, fingers clumsy and hot, he picks it up and tears open the packet then pulls out the syringe, holding it aloft before jabbing it into Lauren's leg with force. He winces, can feel the heat from her body, the slight squirm from her torso as the injection takes hold, pumping adrenaline around her system, doing its damnedest to keep her alive.

He kneels beside her, gently sweeping her hair out of her eyes, and places his hand at the nape of her neck before turning her onto her side into the recovery position, pushing her sideways. And then he prays. He prays and begs and pleads and offers up his life for hers.

His heart thumps while he waits, attempting to hold back the tears that threaten to flow, blinking and swallowing, hoping somebody up there is listening as he implores them to save her, telling them they have suffered enough. No more. Please God, no more.

'Come on, Lauren. Come on. Wake up. Wake up!' He turns to Alice, his features frozen, rigid with terror. 'Call an ambulance. Please, Alice, do it now!'

She doesn't move, sitting instead in the same position, angular and unmoving, watching, waiting. Assessing, impassive. Stony cold.

'Alice! Call 999. Call a fucking ambulance!'

Again, no movement. And then another smile. A fucking smile! The room tilts. He can't breathe. He is wheezing now, holding Lauren, stroking her hair, rocking her, willing her to open her eyes and smile at him, telling him everything is going to be just fine.

'No,' she says quietly, a murmur from between her thin pursed lips. 'No emergency services.'

A bullet ricochets around his head, bouncing off his skull, shattering his thoughts. 'What? What the hell are you talking about? She's dying! Can't you see that my daughter is fucking dying here?'

He can't leave her to get his phone. Alice will kill her. She will kneel down beside his daughter and end her life. He knows it for sure.

There's a sound, a low murmur. Barely noticeable, more like a rasp, before it becomes louder. Lauren's body convulses. Her limbs shift and move. Her eyes open a fraction. Then a sickening roar as she empties her guts over and over, the effort of it causing her to pant and cry. Vomit spills out around them, a pool of sticky bile covering the floor, spreading and pooling.

Peter hauls her up, the top half of her body resting against his, her head bent forward as she is sick again and again, glutinous strands of saliva hanging from her mouth, a groan emanating from the back of her throat.

A stray clump of hair sits in front of her eyes. He pulls it away, gently rubbing at her back, cooing at her that everything is going to be okay, that she is safe now. She shudders and slumps against him. He touches her back, his fingers caressing the nodules of her spine. He is able to feel her breathing, the slow pulsing of her body and almost cries out loud with relief, a rock-sized lump lodging itself in his throat.

He can't bring himself to look at Alice. He doesn't want to try and fathom what is going through her head, what thoughts are festering there.

'Dangerous...' Lauren's voice is a whisper, a hoarse, guttural moan, and he has to lean closer to be able to hear what she is saying.

'What is it, sweetheart? You need to rest up now. Focus on your breathing; that's the important thing.' The room is unfeasibly hot, sweat coating his back, standing out on his forehead, a thin crescent of pearls around his hairline and blooming under his armpits even though he is shivering and trembling, his flesh cold and clammy.

'She's dangerous. Police. Call the police.' Another whisper, her words slurred, almost unintelligible. Almost. But not completely.

He turns, looks at Alice who sits, watching them intently, never moving, her features locked into position as she evaluates the situation. Assessing them, monitoring them like lab specimens.

'Alice, what the fuck is going on? What is wrong with you?'

A shrug. A non-committal countenance, her pale face expressionless, unresponsive. She sighs, lowers her shoulders. Shakes her head dismissively.

He speaks again, more forcefully this time, anger, exasperation, desperation in his tone. 'Alice. Why didn't you help us? And why did you have Lauren's EpiPen?'

Her voice is crisp, almost a bark, but clear and precise as she gives her reply, the words she utters a cold knife that twists in his guts. 'Because I could.'

'Because you could what, Alice? You're not making any sense.' He wants her to have a reason, a good reason, because the alternative is too grisly, too terrible to bear.

'Because I could keep it and watch you struggle. That's why I had it.' She stands up, strides around them, her tiny frame taking on gargantuan proportions, her feet clipping on the wooden floor like a crack of thunder. 'I knew where it was kept. I think perhaps you told me, Peter, and so

I saw an opportunity and I took it. I'm not sure what else you want me to say.'

'She could have died! For fuck's sake, Alice, my daughter could have died while you sat there and watched. Not only did you watch it all happen; you fucking smirked!' A rage builds. He wants to stand up, to unfold his crumpled body and tell her what he thinks of her and stupid, murderous little game but knows that he can't leave Lauren here unattended. So instead, he stares up at her, his eyes narrowed. Tiny slits of hatred and despair.

'Who are you, Alice? Who the fuck *are* you, really?'

A yelp of laughter followed by a prolonged silence. 'You don't know? You really don't know?'

'No, I really, really don't know. Why don't you tell me?' He thinks that perhaps he does know but doesn't want to admit it to himself, is too scared that admitting it will unearth his buried secrets.

Lauren murmurs something, her words garbled. Incomprehensible. She attempts to sit up, her arms flailing, the effects of the anaphylactic shock still battering her system, leaving her weakened, defenceless and exhausted.

'Shh.' Peter strokes her hair, pulls her closer to him, thinking he can protect her against this woman, this individual who is now a stranger to him. What a fool he has been. There is no fool like an old fool and he is the biggest of them all. He thought he knew her. She has been in his bed and was firmly entrenched in his heart but she is in fact a total stranger to him. An imposter in their house, in their lives. What was he thinking? What the hell was he thinking? 'Just take it easy. Let your body rest now.' He murmurs into Lauren's ear, strokes her hair, pulls her even closer to him to shield her from the threat that Alice poses to her. To them both. His eyes have been opened. He's under no illusions as to how dangerous this woman is. This Alice lady. This psychopath. She would have sat and watched his daughter choke to death and not broken a sweat.

He cranes his neck, staring up at Alice, who is parading around them, a predator stalking its next kill. Her usual soft features have morphed into something more sinister, something unrecognisable, her dark eyes full of fire, her skin stretched over the bones of her face like a death mask. Peter sucks in his breath, holds it there, releases it in a burning rush. The look he sees on her face will stay with him, haunting him for an age.

'I think you should leave now. Lauren and I need some time alone and you need to go.'

'Oh Christ. You still haven't worked it out, have you? Peter, Peter, Peter, you are so desperately and worryingly naïve. You have the mind of a child – so quick to trust people, to let them into your life without knowing anything about them.' Her voice is a rasp, the sound of somebody unhinged and unpredictable. Somebody teetering on the brink.

His breathing is shallow. He tries to clear his mind, to think clearly. Rationally. He cooked the food. It was nut-free. Alice took it upstairs to Lauren.

'You put something in Lauren's food.'

Her slow clapping prickles his skin, his scalp shrinking against his skull.

'Well done. You got there in the end. Took you a while, didn't it? But you have finally woken up. Poor, sad little Peter. Dear God, I don't know how you function with that small brain of yours.'

'Why?' The sound of his heartbeat drowns out everything else. 'Why would you do such a thing? You were really prepared to let her die?'

'She didn't die though, did she?' Alice points down at Lauren's slumped body. 'I mean, look at her. She's still here, isn't she? She's still breathing. What's your problem?'

Over the past twenty years, he has been on numerous sales courses, learned how to elicit the correct responses from customers, how to build up relationships and make people comfortable while he takes the lead and talks about his expertise in engineering but for once, he is lost for words, unable to do anything except gasp and stare at this creature before him, this woman he thought he knew. This monster.

'Go. Get out of my house. Leave us both alone. Just fuck off out of here and don't ever come back!'

No movement. She carries on pacing around the room, appraising them, picking over the carcass of their weakened position. A vulture circling, wheeling above them. Waiting. He wonders what she's planning, what her next destructive move will be. He doesn't have to wonder for long.

Alice disappears for a brief second – not long enough for him to do anything, to rouse Lauren and grab at his phone – and returns carrying a knife, the metal blade glinting under the glare of the lamp.

Next to him, Lauren stirs again, her strength returning, her floppy limbs gradually gaining some rigidity. She pushes herself up on her hands and sits next to her father, her skin pale and waxy, her eyes glazed and full of horror.

'Missing child. The news. Alice,' is all she can say before she bursts into tears, places her head in her hands and sobs.

43

LAUREN

I thought I was going to die. I really thought it was the end for me. If Dad hadn't managed to get hold of the adrenaline, then I might not be here. It makes me shudder, that possibility, the thought of dying, slowly choking to death. And all the while, she sat by and watched, doing nothing to help. She was prepared to watch me suffer and gasp my last. I knew it. I just knew that something was amiss with her. I thought she was a gold digger, an opportunist, a sad, old woman who seeks out grieving men. I didn't know that she wanted to kill me. I definitely didn't see that coming.

I need to speak clearly, to tell Dad about Alice, about the kidnapping but my throat is still swollen and sore. I try to concentrate, to get the words out properly, be clear and coherent. I want him to listen. I want Alice to listen. She needs to know that I know. Dad may have been blinkered to her ways and blinded by her charms but I knew. I just knew there was something murky, something sinister going on. And now I've found it.

The news broke while I was sitting upstairs eating the food she gave me. Her weapon of destruction. My plate of poison.

I can hear Dad shouting at her. I listen to the click of her heels as she paces around us, circling and circling wildly, her feet hitting the ground like gunshots. Then I hear Dad gasp and suck in his breath. He is staring up at her; his heartbeat is thick and fast. I can feel it as I sit next to him, his body helping to prop me up. I regain more strength, pushing myself up on my hands. I need to pull myself round, be a force to be reckoned with, not a floppy, useless mess who is unable to defend herself. I won't get caught out again by this woman. I'll do whatever it takes to get her out of this house.

Only when I can look at her, really see her properly, does my stomach sink. She is holding a knife. The blade is pointing at us. Her hand is wobbling about, her eyes glistening, her mouth twisted and menacing. Jade Kennedy is here. Not Alice Godwin. Phillip Kennedy's wife is here in our house.

I saw it when I was upstairs browsing the internet. Her face was there next to a bold headline about a missing child. The police had said she goes under the name of Alice Godwin but is also known as Jade Kennedy. A neighbour had seen the photograph and passed on information about her true identity. That's when it hit me – the thought that I'd seen her elsewhere, the familiarity of her features. Those few times I attended Mum's murder trial. I saw her there. She looked very different with short, dark hair and no glasses. She was also much heavier, sitting on the bench hunched over, shoulders slumped, wearing a dark, frumpy overcoat and a downcast expression. But now that I know, there's no mistaking the cut of her jaw, her piercing, blue eyes. It's definitely her. Here in our house.

'Missing child. The news. Alice,' is all I can manage before the shock catches up with me and I am unable to control the tears that come thick and fast. My chest heaves, my stomach contracts, stars burst behind my eyes as I press my hands into them to suppress the wave of terror that is washing over me. It's such a mess. Everything is such an awful mess. We need to garner our strength, Dad and I. We need to show her that this is our house, that she isn't wanted here and should leave.

Except she has a knife and by the look in her eyes, that dark, bottomless pit of nothingness in them, I know she's willing to use it, slitting us from ear to ear, smiling as she does it.

'Dad,' I whisper, my throat still sore and croaky. 'The news. She's on the news.'

His warm breath filters over to me, reminding me of when I was a child and how safe I felt when I was around him, how he used to pick me up in his big, strong arms and cuddle me into his chest. I want to be that child again, invincible in an ever-changing and increasingly perilous world. Except I'm not. I'm almost an adult and now here we are in this situation, being held hostage by somebody who's clearly deranged and unpredictable. We don't know her. Not at all. And she doesn't know us. Or me. Not the real me. The one who is capable of so much more than anybody knows or realises. But not at the minute. Not like this with my weakened body and an immune system that's trying to fight off a perceived poison I've ingested.

'Who, sweetheart? Who's on the news?' He tries to whisper but I know she can hear him. I can tell by her unwavering gaze, her pinched features that she is listening to every word we say. Despite her proximity, despite her crazed expression, she is tuned in to every single thing that we say and do.

'Her,' I hiss as I attempt to dip my head, to get him to lean in closer to me so she can't hear what we're saying. 'It's his wife. Kennedy. Phillip Kennedy. She's not Alice. She's Jade. Jade Kennedy.'

'Stop talking!' Her face looms close to mine, her fetid, sour breath causing me to back away. 'Stop saying those things! I'm Alice, you hear me? Alice Godwin.' She laughs, her voice oscillating wildly between a childish giggle and a loud aggressive roar. 'Except I'm not, am I?'

She moves away from us, her face creased with laughter as she continues her gawkish, macabre display. A display of madness, of somebody rapidly losing their grip. 'I'm Alice, I'm not! I'm Alice, I'm not. I'm Alice...' Her voice fades. She dances around the room, skipping, swirling, sashaying, the metal blade glinting, before coming to a rapid halt. 'I'm not!' Her hands are still clutching the knife as she spins around, stares at us, her eyes dead and fathomless. Only darkness there. No logic, no rational thought. Nothing but darkness.

'Where is he, Jade? Where's the little boy you took from his parents?' I'm taking a chance, trying to reason with her. I have no idea what she is capable of. I don't know her; I don't know what levels she will stoop to. How far she has fallen. Although judging by the blade she's holding, I have a fair idea. I'm trying to appeal to her better nature, the softer side she showed us at the beginning of her relationship with Dad.

I need to do something. It's not just about us. There's another family out there who is missing their child. Where is that boy? What the hell has she done with him?

There's stillness in the room, a sharp moment of reckoning as we wait for her reply. Then a noise. Not a voice. Not at first. A dull, clicking sound followed by a slam of a door. Then the voice comes and I go faint once more.

44

JADE/ALICE

They've called somebody. I don't know how they did it or when, but I do know that whoever it is coming through that door will have to be dealt with. I can't come this far and then lose everything before it's finished: before I've had a chance to reveal my hand and show them what I'm capable of.

The words are out of Lauren's mouth as I spin around, blade outstretched. There's a screech, a deathly hollering from both Peter and his daughter when I catch the intruder with the knife, the sharp blade sliding across their skin, cold metal against warm flesh. I watch transfixed as they slump to the floor, arms covering their midriff, small trickles of blood seeping from between their fingers. A rose hue of blood blossoming and oozing out of her. So much of it. It's both wonderful and utterly grotesque. A mesmerising sight.

'Grandma!' Lauren screams, her face deathly pale.

'Oh my God! What the hell have you done?' Peter is up on his feet now, racing towards me. I'm too quick for him. He's tall, broad shouldered. Solid and cumbersome. I'm lighter, more agile and able to dodge his towering approach.

Clutching the knife, I slalom out of his way, watching as Lauren attempts to slide over to the bleeding woman, her limbs floppy and weak after her own near-death experience. She throws her arms around the older woman's body and sobs. Something nips at me, a usually concealed emotion. An unfamiliar emotion. Guilt. It's a new sensation. I don't care for it. I push it away. This is on them. They gave me no choice. Everything that has happened so far in my life has been thrust upon me by other people. They put me here. *They made me do it.*

My childhood, my marriage. My life. All taken from me. You can't just do that to people, can you? Rob them of things that are rightfully theirs: my parents, my husband, my short-lived relationship with Tom, all of them saying the same thing – that I should be locked away, kept separate from other people.

My past creeps in, bites at me, my mind debilitated by this turn of events, the appearance of this woman in the house. I close my eyes, trying to escape the memories: that child. My sister. All these years on and still her face haunts me, how she clawed and fought as I held her under the bathwater: the desperation, the fear, her bucking body, her bulging eyes. Her open mouth and thrashing limbs. The way she looked at me, blaming me even though it wasn't my fault. She made me do it, you see. She made me hold her down until she stopped fighting. That's what it was. A silent request. I had no choice. I didn't enjoy it. It was gruesome, difficult. Not a natural thing to do, but I did it anyway. I had to. That's what people don't understand. I simply had no choice. There was no other way.

She's at rest now, just sleeping. That's all it is. A long and peaceful slumber. An eternal one. No having to endure this cruel world. No having to endure the temperaments of others. No having to be subjected to their unsubstantiated accusations and hatred and sharp, unforgiving words that cut deeper than they will ever know.

A sound penetrates my thoughts.

It's Peter. He's running at me, his face contorted with anger. I've hurt that lady and he is furious. But so am I. He needs to remember that. I had a life until Sophia Saunders ruined it. Until Peter made her so miserable that she turned to somebody else for succour and sex and happiness.

I hold out the knife to stop him, my body bent low. I jab at his middle, slashing the air repeatedly, trying to connect with him. He moves back and forth, the two of us dancing around each other until a voice stops him in his tracks.

'Dad, we need an ambulance. Grandma's dying. Please, somebody help her!'

I shake my head and nod at him to sit down. Just to assert my authority, to let them know that I'm in charge here and not about to be browbeaten into following their rules, I step closer and slide the knife across his forearm, catching him unawares while his attention is focused on his daughter and the older lady.

He lets out a yelp. Blood bubbles out of the wound in a straight line; small strips of crimson running over his arm and dripping onto the wooden floor, pooling and growing, combining with the vomit. Bodily fluids everywhere, spreading and congealing, dark and ominous. The colour of death.

'Sit the fuck down.' Gone is the diminutive voice I previously used in his presence, the peaceable little squeak that he liked so much. I am almost growling now, my anger palpable. It's driving me on, that fury, forcing me to do things that I know I shouldn't do. I can't stop it. I never could. It's who I am, as much a part of me as breathing, chiselled deep into my DNA.

I jab at the air, watching as Peter eventually backs away and drops down next to the two other women.

'Who is she?' I point at the bleeding body and nod at her. 'Why is she here?'

'It's my mum,' Peter says, his voice a thick, strangulated noise. 'She's badly hurt and we need to call an ambulance.'

'I asked why she's here. Who did she get in touch with before coming here?'

'She didn't get in touch with anybody you mad bitch and she's here because she's part of our family!' Lauren has regained her strength and is shouting at me now. I smile, my laughter fizzing up inside of me, fighting to be out. 'I swear to God,' she continues, 'you are a fucking maniac and should be locked up for the rest of your days.'

The smile fades from my face. Frost burns at me, ice slithering through my veins.

'I beg your pardon? What did you just say?' My heart bounces around my chest. Saliva fills my mouth. I start to walk towards her, the weight of the knife in my hand a reassuring sensation. Hefty and powerful. I could do it right now. I could lean down and push it deep into her ribcage, watch her beg for mercy, then smile as she dies, right here on the floor. But I won't. Not just yet. We need to talk, the Saunders family and I. They need to know what Sophia did to *my* family: how her sluttish ways tore me and my husband apart.

'You should have loved her more. Made her feel wanted. You drove her into the arms of another man.' I brandish the knife in the air, the glint of the blade mesmerising me.

'What?' Lauren meets my gaze, her voice a metallic screech. Sharp. Incredulous.

Peter attends to the older lady, cradling her head, telling her she's going to be just fine. She isn't. None of them are going to be fine. I'll make sure of it.

'Sophia. Nobody from a happy marriage has an affair. He drove her to it. You too. You both drove her away.'

Lauren laughs, shakes her head, closes her eyes and breathes deeply. I can almost hear it – her exhalations, the rush of air that leaves her lungs. In, out. In, out. Out, out, out: small, desperate, dry gasps until they are empty. Devoid of oxygen. Until she is dead.

She looks at me, hisses. 'Where is the little boy? What the fuck have you done with him?' Her teeth are small, white fangs. Foamy specks of saliva gather on her lips.

'He's fine. Safely tucked up in bed. Not that it's any of your concern. He's nothing to you.' She's trying to catch me off-guard, hoping to deviate from our current situation. I can read her thoughts, see through her flimsy act. She is a child. A pompous, overbearing woman-child, her experience of life deeply limited. Cushioned from everyone and everything, she is no match for me.

'You do know that your face is currently splashed all over the news, don't you? Women who kidnap children don't fare well in prison. All manner of terrible things happens to them.' She smiles at me. I return the gesture, wondering if she will still be grinning when she is bleeding to death, her face slashed and torn, her neck ripped wide open.

I step closer, myriad voices in my head urging me on, telling to do it, to stab her first and then finish off the others. I push them away, those sounds, the voices, and continue walking towards the heap of bodies on the floor before me, those terrified, trembling people who thought they knew me. Nobody knows the real me, the one I hide away. The one who wants to hurt people, to maim them. I lock her away, stuff her out of sight, but she always manages to scramble back out, showing everyone that she is made of stern stuff, that she won't be silenced.

The pool of thick scarlet inches closer to my feet, trickling into the cracks of the flooring, filling the air with a sour, metallic tang that hangs in the back of my nose and my throat. The stench of death as it creeps closer, that's what it is. She's on her way out, the older woman. Soon she will be gone, leaving me with less to do. Fewer people to punish. And then I can leave here, be on my way. I can collect Luke. We'll leave this town, head off together and start a new life, just the two of us. I have money and now I have a son. He is my new family, my little boy. I need nothing and nobody else.

'I know you, Jade Kennedy. I know all about you. So does the whole of the UK now you've stolen somebody else's child. I always suspected you were unhinged. It took me a while to see through your little act but I see you now. I see you for who you are – a pathetic, desperate individual with nobody and nothing.'

My laughter rings through the room, bouncing off every surface and wiping the superior smile off Lauren's face. 'You think you know me?' I get down on my haunches, the knife poised just inches from Lauren's pretty little face. I think about how she would look if I carved her up right now, how much blood she would lose, how much glee it would give me, the excitement that would shoot through my system, threading its way through my veins, blooming and warming me. 'You really think you know all there is to know about me?' I take the blade and trace it over her throat, circling it around her neck before resting it in the hollow of her clavicle. 'You know nothing about me or my life. Nothing at all.'

Her groan is soft, a gentle whimper, her eyes never leaving mine. 'So come on then, *Alice*, tell me what I'm missing here. What don't I know?'

A sob forces me to turn around. The older woman is lifting her head, trying to speak. Peter is stroking her face, his hand pressed against her abdomen to stem the flow of blood. I think about how it would feel to press this knife deep into his back, to feel his blood as it pumped through my fingers, departing his body, leaving him an empty husk of a man. Goosebumps rise on my skin. A wave of pleasure runs through me, spasming in my muscles and chiselling its way into my bones, happiness and contentment solidifying inside me, anchoring me to this moment. Oh, God this is glorious. Better than alcohol, better than sex. It thrills me like nothing I have ever experienced and I want more if it, this feeling. I never want it to end. It completes me. So much power. So much glorious control and power.

'What don't you know? Oh, there is so much to tell, dear girl. So many secrets. A lifetime of them.' My voice is a distant echo, a ghostly whisper in my head. I want to tell her. I want to tell her everything but then she will be privy to all there is to know about me. I will have nothing left to hide. I will be empty, the core of me devoid of everything I hold dear. And I need something, a small, special something to remind me of who I really am.

I close my eyes, just for a second, to allow the feeling to pass. My skin is being touched, softly at first, then with more force. I snap open my eyes and I'm falling.

45

PETER

She's going to die if he doesn't do something. He can't let that happen. He's bigger than Alice, stronger. He needs to do something. Anything.

His mum is moaning softly in his arms. He looks down at her, terrified every breath she takes will be her last. She seems so tiny laid there beside him, her face grey and lifeless. Helplessness smothers him: that knife, Alice's demented frame of mind, all forming a barrier between him and his family getting out of here alive.

And then he sees it – Alice is losing focus, her eyes clouding over, her features slackening as if all of her thoughts are currently tumbling out of her head and leaking out into the ether. He nods to Lauren, an imperceptible sign that she notices. She edges over to her Grandma, places her hand behind her neck to support her head and leans down to stroke the older lady's face, replacing him as he slides away.

He is freed up, able to do something – anything, to get them out of this situation. He moves, a shuffle at first, gaining some distance, more speed and then with hands outstretched towards the handle, he lunges at Alice, knocking the knife clean out of her hands. It hits the floor with a muted thump, spinning out of her reach and landing close to where Lauren is sitting with her grandma.

Alice lets out a roar – elongated, frenzied, like the cry of a wounded animal. Peter pushes her backwards and sits astride her prostrated body, holding her fast, pressing down on her, thinking how demented and damaged she is, how ugly it must be inside her mind, how fractured her world is. Her skull bangs against the floor as she bucks about trying to free herself. He grabs at her arms and pins them above her head but still she continues thrashing and flapping, pushing back against him, her strength inhuman, her eyes savage.

'Stop it!' His voice is close to a sob, energy, adrenaline coursing through him.

'Fuck you, Peter Saunders and fuck your daughter and slut of a wife!'

He ignores her words, words designed to rile him, hoping that Lauren has the sense to move the knife and is using it to protect herself. He can manage Alice. Lauren needs to take care of herself and her grandma. To do what needs to be done should Alice manage to wriggle free.

The air close by him shifts, an indiscernible movement. He prays Lauren is being wise, not doing anything foolhardy that could endanger them all. Not when he's finally managed to get Alice under control.

'Shut up. Lauren's going to call the police.' His voice is loud, powerful, the command for his daughter obvious in his tone. 'Just stop with your stupid games and stop trying to free yourself. You're not going anywhere.' His face is close to Alice's now, their breathing meeting and merging in an invisible, foul-smelling haze as fear and fury swamp them both.

'This is for you, Peter. Just for you.'

For one terrible moment, he fears she is going to kiss him. Instead, she spits in his face, a globule of hate-filled saliva that lands in his eyes, marring his vision. He tries to keep hold of her but his grip loosens, just for a split second and before he can stop her, she wriggles out from under him and catapults out of view.

'Lauren!' Peter spins around, terrified of what he'll see. Visions of Alice slitting his mother's throat, sticking the knife deep into Lauren's guts fill his mind.

Alice is scrambling around on the floor, trying to find the knife. Lauren is holding her phone, her eyes glassy. She is speaking into it, her voice low, clipped as she punches in the number and speaks, asks for help.

'No!' Alice throws herself at Lauren and manages to snatch the telephone out of her hand. She smashes it onto the floor over and over before throwing it to one side. 'I said no calls to the emergency services! Are you deaf or just plain fucking stupid?'

He drags Alice away, a wrestle ensuing as he attempts to restrain her. She's powerful, there's no denying that fact, but he's bigger, has a greater inner core strength, greater muscle density. For such a small woman, she seems to have unlimited reserves of energy, her fists pummelling at his chest, her torso squirming and twisting until eventually, exhaustion gets the better of her and she slumps against him, spent, her skin flushed pink with the exertion.

She is panting heavily. Peter grabs at her wrists, holding them fast. 'String, Lauren. I need some string! Anything at all that I can use to tie her up.'

Lauren's voice is a shriek. It pierces his concentration, tugs at his emotions. 'Grandma is dying, Dad! We need an ambulance.'

He catches his breath, knows he doesn't have to turn to face them to see that it's true. 'Get my mobile. I'll hold her here. You ring 999.'

Again, as if she has been suddenly injected with a short burst of energy, Alice struggles, her bony limbs writhing and pulling. He holds her tight, sweat coursing down his back. In the next room, he can hear Lauren hunting for his phone.

'Next to the microwave! It's next to the microwave, Lauren. Hurry!' Heart thumping, stampeding through his chest, he leans closer to Alice to hold her in place, pressing his entire weight onto her. Bone, muscle, sinew, meeting, melding together, suctioned together by sweat.

Lauren's voice filters through from the kitchen, desperation and screamed obscenities echoing as she tries and fails to punch in the passcode.

'Two six one three!' He shouts through to her, wills her to get a move on. His mum cannot die like this. He won't let it happen, silently vows to use every little bit of strength and ingenuity to get them out of here alive. 'And then come and find the knife, Lauren. We need that bloody knife!'

He listens to Lauren mumbling, her voice muffled and indistinct above Alice's growling and shouting, the thump of her feet against wood as she batters them on the floor, the gnashing and wailing and shouts that she will kill them all. Then a worrying silence. An unexpected slump as she watches and waits.

At the edge of his vision, Peter can see Lauren as she walks back into the living room, the phone clasped in one hand and another serrated knife in the other. Two knives. Jesus. They've already had enough blood spilled in this house. Too much. They don't need any more.

The blade wobbles about, glinting and flashing as she holds it aloft. Her voice is a murmur, soft and frightened. Pleading. It rises slowly, her strength rapidly returning. The old Lauren. The wilful, capable Lauren. She barks out the details to the person on the other end of the line, telling them to hurry. Screaming at them. A command, not a pitiful request.

And then Alice springs to life once more. Just when he thinks it's over, that it's coming to an end. Like a rabid dog, she lets out a howl, her teeth bared. Kicking out and writhing, she manages to break free, but not for long. Long enough, however, to catch his daughter unawares. The phone drops to the floor, slipping out of Lauren's fingers, but she manages to keep hold of the knife. Underneath the sideboard, Peter spots the other one, the original weapon, the silver tip protruding out from beneath the curved, wooden legs of the old, oak unit. Alice sees it too. They both move forwards, their movements, their bodies synchronised, but he's too fast for her, a split second only separating them. He grabs it with both hands, waves it at her, telling her to back the fuck away.

It takes a matter of seconds to catch her, to wrap his arm around her waist and drag her over to a chair. He holds the tip of the blade to her throat, muttering that he will slit it in a heartbeat if she tries to escape again. He means every word of it. He'll kill her if he has to. He will gladly run the knife across her throat and watch her bleed out.

'My belt, Lauren! Take my belt off and tie her hands to the chair.' She falters, stays put, eyes wide. 'The belt, Lauren. You need to do it now. If we don't hurry, Grandma is going to die.' He's trying to keep his voice even but his own fears and anxieties are bubbling up, slowly rising to the surface, trying to pull him under.

Hands grab at his midriff, a tug at his waistband, leather being freed from his stomach. Lauren is beside him. She wraps the belt around Alice's wrists, looping the buckle through the back of the chair, pulling at it tightly. Securing it. Saving their lives.

'Make sure it can't come off. I don't care if she cries out or if her blood supply gets cut off. Just tie her fucking hands together so she can't escape.'

It feels like hours, time too difficult, too ethereal to measure. It's only seconds; he knows that. Seconds to restrain this insane creature, to put a halt to her crazy mission to kill them all, but it feels like an eternity.

He steps back, spins the chair around to look at Alice's face, to study her expression, try to work out what is going on in that addled brain of hers. Maybe it's better he doesn't know. Some things are best left unknown and unsaid.

'Lauren, call 999 again. We need an ambulance and the police as soon as possible.'

She is smiling at him, this Alice/Jade person, a lopsided grin that turns his skin to winter, ice flooding through his veins. 'Well, well, well. The sad little man finally grew some balls and managed to pin me down. I'll tell them it was you who did it when they do finally arrive.' She nods over to his mother, the crumpled heap on the floor and winks at him. 'I'll tell them you turned on us all, that you're a madman. Once they see the bruises on my arms and my body where you attacked me, then they'll know who to believe.'

He wants to laugh at the absurdity of it, isn't even sure how she has the temerity to talk such shit. Her thoughts are on a different plane, so far removed from reality that she may as well be on another planet, in another galaxy.

'Stop talking, Alice. We've heard enough from you. Just shut your fucking mouth, okay?' A dry bark from him. A lacklustre comment. He's all out of energy.

Snot and blood trickle down from one of her nostrils, slipping over her top lip and dispersing over her gums and teeth, a glistening, silvery streak of gelatinous fluid. She grins, her face a mask of hatred. Twisted and perverse.

'Shut my mouth? Oh, I don't think I can. There's so much to be said, don't you think? So many secrets still untold.'

He shakes his head, unwilling to become embroiled in any of her stupid, warped games. He refuses to be manipulated by her any more. Enough is enough. God, he has been blind. So fucking naïve and blind. He should have listened to Lauren, should have removed those blinkers and taken a long, hard look at the situation, assessed it objectively, but he didn't and now they're all paying the price. His mother is dying and it's all his fault. Alice is right about one thing – he was too childlike, too trusting. But not any more. He sees who she is now, this Alice person. This Jade Kennedy. He sees straight through her, knows exactly who she is, what she is capable of and will have no hesitation about sticking this knife in her neck to save his family.

46

JADE/ALICE

They'll be here soon, the police, and when they arrive, everything will be over. I will lose it all. All the things I've worked for over these past twelve months will vanish, everything I have clawed and strived, and fought tooth and nail for will be taken from me. And what will happen to Luke then? My little Luke, the boy I deserve. My boy. Who will take care of him then? What will become of him?

My options are rapidly diminishing. I can, however, do as much damage as humanly possible before they turn up with their rough ways and punitive measures. I can tell the Saunders family what I think of them. Tell them who I really am. Let them know exactly who and what they are dealing with.

Peter is standing before me, observing my every move. Lauren is on the floor with the older woman, whispering into her ear, smoothing down her hair. Trying to stop her from dying. It's pointless. I felt that knife as it caught her, the satisfying swish of metal cutting through flesh. She can't have long left. I wonder how long it takes a person to bleed to death – half an hour? One hour? Two? I once read that the battlefields of the Somme weren't littered with dead bodies but dying ones; battered, torn men who took days and days to die, their blood slowly leaking out of their bodies. I don't imagine Peter's mum has the same strength as those soldiers. I imagine she will die pretty soon, her organs shutting down, her heart beating its last. But she isn't dead yet. She is suffering and so are they, sitting here, watching the life ebb away from her. That in itself gives me a great deal of pleasure.

As if he can read my thoughts, Peter shouts over his shoulder, never taking his eyes off me. 'Lauren, call 999 again. Hurry!'

I hear her scramble for the phone, listen to her speak, then catch the faint sounds of sirens in the distance. They are already on their way. Almost here.

'I guess you've seen through me now, haven't you?' Gone is the sweet squeak of a voice I've used in his presence, replaced now with my usual, dull, dour tones. My embittered, gravel-like deliverance. It runs through me, that feeling of sourness, of being forgotten, discarded. Treated like dirt. A lifetime of it. I have suffered a lifetime of hatred and rejection and I am done with it. This is my time now. A time for revelations and revenge. 'Well, this is the real me.' I sigh, stare down at my feet, inspecting them. 'Have you any idea what it is like to be viewed as worthless?' No reaction. Not a sound. Just the hard stare of a man who thought he knew it all. A man who thought he had it all and now doesn't. Serves him right. They deserve each other – him, Lauren, that interfering old hag laid on the floor. They all deserve one other, every single one of them, with their sad, insular little ways; their lives a thin veneer of gloss that radiated shallow, superficial sadness. They don't understand real sadness, not the grinding misery I have had to endure. They have no fucking idea. 'No, I'll bet you don't. Not you with your perfect little family and perfect house. What would you know about being ignored and cast aside, about being branded a failure? Life has always gone your way, hasn't it? Even losing your wife didn't dent your existence, did it? You managed to carry on with everything, holding down a good job, living here in this lovely house with your perfect child and textbook mother popping in every so often to make sure you're both managing. How bloody marvellous for you, eh?'

Outside, the sirens grow closer. I don't have much time left. It's almost at an end.

I can hear Lauren sobbing, her hands draped over her grandma's body. Long, slim fingers, hair floating. Head dipped. Her tears are futile. Futile and useless. We've all shed them in the past year, me included, but what is the point of them? A good bout of crying leaves you breathless and exhausted. So I found a better way, a more productive way. A way of venting my anger, an outlet for my misery. I worked out how to redress the balance, to show them how it feels to be lonely, to feel as if the whole world is against you. And I have done just that. Sometimes, it was in small ways like breaking the window and ruining Sophia's books. And then there are times such as this, where I have had to really slap them in the face to get their attention.

Peter starts to speak. I sigh, turn away, close my eyes, suddenly exhausted. It's been a busy day, a trying day. Fatigue swamps me. Everything begins to slip away.

I hear the banging on the door, the loud voices, the shouting. I feel the vibrations on the floor as they enter the house, the charge of heavy feet, the throb of energy as they push through into the room. And then Lauren screaming, Peter shouting, my own heartbeat ringing in my ears.

It's happening. They're here. It's over.

47

LAUREN

'Oh, God, please help her! Somebody, please help her.'

I am ushered away, strong arms wrapping themselves around me. I see medics and police officers kneeling at Grandma's side. I try to move back to her, shouting that I don't want to leave her but I'm held in place and unable to move, their hands holding me fast, rooting me to the spot.

We're all under suspicion. None of these people know what has taken place in this house. Officers cuff Dad and untie Alice. She struggles and tries to get away. I watch her through misted vision, silently willing her to show her true colours, to let the police see who she really is. She spits and fights, shouts and swears as they hold her down and place handcuffs on her wrists as well. Still, she squirms, still she protests, screaming that I was the one who did this, that I attacked Grandma and then attacked her. I almost laugh at the absurdity of it, the ill-thought-out stupidity of her claims.

My face flushes hot, my skin grows cold, a howling gale blowing through my veins as I'm forced to listen to her mad ramblings, the wild accusations of a woman unhinged.

Bodies surround Grandma, the hustle and movement of people trying to save her life. I close my eyes and pray, reciting the words I was taught in school and have never since repeated, saying them over and over until I feel movement nearby, hear the squeak of shoes against the flooring and then watch as she is strapped to a stretcher and carried outside.

Vomit and blood swill at our feet, the stench hitting the back of my throat with a swift punch, dragging me out of my stupor.

People everywhere, authoritative voices, shouts, commands barked out, bodies moving and pushing, and then the heat. So much heat. A wall of it. Yet I'm cold. Freezing, actually. I shiver. Sickness rises, swirls in my gut. I try to ask for help but nothing comes out. I try again but my words get lost amidst the noise and the confusion. My head pounds, crystals stab at my skull before I take a deep breath and everything goes black.

48

PETER

It's funny, he thinks, how the human brain works. And what can happen when it doesn't. What dreadful atrocities can take place in the absence of all compassion and logic. He's seen both sides of the coin, been married, in love, deliriously happy, and then subjected to the heartache that ensues when it comes to an end, when all life drains out of it and you are left bereft and rudderless. No sense of direction, no end in sight.

And then there was Alice. He put it down to grief and guilt, being sucked into her little game. Stupid. So stupid and blind and humiliating. A hard lesson to learn.

He feels foolish but is trying to get over it. He was deprived of all reason, pulled towards her by lust and a need to get settled again, get his life back on track. That's what he keeps telling himself. He's an educated man, practical and sensible, so how did he allow it to happen? He has no answers except to say, she was exceptional at spotting his vulnerabilities and exploiting them mercilessly. He has learned a solid lesson. One he won't ever forget.

His mum is recovering. Still in hospital under observation and awaiting discharge, she is coming to live with him and Lauren until she is completely healed both mentally and physically. He anticipates nightmares and restlessness and fear. From all of them. It's going to be a long road back to normality. Whatever normality is. It feels like a lifetime ago since their little family has led an easy, comfortable way of life without any heartache or acrimony, but he's prepared to work at it, to restore a kind of loving routine back into their everyday existence.

Lauren has changed her mind about her studies, now preferring criminology rather than English. Both fascinated and repulsed by Jade Kennedy in equal measure, she has talked endlessly about what drove her to do what she did, what was going through her mind and mainly, how good she was at initially fooling them. At fooling him. Lauren had an inkling long before Peter did. He was too wrapped up in the idea of falling in love again to see beyond her charms. And my God, he tried so hard not to love her but a year of turmoil and sorrow had wreaked havoc with his senses and he lowered his resistances, allowing himself to get sucked in, crashing hard against the rocks when it all came undone.

And now, they're being forced to go through the whole court process again. After doing their damnedest to avoid it the first time around, they've decided that they are going to attend this one. He wants to stare into Jade Kennedy's eyes, try to see inside her head, work out what she is thinking. What drove her. See who she really is.

They're on the mend, their little family. They still have some way to go but this journey that lies ahead of them will be easier than the last road they navigated. Smoother, easier. Fewer potholes and deviations.

The guilt is still the hardest thing to deal with. It follows him, trailing in his shadow, watching, waiting to bite at him, to take chunks out of his soul for what he did that night by the riverbank. But that is something he is going to have to learn to deal with.

49

LAUREN

I'm sitting here reading about an antibody jab that works as a cure for peanut allergy sufferers. It's not yet fully available for the general public but it's a tiny ray of hope for people like me who, when faced with a plate of food of provenance unknown, take a tentative bite, unsure if it will be their last.

Jade has shown no remorse for her actions. If anything, she has apparently been intrigued by my condition, asking prison officers how much it would take to kill a person and how long it would take for them to die. I try not to think about that day, the possibilities of what could have happened had she not relented and given Dad the EpiPen. I try to not think about her at all but it's almost impossible. Psychiatrists have assessed her, found her fit to stand trial after throwing out diagnoses like borderline personality disorder and schizophrenia.

Personally, I think that is bullshit and an insult to people who have those illnesses. I think Jade is just evil, her mind incapable of emotion.

How do I know that? Perhaps it's because we are more alike than she will ever realise. We all have our flaws, our hidden identities, parts of us we would rather keep concealed. Until they're required to show themselves, that is. I saw it in her – parts of me. The darkest parts. The uncontrollable parts.

I think that's why Dad couldn't spot it, her rotten inner core. He's too unassuming, too blithe and breezy. So blithe and breezy that he couldn't finish what he started that night all those months ago on the riverbank. The evening I followed him, a shadow darting in and out of the shrubbery, a ghost in the night.

He saw Mum with Phillip Kennedy, saw them argue, saw the push Kennedy gave her and then watched as he walked away. Mum wasn't injured. No bruises, no bleeding, no broken bones. Only her pride was damaged as she picked herself up off the floor and tried to regain some of her dignity.

I wanted him to do it at that point: to end her life there and then. Is that a terrible admission? I wanted Dad to kill her. It needed to stop – her behaviour, the way she humiliated him, dragging his reputation through the dirt. I visualised him placing his hands around her neck and squeezing tight until her body became floppy and lifeless.

Except he didn't. He moved, caused a rustling sound.

She turned, saw him, narrowed her eyes in disgust, called him a name. Something vicious, something demeaning. And then she spat at him. So he hit her across the face. She staggered, eyes wide, and fell back into a tree, her head smacking against the trunk before sliding to the ground in a heap.

He fled. I knew he would. Fear and guilt sent him running in the opposite direction. But not me. We are very different, Dad and I. I stepped closer, obscured by the dense foliage, was able to see that she wasn't dead, her breathing gaining in momentum, growing stronger with every passing second. Her ability to resist would soon reveal itself as her strength returned. I did it quickly. Cleanly. The heavy branch was short and squat, more of a log, its end smooth and substantial. I held it tightly, swung it, catching her on the side of her face and then once more on the top of her head. Just to be sure. I heard the crack, saw the life drain out of her, and waited. No rising of her chest. No breathing. It was over as quickly as it began.

I'd like to say I was upset, nervous, sickened by my actions. Except it would be a lie. I wasn't anything. That's how I know Jade and I more alike than we care to mention.

With my foot, I rolled her down the bank, kicked the leaves over her body and left, throwing the log into the river, watching as it got carried away by the current before disappearing altogether. And the rest, as they say, is history.

My letter to Phillip Kennedy will serve as my defence should anything ever crop up in the future, should any prying eyes who saw me that night suddenly decide to speak up. Why would I write to him if I thought he was innocent? He's as good as guilty. He was there that night. He started this whole thing. I may have killed her but he set the whole thing in motion. He's in the right place. I feel no guilt. All I feel is relief.

On a different note, my life has taken an upward turn. Dad is still alone but I'm going out with Josh tonight and have been almost every night since Jade's arrest. He has proven to be a great friend as well as an amazing boyfriend. I think maybe he is attracted to my strange life and the impending court case. He tells me nearly every day that he really likes me, but he would, wouldn't he? That's because he doesn't know me. I'm not sure anybody does.

How well do any of us know our family, our friends, our neighbours? Every bit of confidence we have would be eroded if we could see inside their heads, pick our way through the debris of their thoughts. I can tell you with absolute certainty, you wouldn't want to see inside mine.

50

ALICE/JADE

Jade Kennedy. I am refusing to answer to that name. They call me by it all the time – Jade this, Jade that. Jade, Jade, Jade. She doesn't exist. Not any more. I'm Alice. Alice Godwin.

They think they know me, these people. They don't. Day after day, they try to get inside my head, to delve into the darkest corners of my brain and work out what I'm thinking; what it is that drives me. I won't let them in. I'm good at shutting people out and keeping the secrets in. It's what I do. I've been practising it all my life.

They tell me that they've been speaking to Jack Downey and that I am being charged with the kidnap of his son, Fionn and extorting money from him. I laughed. Fionn doesn't exist. He's a ghost of the past, somebody I used to know. Luke was sleeping peacefully the evening the police raided my house to find him. He was healthy, happy, unharmed. They should have let him be, allowed me to see him one last time but they didn't. Such cruelty and heartache. That boy was all I had, and now he's gone. As for the other fabricated claims – I wish them every luck. No contracts changed hands, no ATMs used. Just the cameras in the Downey household showing Jack handing me my wages. What does it matter anyway? I'm in here for the long haul. I know that. I stabbed an elderly lady. People don't take kindly to such perverse acts of violence. Me? I don't mind them either way. It's part of life, part of our existence – survival of the fittest. I did what had to be done and now it's over.

'It's Luke,' I told them, as they sat at the table, their eyes fixed on me while they waited for my answers. 'I don't know anybody called Fionn. Luke is my son. Use his proper name or don't speak of him at all.'

Sometimes, they roll their eyes when I reply to their statements, their rhetorical questions. They think I can't spot their techniques, the tricks they use to try and elicit the correct responses from me. Responses that would undoubtedly lengthen my sentence, stripping me of my freedoms, depriving me of natural light and all the things we all take for granted day after day.

And then other times, they bang their fists on the table and shout, but only when none of the doctors are present. The head doctors as I like to call them. They are all a little more erudite and peaceable. They don't have to resort to yelling and violence to get me to speak, to get me to open up about my past. They too, play their little mind games, asking me to tell the truth and telling me that they're on my side. I don't necessarily believe that but because I have a little more respect for them, I do try to speak openly and tell them of my thoughts, how they claw at me, daring me to do things.

None of them really listen to what I have to say, however. If they did, their lives would be so much easier. They wouldn't have to probe and delve. It would be there for them, my thoughts an open book. They could pick through the unimportant stuff and get to the nub of my life. The bits that matter.

Everything stems from our childhoods, doesn't it? Such a delicate period of our lives, our brains still forming, being constantly moulded and shaped like plasticine. Am I blaming my parents for the way I am? Perhaps. Should I hold it against them – the way they blamed me for my sister's death? Who knows? I am acutely aware, however, of how they were able to see through me, to see inside my head. There was no hiding my dark thoughts in their presence. Which is why I choose to be somebody else. Anybody but who I really am. The real me is dirty: murky and damaged. Even my mother and father could see that. They tried to rail against it, to reconfigure and transform me, turn me into someone different, a better person. Less damaged. They failed. So I am now a new me. An improved me. We all strive to better ourselves, don't we? Even me. I still see my sister's face that day, her eyes staring out, wide and full of terror as I held her under the water. I hear her voice in my head asking me why I did it and I have no answers, nothing to give her in return. I just know that it felt like the right thing to do at the time. My parents were naturally distraught and even though I protested my innocence, I could see that they knew. They had always known something was going to happen. It was just a matter of time.

None of these people listen when I tell them that I'm not really here anyway, that I'm already dead and buried and lying in the graveyard of St Martin's Church. They sneak glances at one another and suppress their heavy sighs. The police think I say these things to increase my chances of getting a more lenient sentence, maybe even getting admitted to a mental health unit rather than a prison. In truth, I couldn't care less where they send me. Anywhere that is not with Luke is a prison to me. I had him and now I don't. Just like I had my sister, and then I didn't.

Luke had the same eyes as hers. I think about her more and more lately, our time together, how we used to play as children, her smiles, her laughter. Her inevitable death.

The detectives working on my case are investigating the murder of woman after a body was found in a churchyard in York. They say she had connections to me. I don't know who she is, know nothing about her. People die all the time. How can I be held responsible for something I know nothing about? My solicitor is constantly asking me to just be truthful and tell them what I can remember. I am being truthful. I remember nothing at all. Maybe they should ask Jade about such things, if they ever find her, that is. She is dead to me. As if she never existed.

Apparently, a taxi driver identified me as being in his cab on the day she was murdered. They speak of CCTV footage and how they have found DNA linking me to the body.

'I know nothing of it,' I said, when they asked if I had anything to say on the matter. 'Why don't you find this Jade Kennedy and ask her instead?'

Such responses infuriate them. That's when they start banging on the table and shouting at me. It doesn't faze me. It never has. I'm immune to such reactions. They wash over me, their words leaving no trace. I've had a lifetime of it, am impervious to their insults, their insistence that I'm nothing but a liar. The detective leading the case is starting to look tired. I told him he needs a break and should take a few weeks off in the sun.

'Get yourself off on holiday,' I told him as I gave him my best smile and cocked my head to one side sympathetically. 'Or this job will be the death of you.'

He didn't like that particular line but a few other people in the room laughed. I think they like me, those other people. Just like Peter liked me, they are warming to my charms, getting used to my subtle humour and slowly realising that somebody as quiet and gentle and demure as me couldn't possibly have committed those atrocities. It just isn't possible, is it? I'm Alice Godwin – a dead woman. And what possible harm can the dead do to the living?

ACKNOWLEDGEMENTS

This was a difficult book to write. Some novels flow easily; others take a little while longer. This particular story required a lot of changes and some heavy editing and a lot of blood, sweat and tears but I got there in the end!

I can't begin to imagine how lonely it must have been for writers back in the day, pre-internet, sitting at home week after week, seeing nobody and speaking rarely to other writers. We now have the ability to communicate with each other to solve problems, chat or offer a shoulder to cry on. With that in mind, I would like to say a big thank you to Anita Waller and Valerie Dickenson (Keogh). I value our chats very highly and would have been lost without you two lovely ladies over the past few years. Here's to the next few months and many more books between us!

Without readers, reviewers and bloggers, my books would be nothing, so I would like to take this opportunity to offer my sincerest gratitude to anybody who has taken the time to read any of my novels. They are all my babies and I appreciate that you've taken time out of your lives and am also humbled that you've chosen to read something that I have written. Thank you.

A final thank you to the staff at Boldwood Books for republishing my book and for all your assistance with the many hiccups and snags along the way. A special thank you to Emily Ruston for her hard work and moral support. Emily, you are a gem.

I hope you enjoy reading my book and can be found at:
Twitter: @thewriterjude
Facebook: @thewriterjude
Instagram: @jabakerauthor

I look forward to hearing from you!

Best wishes,
    Judith Baker

ABOUT THE AUTHOR

J. A. Baker is a successful writer of numerous psychological thrillers. Born and brought up in Middlesbrough, she still lives in the North East, which inspires the settings for her books.

Sign up to J. A. Baker's mailing list here for news, competitions and updates on future books.

Follow J. A. Baker on social media:

facebook.com/thewriterjude
x.com/thewriterjude
instagram.com/jabakerauthor
tiktok.com/@jabaker41
bookbub.com/authors/JABaker

ALSO BY J. A. BAKER

Local Girl Missing

The Last Wife

The Woman at Number 19

The Other Mother

The Toxic Friend

The Retreat

The Woman in the Woods

The Stranger

The Intruder

The Girl In The Water

The Quiet One

The Passenger

Little Boy, Gone

When She Sleeps

The Widower's Lie

The Guilty Teacher

THE *Murder* LIST

THE MURDER LIST IS A NEWSLETTER DEDICATED TO ALL THINGS CRIME AND THRILLER FICTION!

SIGN UP TO MAKE SURE YOU'RE ON OUR HIT LIST FOR GRIPPING PAGE-TURNERS AND HEARTSTOPPING READS.

SIGN UP TO OUR NEWSLETTER

BIT.LY/THEMURDERLISTNEWS

Boldwood

Boldwood Books is an award-winning fiction publishing company seeking out the best stories from around the world.

Find out more at www.boldwoodbooks.com

Join our reader community for brilliant books, competitions and offers!

Follow us
@BoldwoodBooks
@TheBoldBookClub

Sign up to our weekly deals newsletter

https://bit.ly/BoldwoodBNewsletter

Milton Keynes UK
Ingram Content Group UK Ltd.
UKHW040717080724
445163UK00001B/3